FOR ANOTHER WOMAN

By
JEAN DEGARMO

Chapter 1

There was no way around her. No place to hide. Russ Shaw's mother told him to stop by the Birch Hill Lodge on his way home from work, so he'd better do it. She'd hunt him down if he didn't. Even in a November storm, with the wind off Lake Huron cold and cutting, she'd search for him. And she'd find him.

It was six-thirty by the time he walked through the heavy doors of the Lodge, and right away the heat from the dining room made him dizzy. Maybe that was her plan: light the three fireplaces, hoping he'd pass out so she could drag him into her chambers and torture him slowly.

His first clue of danger was that there were too many customers for a Tuesday night. A variety of faces invaded the rustic interior and blurred into a mass of flesh—voices high and low, surrounding him, pushing him—as he walked through the maze of tables toward the hallway leading to her office.

He was nine years old when his parents built the Lodge. Now at thirty-four, he hated everyone and everything associated with his mother's business: the staff, the food, the loud classical music.

"Hey, Russ. I heard they're laying off workers at the quarry," someone said from a dark corner. He couldn't identify the person by candlelight and thought about turning back for a closer look, but he decided it wasn't worth the trouble and moved on.

If his employers were laying off people at the limestone quarry in Rogers City where he had worked for the past fifteen years, they'd better check his outstanding record first. Better get the facts. Then again, collecting unemployment checks might not be a bad idea. Sleeping in late and sitting around the house while Libby waited on him wouldn't be bad either. That is, until he would need to ask JoAnne for financial assistance—and he would rather jump onto the icy surface of Grand Lake than ask her for help.

But it was impossible to imagine ice when the sweat was collecting around his eyes. He lifted his ball cap and slapped it back onto his head...*so hot*...and yet, he would wear the hat to protest her and her coveted Birch Hill Lodge.

Be polite to the customers, he could still hear her say back when he was a teenager and spent his summers as a fishing guide. He was polite all right; he was so polite he wouldn't speak at all. He would lead the tourists into the shallow sections of the lake where the fish would not live, much less feed.

He opened the door to her office, leaned against the frame, and crossed his arms. "What do you want?" he asked her crooked back. "I told Libby I'd be home in time for dinner. If I'm late, it's your fault."

"Fault!" JoAnne said, her voice full of static. She put a purple-spotted hand to her bent hip and turned from the filing cabinet. Her eyes were black slits inside her pasty skin, and her upper lip quivered like a dying night crawler. She was skinny and bony and dressed in gray. "*You* are the one at fault!" she insisted.

Her lips, that *looked* like withering night crawlers when she spoke, and her complexion, like crumbling earth, reminded him of fishing and his youth. He remembered the afternoons he ran away as a boy, running and hiding, deceiving her, in search of minnows and frogs.

He also remembered walking up the road from Lotus Pond into the sanctuary of the woods, hoping to find his grandfather—a quiet, kind man with a mangled left knee. He shook his head to lose the memory. He got in trouble for daydreaming as a child; he'd probably get shot for it now.

And he could tell she knew what he was thinking when she looked straight into his eyes, her expression radiating one holy law. *Nothing comes before the Birch Hill Lodge. Not frogs, fishing, or conversations with a limping old man.* She snapped her fingers. "Fault?" she said again. "You arrogant fool! You should know all about *fault!*"

For once in his life he wanted to study every side of her, but it wasn't meant to be. Not now. Not ever. She'd shake with rage and call him names at the very notion of him leaving her, if only for a minute.

Abruptly, she balanced a pair of glasses upon her curved nose. She wore the glasses as an exclamation mark for her delusional mind. She was out of reach. Too complicated for him to understand.

He flashed back to the year he turned seventeen and told her he wasn't going to college, wasn't taking business courses as she had demanded. "Then you can be a hopeless loser on your own," she told him, her eyes wild and red. "And don't come to me later for a handout. Don't bother asking your father for one either. I run the finances around here!"

Standing up to her twenty-odd years ago motivated him to take control of his life, but later on, she proved to be right: he needed an education, a direction. He ended up working temporary jobs until he had no choice but to accept his grandfather's help behind JoAnne's back. Only with Grandfather's connections was he able to land a job as a machine operator at the limestone quarry in Rogers City, thirty miles north of Grand Lake.

It was a good-paying job that suited him, but now, according to some stranger sitting in the shadows of the Birch Hill Lodge, layoffs were pending.

Maybe the stranger is a ghost.

Maybe losing his job was JoAnne's lesson to him for not listening to her, for not doing what she had *wanted him to do* with his life.

He had a wife, Libby, and a five-year-old daughter, Olivia, to support. He had bills to pay, debts, house repairs, and before too long, he would need a new truck. He knew she sensed his frustration when she clicked her tongue against the roof of her mouth as if to say, *I told you so, Stupid.*

He wanted to grab her and rip her apart, squeeze her scrawny neck. He wanted to force her to give him his trust money from his grandfather and the deed to his grandfather's land. Grandfather had been sickly and delirious, but she talked him into making her executor of his will in order to protect his assets, or so she had claimed. Russ suspected she had pushed him down a flight of stairs, causing his debilitating limp, and eventually, his death.

Breathless, he needed to get back to sturdy ground. She had the ability to stare him down with her piercing black eyes; they punctured like arrows, straight into his conscience. Her aim, on target ninety-five percent of the time, made him realize he'd never be able to keep secrets where they belonged. She'd intercept them as soon as he made them.

He watched her, thinking about how she used to wear her shiny hair, bunched up with two rows braided together into a tight knot. He had wanted to pull the pins out to see how long her hair was. To her shoulders or to her waist? After her husband, Aaron, had been dead for two months, she changed her appearance, at the age of sixty-nine. She cropped off her hair, flattened it against her weather-worn face.

He didn't care about her hair now, or her bad heart either. He only wanted the money she owed him. And Grandfather's land. He wanted retribution for his father's untimely death. Aaron, whether it was in raising children or running the business, never intervened with JoAnne's rules. He was a poor excuse of a father, only present physically, hollow mentally and emotionally, until sometimes Russ *believed* what JoAnne was forever saying behind his back, "He is a waste of my time."

She had accepted him into her life only because he was tall and good-looking, and thanks to his parents and maternal grandparents who had made a fortune in the logging industry, he was also wealthy. Aaron acquired thousands of acres of land from his family—a valuable commodity worth two million—by the time JoAnne got her hands on it.

She refused to let go, even when developers wanted to buy some of the property to expand Harbor Enterprise and surrounding areas. They wanted to build summer cottages, a pizza parlor, a tavern, a gift shop. She refused to sell by sheer strategy and willpower. She was a fuse forever lit.

Thinking of his father dead on the Birch Hill grounds after mowing in the summer heat made Russ want to drive a knife into her rickety arthritic back. Shove the knife in and twist it a couple of times, but she turned and drove her sharp, black eyes into him further than he could ever hope to stick a knife.

"I'm looking for my attorney's new phone number," she said, every word sparking in the air. "You know Jerry McPherson, my attorney and your best friend? You want to know why I need *him*?"

"No," he said. "Tell me why."

"Because someone has started a storm of trouble, and that someone is going to pay!"

A storm of trouble. Russ imagined dark clouds and a fierce wind spinning off Lake Huron. A storm of trouble whipping pins of ice around their legs, suffocating them with currents of her fury.

He waited for her to say it. He waited for her body—sun-scorched, stiff, and rapidly becoming deformed—to leak the name. *Libby.*

"You're unbelievably stupid and ignorant!" The delivery of her words had been so brazen and loud. She shook her head and continued in one breath, "Betraying Libby just like the imbecile you are!"

He squinted at her, hoping to see inside her, or better yet, make her vanish entirely, but the more he squinted, the larger she became. Soon enough, she filled the room like a growing fog. She made him swell and stammer and want to run away…like a child.

He said, "What I do with my life is none of your business."

"That's where you're wrong. I've told you, I have a life planned for you. You break it off with the whore you're sleeping with, and you do it now! Or you'll never get the money. You'll never get the cottage. And what's more, when I find out the vulgar details, I'll go straight to Libby, and you'll lose her too. You'll never see your daughter again!"

Russ's skin turned warm when his fear drifted away, like Aaron floating along the road toward his car. He took another step forward. He was going to grab her arm but clenched his fists instead. "You've got nothing better to do than make up lies to tell your friends," he said. He stared her down into her leather chair. "Say one word to Libby, and you'll regret it!"

JoAnne slapped the arms of the chair. "You stupid, stupid *boy*! Didn't you hear a word I said! I have people investigating you. If you don't believe me, ask Jerry McPherson. Next, I tell Libby. I promised her mother, Susan, that if anything happened to her, I'd take care of Libby. I'll eliminate *you* if it means taking care of Libby!"

Russ thought she was going to have a stroke. Her veins spasmed beneath her skin, ready to pop out of her neck. "What if I can prove you knocked Grandfather down the stairs?" he asked, "Or that you threatened him to get power of attorney? You've got nothing on me!"

He turned and walked out the door, expecting a rock to shatter his skull, a blade to slice into his back, or a bullet to rip through his ribs. And he worried he might pass out; it was suddenly too hot to be near her, so unnaturally hot.

He walked down the long corridor toward the exit. He needed air and he needed it quickly. Outside in the parking lot, the breeze touched him. *I will comfort you,* it said, and then, *A storm of trouble is brewing.*

He climbed into his truck and thought about turning it toward the pier. He pictured himself driving off the dock, straight into the mouth of the harbor. He would sit tight and sink into the depths of oblivion, pitch-black and silent, hear and feel nothing except the echo of his heartbeat seconds before the clamp of death.

The things Libby didn't know.

The things JoAnne would tell her. Life could be over for him if he wanted to step on the gas pedal, and then it wouldn't matter if JoAnne talked. But as the night closed in on him, the stars burned off his hallucinations, and he knew without a doubt he couldn't leave Libby.

Above even that, he couldn't let JoAnne win.

Chapter 2

As Russ drove toward Grand Lake, he looked at his watch and noticed it was almost eight-thirty. He was late for dinner, and Libby would be mad, exactly what he had hoped to avoid. He worked hard every day, and when fall finally arrived—his favorite time of the year— he spent his free time hunting. He would take off for the woods behind his grandfather's cottage on the other side of the lake and hunt grouse, sometimes from early morning until late afternoon. He would deer hunt in November and late December into January; and in February, he would ice fish on Grand Lake.

But now JoAnne might force him to take stock. She would hire people to follow him. She would rearrange his thoughts and revise his feelings.

Before turning onto the road toward the lake, he stopped at the small store on the outskirts of Presque Isle to buy a pack of cigarettes. After he bought the cigarettes, he drove his Blazer along the winding road through the trees, past summer cottages and winterized homes built along the shores of Grand Lake.

He had lived in Presque Isle County all his life. When JoAnne and Aaron acquired the Lodge from Aaron's parents, they added an upstairs to the first section and then a dining room and huge kitchen; they even built twelve small cottages among a grove of pine and cedar trees for guests who requested privacy.

Russ, his parents, and his sister Andrea lived in a trailer while the Lodge was expanding. He recalled shivering constantly because the trailer was drafty, the walls too thin for northern winters. He could still hear the wind whistle through the seams of the ceiling and doors. Thinking of this, he turned up the heat in the Blazer.

Now that it was November, Grand Lake would soon cover over with ice, and there would be no more taking Grandfather's wooden Lyman boat out on the lake to float away in peace. It was time to ready the plow on his old truck and close the boathouse.

Russ's grandparents built their wealth through the logging industry and had invested wisely—mostly in land and the stock market. When they first settled at Grand Lake, property was cheap, and investors bought acreage quickly, knowing the land would be sold years later at outrageous prices. Buyers would convert the beaches and the surrounding woods into resorts, an abundance of vacation cottages, clubhouses, restaurants, and elaborate retreats like the Birch Hill Lodge.

Summer was their best season. Summer fees tripled their investments. The more money Aaron's parents made, the more land JoAnne bought. Among her prized parcels was one hundred acres next to the Harbor Resort near Lake Huron. The owner of the resort wanted her to sell to him, but she held her ground and played him as if he were a piece on her game board.

Thomas Bishop *was* the prized piece. He was the owner of the Harbor Resort and a ruthless scoundrel as well, making him the perfect opponent for her. It was rumored that Bishop had several illegitimate children throughout the state of Michigan, and a few in Wisconsin and Ohio. Every now and then, a person would appear out of the blue with papers and blood tests to prove kinship to him, and not only would the mother of the child feast on a substantial financial banquet, the entire community would take note, particularly JoAnne. She knew that sooner or later, Bishop would agree to her price. She wanted the Harbor Resort more than he wanted the one hundred acres she owned that surrounded it. She intended to buy his one-hundred acres for her property portfolio sometime within two years: by December of nineteen-ninety-four.

When Russ thought about the thousands of acres of land his parents owned, it made him furious that JoAnne also wanted his grandfather's property, which consisted of ten acres and a small cottage.

But it was prime property on Grand Lake and worth more than Russ could imagine. He wanted the land and cottage because he had always loved it *and* his grandfather. JoAnne wanted the property solely for profit.

Russ didn't know she had control of the land before she found out he was having an affair. Once the details of his indiscretions were confirmed, she refused to sign the property over to him, even though she had promised her father before he died she would manage the property and the sixty thousand dollars for Russ until he decided what he wanted to do with his life.

Russ knew his grandfather hid a third copy of the will. Grandfather told him he would hide it in a strongbox with other important documents. Now all Russ had to do was find the strongbox.

It was also odd that Andrea left town years ago without an explanation. She had been living with a man named Edwin Mayfield, an illiterate type who JoAnne highly disapproved of. Andrea ended up leaving Grand Lake with Mayfield. Russ always wondered if JoAnne had anything to do with their departure. Maybe she paid them to relocate. Andrea was now in her twenties—twenty-eight, Russ speculated. She was six years younger than Russ, and Russ was thirty-four.

He flicked the cigarette out the window into a shallow mud puddle. He pulled into the long driveway, a driveway he would soon have to plow in order to keep it open, so Olivia could stand by the gate and wait for the school bus. Off she would go to Alpena, a thirty-minute drive to kindergarten.

Their house was a winterized two-story log structure with a front porch that stretched the entire length facing Grand Lake. Russ loved this house almost as much as he loved Grandfather's cottage; both were tucked back among the cedar and birch trees.

If he had a choice, he would live like a hermit, far into the woods. But Libby insisted on living near people; Libby wanted Olivia to make friends and have a social life. They compromised by choosing a home eight miles away from the community, but close enough to the Birch Hill Lodge, the harbor, the church, the grocery store, and if need be, they could drive into Rogers City or Alpena to shop.

He parked to the left of the boathouse. Libby had parked her minivan too close to the path. She always rushed to get home from wherever she happened to be in time to meet the school bus, and because she was usually late, she parked anywhere in the yard that suited her.

All the lights were on inside the house, which irritated Russ even more. They were wasting electricity due to her running late. The thought of wasting electricity prompted him to worry about having *no* electricity if JoAnne got her way and ruined him—if the *ghost* in the dining room of the Lodge had been right by claiming the quarry was laying off workers.

It was a good thing the stars were shining. The moon was almost full, casting golden rays to light up the ground. Nonetheless, he almost tripped over a toy rake. Too much clutter in the yard. Again, he blamed Libby.

He knew something was up as soon as he opened the door and found Beverly Weyman sitting at the kitchen table. She was spooning sugar into a coffee mug. "Russ," she said, "we were about to call the sheriff."

In slow motion, she lifted the mug to her lips and sipped. "Where's Libby?" Russ asked. He was used to Libby greeting him at the door.

"Upstairs, putting Olivia to bed." There was another sip of coffee, and this time, her long eyelashes stayed downcast. "She'll be right back."

Beverly was tall. Five-eight, as opposed to Libby, who was five-four. Her hair was professionally highlighted, even Russ could tell. Blonde streaks blended with brown curls down to her shoulders, framing the sides of her face. She wore expensive clothes, coordinated colors and textures. Tonight, she wore designer jeans, a burnt-orange sweater, tan suede jacket, and high-heeled leather boots. Her hands were slender and pearly. The color of her nails matched her ruby earrings.

Russ looked away from her when Libby walked into the room. And because Libby was a woman of conviction, especially when beholding her territory— the kitchen—she offered an impressive contrast to Beverly Weyman.

Beverly might have been a fashion expert with every hair in place, but it was Libby's personality that shined. Unfortunately, tonight it shined with rage. Libby's alabaster skin had somehow stretched into the most determined expression of self-control Russ had ever seen on her, and he had known her for twenty years.

She wore a red flannel shirt and blue jeans that were not tight like Beverly's but shaped her hips well enough, and her hair, that thick auburn hair, was pulled behind her head and clamped in place with a black cloth band.

Her face enchanted him, no matter the time of day or night. Her arched eyebrows, flashing green eyes, and red heart-shaped mouth told him she was more than just frustrated.

She was on edge. About something, or someone.

And she had the ability to light up a room or cast a shadow over everything—as she was doing now. When her small hands fell to her hips, she said, "You promised you'd be home in time for dinner! Did you forget Beverly and Scott were coming tonight?"

"Overtime at work," he mumbled, one syllable at a time. "I need the overtime," he added, thinking *that* should have been common knowledge.

"We had chicken alfredo," she said, as if the menu itself defined the last of her patience. "I guess I could warm up some for you." She turned to glare at him, a reaction so out of character for her in front of company, he almost tipped backwards.

"Scott will be back to get me any minute now," added Beverly. She sipped and looked down at the red-and-white checkered tablecloth. "Any minute," she repeated.

Scott was three years older than Libby. Or was it five? Russ couldn't remember. "He went on an errand?" Russ asked, wondering if he went to buy Beverly more cigarettes.

"Yes," Beverly said. "And I wish he'd hurry up. He wants to drive past some houses that are for sale. I guess I'll have to check out the one he has his eye on."

"You're thinking of moving?" Libby asked, ignoring Russ. "But I love your house by the bay."

"Scott thinks we need a bigger house," she said. "He wants to move closer to Alpena. He says the winters are too hard out here with Grand Lake on one side and Lake Huron on the other."

Libby pondered the long winters. "That's true," she said, imagining thick blankets and huge heating bills. "Winter *is* coming."

She looked at Russ, as if shocked by his presence. "You might want to take off your coat and come to the table!"

To him it sounded like, *Why are you standing there naked, you fool?* He glanced downward to be sure he had clothes on. "I can't stand around in my own kitchen?" he asked her. "Maybe I'm too froze to move!"

"You mean frozen," Libby corrected, rolling her green eyes upward as if she could faint over his grammatical flaw. Next, her eyes scanned the room evenly and completely. "And if you're so *frozen*, why are you dripping all over my floor?"

Like a child obeying authority, he took off his coat and draped it over the back of a chair. For now, he had to concentrate on avoiding Beverly's eyes. He had known Scott since grade school. Libby, Scott, Russ, and Jerry McPherson had all attended the same schools in Rogers City. They had been friends for years, but Beverly didn't come into the picture until later. To this day, Russ wasn't sure where Scott found her. More than likely, he met her when he moved to Ann Arbor to attend college. Jerry went to Michigan State too. That was it. They met Beverly when Scott was in his second year of college. Scott sold furniture throughout Michigan and the surrounding states. Scott and his fancy business degree, and yet he went around selling cheap, low-grade furniture to hospitals and hotels.

Beverly was educated in medical research and had acquired a technician's degree, but the past two years she worked at a gift shop in Alpena. So much for ambition.

He watched Libby fix him a plate. Chicken alfredo tonight, with the steam rising and the powerful scent of garlic drifting through the house. Libby put down the plate before him with a lift of her chin that warned, *You had better eat this, by God, or I'll dump it over your head.*

Russ picked up a fork and stirred the mound of rubbery noodles. "So," he said. "Beverly, you look tired. Let's hope Scott hurries back." He noticed her gold bracelet was punctuated with small diamonds. He wondered how much it had cost.

"Is it hot in here?" he then asked both women. "Must be contagious. JoAnne had all the fireplaces going full-blast at the Lodge tonight. Maybe a storm is on the way."

A big storm of trouble.

"Speaking of the Lodge," Libby interjected, "Olivia's getting off the bus there tomorrow after school. JoAnne's going to watch her for me. Beverly and I are going shopping."

"For how long?" he asked. "I mean, this won't become a habit, will it?"

"For the *whole* afternoon, Russ. I have a right to get out with a friend now and then!"

"Jesus," he said. "No one said you didn't." He looked at Beverly, who was inspecting her manicured fingernails.

He decided the idea of JoAnne spending time with Olivia was too dangerous, a lot like Aaron's habits had been. Furthermore, Libby seemed to care less that he was late because of JoAnne.

"JoAnne wanted to ask me about Jerry McPherson," he said. "He moved, so she wanted his new phone number. She wanted me to fix one of the heating vents in the dining room too."

His explanation made Libby even angrier. "JoAnne would already have his phone number, Russ. He's *her* attorney, and he has been for years. I don't buy that one. Want to try another?" The way she had said "that one" annoyed him.

The way she stood with one hand pressed to her hip annoyed him even more.

There was a crunching of gravel coming from the path outside; it had to be Scott. He had a loud voice, a voice that entered the kitchen before his body did. "Sorry I took so long," he said. He always appeared to be happy-go-lucky, as if nothing could possibly hurt him, ever. He said, "Can you believe everyone in town was out buying gas tonight?"

"That's about eight people," said Russ. "Eight or maybe nine people in all of Presque Isle County."

"Sit down and have a cup of coffee," Libby told Scott, ignoring Russ's sarcasm. "It's cold outside. Take a break."

"No, we'd better git going." Scott would always say "git" to poke fun at the locals, Russ in particular. He turned to Russ. "As soon as you finish, brother, I need you to walk me out to the car. I need your opinion on something mechanical."

Russ hated it when Scott called him *brother*. He wanted to point out that they were *not* brothers, that he—Scott—was Libby's brother, and that's where it ended. "Why don't you talk to a mechanic *if* you need a mechanic," he said. He stabbed at the mushy noodles again. "Besides, I'm still eating."

Scott put his palms flat against the table; he was so close to Russ's face, Russ felt the chill of the night air emit from his gray overcoat. "I need your opinion *now*," he said in a scratchy voice. "*Now*," he repeated, his breath singed with whiskey.

When Libby went for the coffee pot, Russ stood up; he turned to Scott but said to Libby, "Get your brother away from me!"

"Can't you just *help* him?" Libby said, completely unnerved. "What *is* your problem?"

Russ reached for his coat, pulled his cap from the left pocket, and slapped it onto his head. He tipped his hat to Libby and followed behind Scott's fading back, the ironed trousers, the shiny shoes, and the buzzed-off head of hair.

When they hit the cold air, Russ walked slowly, yet Scott was already up the path, standing next to his red Impala. He opened the door, slid inside, and waited for Russ to do the same.

"What exactly is this mechanical problem?" Russ asked him, looking the vehicle over.

"Get in."

Russ cupped a hand to his ear. "What?"

"I said go around to the other side and *get in*. Do it!"

Russ walked around to the passenger's side, opened the door, and slid into the seat. Scott held a small leather case in his hand. He unzipped the case and pulled out a gun. Russ was a collector of firearms and knew a .38 Special when he saw one.

"I bought this the other day," Scott said, "for Beverly's protection at the house."

Scott turned the revolver over in his hands. He touched it carefully and provocatively. He held it sideways and fingered the safety. "I heard a rumor about you," he said. "A rumor I don't like."

"Is *that* right?" Russ asked.

"I heard you're having an affair," Scott said matter-of-factly. "Heard it from four people, so far."

"That's news to me."

"Here's more news for you: if you don't end it, *I will.*"

"Sounds like a threat," Russ said, feeling his way around the subject like testing the waters of JoAnne's wrath. "I don't like threats. Maybe you should mind your own fucking business."

Scott put the gun back inside the case. "Libby *is* my business," he said. "You hurt her, you deal with me."

Russ pushed open the door and stepped into the cold night. He understood all too well. Scott Weyman had threatened him with a gun, and somehow Russ knew he would use it if he had to protect Libby.

Seems everyone, including his own mother, made it their mission to protect Libby.

Chapter 3

Russ walked back into the house with his head held high. Before he even saw her standing at the counter, Libby asked, "Where's Scott?"

"Outside, waiting for Beverly." Russ knew it was imperative to get Beverly Weyman out of his house. He watched her prepare to leave. He even helped her out of the chair to send her on her way. She picked up her purse and buttoned her jacket. He knew she wanted to ask him if anything was wrong, but instead of saying something, he held the door open for her and saluted as she walked by.

Libby stayed at the counter as if chained there. The counter, the entire kitchen, in fact, seemed to be her permanent post. She was already rinsing off dishes and stacking them in the draining rack. There were tiny lines near her mouth that Russ had never noticed before. She paused rinsing and put a soapy hand to her brow. A second after the door closed behind Beverly, she turned to look at him.

She knew.

There was a vision of Beverly in his mind at the same time he looked at Libby. Beverly so graceful. At first glance, she reminded Russ of a timid doe. But

Beverly disappeared down the pebbled path, driving off into the night…with Scott. To clear his mind of her, he concentrated on the kitchen—the knotty pine walls, the yellow and red curtains, the wife at the counter. He went back to the table and sat down. He watched Libby work, knowing from watching her do the dishes many times before that she was on the last phase of the task, folding up the dish towel and putting it across the draining board.

"What did JoAnne *really* want?" Libby asked.

"I told you. The ceiling fan in her bedroom."

"Oh, I thought you said the heating vents," she said.

"That too. And she wanted Jerry McPherson's phone number."

Libby pulled at the black band and re-tied her auburn hair near the nape of her neck. It was warm inside the kitchen, and she wiped her chin with her sleeve. It was a gesture he had never seen her do before. She was the type to seek out a tissue, foremost. "I see," was all she said.

To change the subject, he asked about Olivia. Olivia was usually the main and sometimes only topic between them. The words JoAnne spat at him earlier that night echoed now. Something about never seeing Olivia again. He would kill anyone who tried to stop him.

Libby leaned against the stove and crossed her arms. Her eyes, listless because of the long day, were incredibly green. He thought of emeralds and wished he could give her a box full. "Is there something you want to tell me?" she asked. "Anything I should know before I hear it from someone else?"

"What do you mean?" he asked.

"I know all about it, Russ." She took great care with shaping her words. "In fact, I've known about it for some time. The layoffs. Are you okay?"

He adjusted his cap, which was still on his head but tipped at an angle. "Sure, I'm fine. Haven't heard my name come up yet."

"Well, let's just hope your job is secure for now," she said. She smiled at him and turned toward the hallway. "Are you coming to bed?"

"In a bit," he said, trying to steady his voice.

Was he deaf? Or, maybe he hadn't heard her right? Her footsteps tapped all the way up the stairs and to the left above him—tap, tap—into Olivia's room to make sure she was covered up. He needed a drink. Yes, a drink; and he would make it a stiff one. He went to the cupboard and searched, but there was no liquor. He went into his study, the small room off the kitchen, where he knew he would find a bottle. It was cold inside the office, but they always closed the office vents when it was time to turn the furnace on in the fall. That goddamned JoAnne. She's probably the one who told Scott.

He sat down at the desk that used to be his grandfather's, opened the top left drawer, and found a bottle of Scotch. He dialed Jerry McPherson's phone number. He waited while the line rang six times. "Jerry? It's me, Russ. *What?* Why are you in bed this early?" He glanced at his watch. "It's only ten-thirty. Listen, I got to talk to you tomorrow, maybe tomorrow night after work. No, I'll come to your place. JoAnne's messing with me. I don't know. Something strange is going on. Yeah, I know you're her attorney. Thanks for the warning!" He took a quick drink while listening to Jerry drone on and on about lawyer-client ethics. "Are you finished?" he said in response to Jerry's rambling speech. "Why are you representing her anyway? *To hell* with the money! Oh yeah, sure, I'll keep my voice down!" But, in fact, he knew Jerry was right. He must compose himself. His voice could carry up the vents to Libby, who might be cozy in bed but still able to hear every word he said.

Russ took another sip. "Listen. You tell her to get another attorney. I need you. She's threatening me about my grandfather's estate again. What? I want what he left to me! You said before that you'd help me. What kind of friend are you anyway? No, I'm not drunk. But *I am* having a drink. Don't tell me what to do. JoAnne called me to her office tonight for a chat. Sure, she called me at work, do you believe it? Like I can just hop off the forklift any old time to take a call from Mommy. I know! She's nuts! Anyway, I go there, and she tells me she knows all about an affair she thinks I'm having. No, goddamm it! You think I'm *that* stupid? Anyway, she claims to have proof, and she says she'll tell Libby and cut me out of the inheritance. Tells me I can't have Grandfather's property and trust." He started to knead his forehead, so foreboding and tangled became his thoughts. He lowered his voice, first from fear that Libby might hear him, and then because it was inducing a migraine.

He said much quieter, "Okay, I'll be there tomorrow evening." He hung up.

Jerry could always calm him down. Jerry would help him, he knew. But Jerry didn't appreciate theatrics from his clients; he expected center-stage for himself.

Russ turned off the yard light and the kitchen lights and climbed the stairs two at a time. He knew Libby had already checked on Olivia, but he had to look in on her as well. When he entered her bedroom, he found what he had always thought a childhood should be: calm and peaceful, stuffed animals, *sweet, gentle dreams.*

Russ touched his daughter's dark-brown hair. She breathed so softly he had to bend down to make sure she was alive. Her small body, wrapped in the quilt Libby made for her a year ago, looked like a doll's. Or an angel's. He knew if he tried to move her, she would wake up. He wouldn't want her startled by his ranting and raving. *The way my parents used to do almost every night of my childhood.*

As he turned to leave, he felt something heavy at his boot and knew right away it was the black Labrador, Pat. He reached down to scratch behind Pat's soft ears; he could see her shadow against the dim glow of the night-light and hear her heavy tail thump a greeting against the wooden floor.

He walked out of Olivia's bedroom and turned left down the hallway toward the master bedroom he shared with Libby. They had lived in this house for most of their marriage—they had Olivia for five of those years, and Pat was getting up in years. Pat was eight. She was

Libby's dog and part of the package when Russ married her.

He walked into the bedroom. The back-up electric furnace—the one they used along with the wood stove—kicked on to the soothing murmur they had grown accustomed to throughout the long winter months; it lulled them to sleep at night.

Libby was in bed with her back to him. She usually started out facing the wall by the bathroom. Her thin body beneath the covers moved up and down with her breathing, but Russ knew she wasn't asleep. He sat down on the edge of the bed and pulled off his boots. Libby wanted him to take his boots off at the door, which was sensible enough, but he always forgot. Tonight, in particular, he hoped he hadn't tracked all over the house. After all, if he knew one thing about Libby, it was that she was a meticulous housekeeper. She didn't like messes, and she detested mud.

He took off his shirt and tossed it into a corner. He couldn't remember the concept of a laundry basket. Off went the clothes, thrown to the floor and scattered around, every time. He wanted to take a shower but decided to wait until morning. He was too tired to walk to the bathroom, much less get wet, lather, dry off. Just too tired. And there was a strong possibility he might drown beneath the steady stream of running water anyway, and then there would be no one to provide for Libby and Olivia and Pat.

He fell backward onto the bed, wearing only his briefs. The bedside lamp cast dim shadows throughout the room—a woman's bedroom, decorated Libby's way with beige and peach-colored designs on the wallpaper, tan and orange lamp shades; and light-peach carpeting, not at all what he would have chosen. He liked dark colors and rustic tones. He preferred simple and plain and comfortable. *But this is what Libby had wanted.*

What Libby wanted now was to talk. He could tell by the way she caressed his arm. She moved her fingers up and down his wrist. "Russ?"

He would have laughed any other time, but tonight, he was too tired. She said his name again. "Russ, I went back to the doctor, but he said the same thing as before."

He repeated, "Same thing." He drifted away from her, exhaustion pulling him down until he could barely hear her. He touched her flannel nightgown, wanted it off but had no energy. She said, "I can't have any more children."

The same thing the doctor told them months earlier. The same thing two other specialists told them. No more children. And there had been numerous, costly tests to prove it. Russ recognized Libby's receding voice, as if they were on the opposite sides of a mountain. Like all the other times she had said it with a sad voice, he stroked her soft hand and said without meaning it, "Sorry, honey. We'll adopt if you want."

He was on the verge of sleep, yet he knew exactly what to say to her. She rolled closer, put her arms around him, and told him she would love him always no matter what happened. "Whatever you want," he said. "I love you too."

And then the nightmares came.

Chapter 4

Libby woke up twice during the night because of Russ's nightmares. He kicked the covers off, muttering that something horrible had happened to his grandfather. He thrashed from side to side. He yelled for Olivia.

By morning, the sheets were damp with sweat, and Libby awoke to the sound of running water in the shower. She listened to him step out of the shower stall, humming, banging things around as if to accent the mystery of himself.

He ended the commotion by dropping something on the floor. Maybe his shaving kit. More than likely, he knocked her hair dryer off the counter again.

She tried to focus her surroundings. She was exhausted from the nightmare-ordeal and had trouble getting out of bed. But she had to get up to fix breakfast and wake Olivia up for kindergarten.

Russ came out of the bathroom wrapped in a light-blue towel. He pulled a comb through his wet, wavy hair. Behind him, the steam lifted into a circle.

"Stay in bed," he said, walking toward her. He reached for her, but she was already out from under the covers.

"I have to wake up Olivia," she said. In truth, she didn't want him to touch her.

He had changed a lot over the past year and a half. He seemed distant, lazy with routine and speech. There was a profound change about him in appearance as well, and she had several theories in mind.

She pulled on a terrycloth pink and green robe, tied it, and brushed her waist-length auburn hair before putting it up with barrettes. She watched Russ sit down on the edge of the bed, still combing his wet hair. He was angry over her refusal to stay in bed, but he knew her well. If she said no, she meant it, and no amount of sweet-talk would change her mind.

"You had those nightmares again last night," she said, putting her brush down on the antique oak dressing table—an heirloom from her mother.

"Maybe because of that movie we saw the other night." He was always making excuses; the nightmares were caused by a movie or a television show. "It was a violent one."

"I wish you'd tell me about them," she said. "You weren't in the war. I could understand this if you were. Did something terrible happen to you when you were a child?"

As the only son, he was exempt from going to war, but perhaps he had a war of his own. His false innocence was beginning to annoy her. She knew something was going on with him, but she couldn't prove or define what it might be. She had a feeling he found another woman, that he had changed for another woman. Although, maybe not, he had just now wanted *her*.

She knew she should forget about fixing breakfast; she should forget about finding Pat to let her outside; and she should forget about waking her daughter up so early for school. She should get back in bed and make him happy if she wanted to keep him in her life.

But she was too tired, and she didn't care about making him happy anymore. The nightmares or dreams, or whatever she should call the previous night's disturbance, had been startling, although predictable.

"Any clean clothes?" he asked. "Did you do laundry yesterday?"

She went to the closet to get another set of work clothes. "Remember," she said, "I'll be spending the day with Beverly. Your mom's taking care of Olivia."

Russ threw the comb down on the bed, unwrapped himself, and put on his underwear. He glanced over at her, as if to give her one more chance to climb back into bed, one more opportunity to start her day out right.

He stood up to pull on his jeans. He was gradually changing in phases and segments, and at other times suddenly, right before her eyes. This morning he looked more rugged and unkempt than ever, even though he'd just taken a shower. He never shaved anymore, she noticed. He used to keep himself clean and well-groomed, but not lately. It was as if he were trying out a new identity. For another woman.

As he buttoned the cotton shirt, he smiled at her. "Tonight," he promised. "I'll get you tonight."

"Please come home on time," she said.

"I'll try. I always do." Then he reminded her, "I have to go see Jerry after work. I need to ask him some questions about Grandfather's property."

"I'm going to the kitchen." On her last word, *kitchen*, she turned toward the hallway; Pat was right there and followed her. She was tired of hearing about Grandfather's land. Grandfather this and Grandfather that. The copy of the coveted third will.

Inside the kitchen, she made coffee and let Pat outside. She had a habit of looking out the window above the sink to make sure Pat was still in the yard. The sun was separating through the cedar trees, and she could see Pat's shadowed shape filter in and out of view.

She worried Pat might wander out to the road. The traffic went by too fast, despite the *Slow Children* sign the county put in near the gate. There were always trucks speeding past to and from the limestone quarry in Rogers City and the opposite direction toward Alpena; most of them ignored the speed limits and signs.

She concentrated on fixing oatmeal for Olivia and Russ's coffee, which she would pour into a large travel mug. He liked lots of cream and sugar. She stirred the coffee, thinking about the day ahead.

There was a screech of tires on the road beyond the fence, causing her to jump and spill some of the coffee. She put a hand over her chest. Her legs shook, but she managed to get to the screen door. She whistled for Pat and waited. She heard car motors idling up on the road and a deep voice and car doors slamming shut. Around the corner of the house came Pat, wagging her tail. She'd been down by the lake, not up on the road. "Pat!"

Libby said, holding the door open for her. "Get in here! My god, don't do that again!"

Pat trotted past Libby and headed for her dishes on the floor by the stove; after taking a drink, she left for the living room just as Russ came into the kitchen. He announced solemnly, "I'm running late. Because of your damned chicken alfredo!"

He was so loud, so disruptive of the quiet morning, Libby simply shook her head. Finally, she said, "My alfredo? Last night you said you liked it!"

"That was before the nightmares and before I was on the crapper forever. It's the food that makes me have bad dreams and makes me sick!"

"I knew you hated my cooking," Libby said accusingly. Her luminous eyes narrowed. "Why can't you stop lying and just say what's on your mind?"

He turned from the door to look at her. "Fix something normal from now on—cheeseburgers or sandwiches. Something you can manage without ruining it or adding strange ingredients. This isn't the goddamned Grand Hotel, you know!"

Libby was astonished at his outburst, that he considered her cooking detrimental to his health. Russ acting superior? Suggesting sandwiches? Maybe. But insulting her was a different matter.

Then again, what if Beverly had been up half the night too, sick to her stomach? Libby went over the ingredients in her mind. Did she use too much garlic or oregano? Was the chicken tainted?

Russ grabbed his jacket from across the chair where Libby had neatly folded it, and said, "I'll see you later!"

He pointed a finger in a final warning. "Remember what I said. Cheeseburgers!"

Libby followed him to the door. Her voice trailed after him as he walked down the path. "You asshole! Cook your own dinner from now on! And hey, if you *do* go to Jerry's, what time will you be home?"

"When you see me, that's when," he said over his shoulder. "I can't give you an exact time. You should know that by now!"

As an afterthought, he blew her a good-bye kiss, but her response to the kiss was a slammed door, even though she knew he didn't hear it.

• • •

After Olivia was safe on the school bus—in her usual good mood because she loved kindergarten—Libby had another cup of coffee. She let out Pat one more time, went upstairs to get dressed, did the dishes, and drove off toward Hambert's restaurant.

Hambert's was JoAnne's breakfast and lunch competition and Libby knew she was flirting with danger by taking her business to JoAnne's rival. It was a mystery to Libby anyway, this problem of Hambert's. After all, they were a mom-and-pop establishment, primarily a net for the hunters or an occasional lost tourist passing through the area.

If JoAnne were smart she would worry about the popular restaurant and lounge up at the Harbor Resort. She would worry about Thomas Bishop, not old Mr. Hambert with the large port stain near his nose.

The Birch Hill Lodge served excellent coffee, freshly ground at that, and people traveled for miles to sample the exquisite pasties, pastries, carrot cake, spaghetti, baked lake trout, northern pike, and even more complicated efforts such as prime rib with special sauces or shrimp selections or anything flame-broiled.

But Hambert's made the best burgers.

Libby parked the minivan to the left of the stone walls and wooden doors of the restaurant and scanned the parking lot, only to discover that there was no sign of Beverly's Ford Ranger. She turned off the engine and stepped out of the van. There was a bite to the air, more persistent than usual. The dark skies and shaking aspen leaves meant winter was coming.

She pulled her jacket down past her waist. She walked inside Hambert's, directly to the table she and Beverly considered the best in the house—the small, square one by the back window.

Here they could observe the customers coming and going. If there was gossip to be had, they would have it. Not only that, but the view of cedars and white birch against the deep blue sky was mesmerizing from this particular window. Even today with the wind bouncing autumn leaves off the pavement and the sky turning from purple to black, she felt calm and comforted.

Just as she was about to get up and go to the phone to find out if Beverly had left her house, Beverly appeared. She walked in, noticeable as always, in her corduroy jacket, silk vest beneath, cream-colored blouse, designer blue jeans, and leather high-heeled boots clicking against the wooden floor. All heads would have turned if there were any to turn. The breakfast rush was over, and Hambert's was vacant except for Libby and Beverly and one of the waitresses sitting at the counter near the cash register sipping tea.

Beverly was always wearing something totally unsuitable. She could have just worn old jeans and a sweatshirt on an occasion like this. And a simple jacket or sweater. It's always leather, diamonds or emeralds, the best of everything. She was always trying to impress people, even if there was no one around to impress. Libby also noticed that Hambert was rushing toward them with the coffee pot—now that the ever-so-perfect Beverly Weyman had arrived. Russ thought she was showy and arrogant. She remembered feeling relieved by his answer when she asked him what he thought of women like Beverly. He would never be attracted to all that makeup, he said. Too much eyeliner and eye shadow. Too much everything.

Today she was wearing far too much lipstick. It was purple. Her perfume was too strong too. Old lady is what Russ had once called her scent.

"Hi, Beverly. You look great. New perfume?"

"You like it?" Beverly's smile was forced, Libby could tell.

Perhaps Mr. Hambert would fall at her hideously clad feet, which were much too large for a woman.

Mr. Hambert came up to the table, pouring Beverly a cup of coffee first, naturally. "How are you ladies today?" he wanted to know. His moustache trembled while his eyes moved up and down Beverly's body.

"Cream, please," said Beverly. She shooed him off to get it. "And more sugar packets," she yelled after him.

Beverly folded herself into the booth like a piece of satin. She withdrew a compact mirror from her big leather bag and examined her face. She pursed her lips, checked her teeth, and poked at her stiff hair with two pointed fingertips. "What's new with you?" she asked Libby, trying to sound like she cared.

"Not much since I saw you last night," Libby said, waiting for Hambert to return with more sugar packets. After Hambert put down a small bowl of sugar packets and was out of sight, she added, "I found out from the doctor that I can't have any more children, and I think Russ it having an affair. That's all."

Beverly dropped the compact mirror into her purse. "Oh," she said quietly. "Are you sure?"

"You mean about the part where I can't have any more children?"

"I'm sorry, Libby. I know how much you wanted another baby."

"Enough tests tell me I can't," Libby said, her voice composed. "No more children." She wondered why Beverly wouldn't look her in the eye. Could be Beverly's physical image was more important—her profile, her hair, her lips—even though the only eyes to see her other than Hambert's were those of the mounted deer heads.

Libby counted twenty mounted deer heads with large racks. Those ears, she knew, heard a lot—and not only conversations, but also thoughts. Those ears, although dead, took it all in, and the glass eyes saw *everything*.

A chill went up her spine. She tried to keep her own eyes off the deers' frozen faces. "Russ isn't himself," she added. "Something's wrong. I think it has to do with JoAnne."

"I wouldn't worry about it," Beverly said, appearing bored; she was preoccupied with reapplying her lipstick. "He's probably just tired."

When Hambert came back to the table, Beverly gave him her order: tuna on rye, iced tea. Libby ordered a chef salad and water.

Libby wasn't even hungry. This was just another way of passing time in the woods. After lunch, they would go to Alpena and shop—another method of passing time. She should be home baking or scrubbing or sewing up a new quilt. She should be out looking for evidence of Russ's affair.

Suddenly, Beverly's makeup and compact were put away into her leather bag, which was positioned in the corner of the booth near her curved hip. She touched her bottom lip with a red paper napkin. "I didn't think I'd be able to go on after my baby died," she said. "I wanted to die too. I still do."

Libby touched her arm, which had trembled slightly, but in the next second, Beverly lit a long cigarette. Hambert's had banned smoking two years prior, but Libby knew he wouldn't say anything to Beverly. He was another one of her admirers. He had disappeared anyway, off to the kitchen to oversee the preparation of her sandwich. Perhaps he would fix it himself.

Libby said, "I'm so sorry. I didn't mean to make you think about that. You asked me a few days ago to let you know the test results. So that's it: no more children. I guess I'll just have to accept it."

Beverly stared. It appeared she was looking up and over at an enormous twelve-point buck on the wall. Beverly shifted her sad gaze, and when her long eyelashes lowered to the tabletop, Libby noticed tears.

No one ever saw the baby. They claimed Beverly went into a deep depression and there was only a memorial service for the child—two months old—at the Grand Lake Chapel. The casket was closed. No one ever saw the baby dead, not even Scott, the child's father, though she wondered about that too. Scott had once told Libby that he couldn't produce children.

Beverly said that the baby died in Standish, that she'd been visiting a close friend there and the baby just stopped breathing, something like a crib death. She told Scott she wanted to bury her at the family plot in Standish, but she brought the body to Grand Lake first. Then for weeks afterward, she acted so distressed Scott decided not to press her for details.

Libby wanted Scott to talk to the doctor or the undertaker, to at least find out about an autopsy. She insisted Scott have someone of authority and expertise verify the circumstances of the child's death. But Scott didn't push it. He didn't want Beverly to leave him again. They had been fighting after the baby was born—they named her Christine—and the fighting and tension became so bad, Beverly left with the baby to stay at a friend's house. She wouldn't even tell Scott where they had gone. For several weeks, Scott was a wreck, not knowing if his wife and baby were dead or alive. Then Beverly finally contacted him to tell him the baby had died.

Now in the restaurant, Libby studied Beverly's face. For Beverly to actually allow her makeup to moisten and smear, especially since she had just reapplied it, made her wonder if the tears were real.

Perhaps she had been so overwhelmed by her daughter's death that she *did* go over the edge and bury her in Standish without any ceremony.

Even so, no one actually saw the grave.

Libby was reminded of her mother, Susan, who had drowned in Grand Lake. Libby was sixteen at the time, not so young as to need her mother, but the loss was devastating nonetheless. Susan lost her footing walking the break-wall, yet she was an excellent swimmer. Scott had left for college, but Libby still had two years of high school left before she could leave the area. JoAnne Shaw insisted Libby stay with them at the Lodge, so she could finish high school. She shared a room with Russ's younger sister Andrea and got to know Russ quite well during those two years.

JoAnne told her that her father was a drug addict with a track record of crime, and a lifestyle no one cared to investigate. "That loser, Tim Weyman," she had said. "Nothing but a drunk and a drug-addict, taking up space and ruining lives." Libby remembered reading his name in the obituaries. He had been living in Florida for many years after the divorce, but they still wrote a blurb about him in the local paper when he died.

Libby couldn't stop watching Beverly, how she turned off the tears and brought out the compact mirror again. Beverly checked herself over one more time right before the food arrived. She shook her head, placed the red napkin to her lips, and then to her tiny nose. "We all have our problems," she pointed out stoically. Such a strong soldier. Such faith she has.

Libby picked up a fork and stabbed the green lettuce. She watched Beverly unwrap a straw and shove it into the tall glass of ice tea; then Beverly examined the sandwich, still sniffling from her performance remembering the dead child no one saw lying in a casket.

Libby waited for Beverly to look her in the eye. Never mind the mounted glass eyes, Libby's eyes were the ones to worry about.

"If I find out Russ is having an affair," she said, certain she had Beverly's full attention, "and I find out *who* she is, there will be no place on this Earth for her to hide."

Libby tilted her head and smiled as she continued to tear at her salad. She pushed lettuce and tomatoes around the plate without even taking a bite. Finally, she put the fork aside and looked down at the shredded mess.

"I don't blame you," said Beverly, collecting her bag and jacket. "I'm not hungry either. Let's go shopping."

Chapter 5

Russ couldn't concentrate at work. He kept checking the clock and searching the area around the loading dock, expecting an interruption, a summons to the main office.

He remembered enough of the night before to make him light-headed; he remembered something about houses on fire. It was Grandfather's cottage most vividly on fire. The flames ate the cedar logs before he could react.

Then, he dreamed about JoAnne. She sneered at him, laughed at him; she took everything away from him, including Libby and Olivia—and his house. He dreamed Libby and Olivia went to live with JoAnne at the Birch Hill Lodge where they ignored him. His own daughter ignored him because of her.

His mother. JoAnne Shaw.

By three-fifteen in the afternoon, he couldn't stay at work anymore. He kept seeing flashing pictures, segments of the nightmares.

He knew the school bus had dropped Olivia off at the Lodge. He was so worked up about JoAnne talking to Libby when Libby came to pick up Olivia that he decided to fabricate chest pains and asked the foreman if he could leave early. He had time off coming anyway, he explained, and he needed to see his doctor, pronto.

Outside in the parking lot, he could breathe again. He had inhaled the fumes from the factory all morning long, but after his lungs adjusted to the fresh air, he smelled cedar trees on a cool breeze coming from Lake Huron.

He drove ten miles to a carry-out store, where he called Jerry McPherson from a phone booth. Right away, Jerry confessed, "I talked to JoAnne. She didn't go into detail, but you're right. You're in for it!"

At this news, delivered from her attorney so early in the game, Russ's heart skipped several beats. "What did she say about my grandfather's place?" he asked, choking down the wind.

The phone booth was located outside the store, and the wind whipped hard enough to make the trees around him bend. Debris from branches of oak and maple trees, and even needles off the pines, slapped against his face. "She said you're screwed," Jerry divulged, quite simply.

Suddenly, as was Jerry's custom, he became stern with authority. "Now, don't try and make me talk. You know I can't tell you exactly what we discussed."

"That's bullshit!" Russ shouted while the wind grabbed his jacket and attempted to rip it off his back. He didn't know which was worse, Jerry yelling at him over the phone from his office in Alpena, or the wind trying to shred him to pieces. "You're *my* friend, not hers! And you owe *me!*"

"What do you mean by *that?*" Jerry demanded. "What in *the hell* do you mean?"

"You forget that fracas with Bishop's fifteen-year-old daughter?" Russ began. "Fooling around with a minor? I covered for you. If not for me, you would've landed in prison, a goddamned child molester! I have a daughter! I could kill you for what you did!"

"Watch your step!" Jerry warned, his voice inflamed.

Russ could tell by Jerry's change of tone that if he didn't watch his choice of words, he would refuse to help him at all, and without Jerry, Russ would be sunk. Jerry was the type of person who would never cower or back down. And although Russ had covered for him, the case never went to trial due to lack of evidence.

Even so, the memory of the incident hung over their heads like the stench of acid. Like dead carp on the shores of Lake Huron.

Jerry waited a second or two. "You come to my office around five-thirty," he said. "You hear me? Five-thirty!"

"I'm on my way to find Libby and Olivia," said Russ. "They're at the Lodge right now, and God only knows what JoAnne told them!"

"Calm down and *listen* to me. She's not going to tell Libby anything—yet. Just get here by five-thirty. And keep your mouth shut! Don't tell JoAnne or even Libby that you've been meeting with me. Understand?"

Jerry had said "understand" as if Russ were mentally impaired, as if he, Russ Shaw, needed guidance retaining information and keeping his mouth shut. "I understand," he said. "But if she tells Libby, I'm through!"

"You told me you were innocent of JoAnne's allegations," Jerry said, all worked up. "You'd better tell me everything!"

Russ pictured Jerry leaning forward in his black leather chair. He saw Jerry's thin lips contorting and finally pressing together as he waited for an answer. "She's making up stories, and I can't figure out why," Russ said. "I can't figure out *why*, I tell you!"

"Be here at five-thirty," Jerry snapped one last time. He slammed the phone down, cutting Russ off.

Russ touched his ear. For several seconds, he could still hear the slam of the phone vibrate inside his ear canal. He felt dizzy, off balance. He decided to go inside the store to buy a soda.

He knew the girl behind the counter; her name was Evelyn. She was a few years behind him in high school, and she didn't go to college either, as far as he knew. She was apparently content to help her parents run the carryout store on highway twenty-three, fifteen miles north of Grand Lake. She was born a local, and she would stay a local.

Russ said hello and took the change she handed to him. He was going to ask her what was new for the sake of small talk, but the bulletin board caught his eye. There were eight or nine photographs of Grand Lake properties for sale. Besides the usual amateur photos displaying northern pike and walleye tournaments— folks holding up the winning catch—there were six photos of cottages on Grand Lake posted by two of the local realty companies.

Right in the middle and larger than the others, there was a photo of his grandfather's cottage. It was in color and had a clear view of the front porch, which was Russ's favorite part. He shouted, "JoAnne!" and grabbed his hat from his head. "I'll kill her!"

After Evelyn waited on him, she went back to counting inventory. For the most part, her head was a mop of yellow fuzzy hair, her face was covered with freckles, and her eyes were magnified under glasses. She paused, waiting for him to speak again.

"Do you happen to know who put up this picture?" Russ asked. He tried to control his voice, but he ripped the photo from the board and shoved it at her.

"Yes, it was the realtor from Sunrise. What's his name? I think Connolly."

Russ stuffed the photo into his pocket. "You call me if he comes back with more pictures!"

He walked out of the carryout, leaving the can of soda he had bought on the counter. Once inside his truck, he fumbled with the keys, dropped them to the floor by his boot, and picked them up again, sticking the correct key into the ignition. He backed out of the parking lot, narrowly missing a trash dumpster.

He rolled the window down for fresh air. He turned off the highway and onto the road leading to the Birch Hill Lodge. No one passed him. In fact, the road to the Birch Hill Lodge was all his. Her neck between his hands would be his too. He turned left and zipped into the side parking area. There was Libby's minivan, parked near the stairway that led to the back rooms— the same rooms Russ had lived in as a teenager. The rooms JoAnne occupied now.

He looked at his wristwatch—four-fifteen—and thought about turning around but realized he couldn't. He stepped out of his truck into the brisk afternoon air.

As soon as he walked through to the foyer, he knew that the dinner special was lake trout. The entire lodge stunk of fried fish. He heard silverware clicking and the cash register ringing, its door slapping shut.

He heard music coming from the jukebox. It was nothing with get-up-and-go, nothing that Russ or any normal person would like. It was that loud elevator-type flimsy, repetitious tinny violin music JoAnne insisted was soothing.

There was a woman and a man eating at a round table, but they didn't notice him. If they had noticed him, they would have tossed aside their utensils and napkins and hit the floor. His desire to commit murder was so intense, it sparked on him, head to foot.

He stomped down the hallway and straight for the private dining room. He knew JoAnne was there with his wife and daughter. They were probably eating little sandwiches with the crust cut off. He yelled, "JoAnne!" and stood solidly to the floor as if his steel-toed boots were stuck to the carpeting. "I want to talk to you!"

Libby had a wedge of a sandwich to her lips, but she dropped it to the plate. She stared at Russ as if she might recognize him but wasn't sure if he was a close relative or maybe a long lost one.

Olivia jumped out of her chair. "Dad!" she said. She was happy to see him, as usual. She ran to him with her arms stretched out. She wore blue jean overalls with a red shirt beneath it, and her brown hair was pulled back by a ribbon.

Olivia was so necessary for Russ's sanity, he forgot about JoAnne and reached down to pick her up. He held her and kissed her on the top of the head. After clutching her, he put her back down to the carpet.

"It's my *dad*," she informed her mother and grandmother. "He's *here*," she said.

JoAnne stiffened at the table. "We can see that," she said. She heaved until her black sweater formed the illusion of breasts. She wore black pants as well. Her hair, cut even shorter than normal, had a black band stretched across it near the top of her head like a bandage to keep her skull intact.

Libby had apparently regained her memory of him. She straightened in her chair. "Something wrong, honey?" she asked. "Why aren't you at work?"

Russ didn't hear her. He *heard* JoAnne's brain crank behind dark eyes that didn't blink. "I need to talk to you in private," he told her.

"Oh, Russ," she said in a patronizing tone, "can't you see we're in the middle of dinner? Why must you always storm into a room like a half-crazed maniac? Sit down and eat with us."

"Don't yell at my dad!" Olivia's expression, as well as her voice, warned her grandmother to back off. She even pointed a straw at her. "No!"

JoAnne jerked her head in Olivia's direction, about to reprimand her, but she smiled instead. "Isn't that nice," she said to Libby, "a little girl defending her father." Then she looked right at Russ, her lower lip quivering.

There had been a time when the lip quivering would have sent Russ to his knees, but not now, not at the age of thirty-four and in front of his wife and daughter. He said, "We'll talk *now*."

In fact, he wanted to go over to the table and dump her out of the high-backed chair, queen that she was. But he didn't have to. She dropped the beige napkin on the table and pushed back her chair.

She told Libby, "I must go see what this is all about, dear," frowning apologetically, as if it was her duty as his mother to prevent him from causing a scene, a deplorable show of bad manners and impertinence in her place of business, no less.

Libby leaned to the side and helped Olivia cut up a small steak. She said to Russ jokingly, "Remember where you are."

Remembering where he was enraged him all the more. He waited for JoAnne to go first. He followed her bent back down the corridor, to the left, past a busboy, and onward beneath a crystal chandelier. Finally, when they were under the stairway to the door of her office, JoAnne pulled a key out of her sweater pocket and unlocked the door. "After you," she said pleasantly, her bumpy back arched.

Russ went inside the office and flipped on the light. He waited for her to step all the way inside. He certainly didn't trust her to stand behind him. She walked past him and clamped a gnarled hand against the edge of the desk to support herself. He could tell that she was uncomfortable, and he intended to use it to his advantage.

He stood inches from her face. "You *aren't* selling my grandfather's cottage," he said, the accent on *aren't* very specific. "It's mine, and I want the papers!"

JoAnne started to speak, but Russ put his right hand around her throat, feeling the cords beneath her tough, rippled skin. "Don't fuck with me," he warned her.

She smirked, as if implying he wouldn't go through with it. There was too much he had to settle before settling *her*, but she grabbed his hands and pushed him away. "Don't you ever touch me again, you brazen fool," she hissed. "You have no claim to that land. He didn't have time to put it in your name!"

Russ held a fist up to her nose. "I'll make you wish you were dead before this is over," he promised.

His forehead was blazing hot. He was precariously caught in the middle of wanting to beat her to death and needing to hold himself back simply because she had given birth to him. "Give me the goddamn papers!"

"I said *no,* Russell! You leave immediately and don't bother me about it again! If you don't drop it and accept things as they are, I'll tell Libby you're cheating on her. I found out who, and I even know how often. Or did you think I was bluffing when I told you I hired a private detective?" Now it was JoAnne's turn to raise a fist, but she merely shook it at him. "You hear me, you babbling, stupid boy!"

"Tell Libby and you die, old woman! You'll die before some stranger buys my grandfather's land! *You* hear *me?* I know you pushed him down the steps!"

"I'll call the police if you don't leave here now," JoAnne said. He saw her hand grope the air behind her to locate the phone on the desk. "I'll have you arrested for harassment and assault! I'll have you put away! Get out of my office and out of the Lodge! And you've done it now with your threats. When I'm good and ready, Libby will hear all about your sordid activities!"

Russ thought he might be sick over the realization that he hated his mother more than anyone else on Earth, and yet he watched her calmly. He stepped back.

And took a deep breath.

Watching her, as she leaned against the desk with one hand on the phone. "Libby probably knows by now anyway, you imbecile!" she said. "Not everyone's as stupid as you are. But she probably doesn't know who the woman is. What do you think it would to her if she found out?"

Russ was about to call her bluff and ask her who *she* thought the woman was, but he was stopped by a sharp knock on the door.

It had to be Libby.

He wiped his perspiring forehead off with his sleeve and walked over to the door. He opened it. There she was. Libby, questions clouding her enormous green eyes.

He touched his chest, expecting the worst.

But all she said was, "If you're done, Russ, can we please go home?"

Chapter 6

"What were you and JoAnne yelling about?" Libby asked as she helped Olivia into the van. The wind had picked up considerably and made a struggle out of loading up Olivia's backpack and getting her settled into the front passenger's seat. "I could hear you yelling all the way down the hall."

Russ kissed Olivia goodbye after buckling her seat belt. "Oh, you know," he said, hoping to find words Libby might believe. "She won't give up Grandfather's property. I have to find a way to get it from her. So, I'm going to see Jerry right now."

"She has it for sale?" Libby's eyes sparked, although he knew JoAnne's antics didn't surprise her.

"She's playing me for a fool," Russ said. "If I could find the other copy of my grandfather's will, this whole thing would be settled. There were three copies. She only found two. She doesn't know about the third one. I think Grandfather hid it somewhere in the cottage or outside under some rocks. Who knows? He never got the chance to tell me where. I'm going to go see Jerry," he repeated. "Maybe he can give me some advice on how I can fight her for the property."

Russ could see that Libby wanted to leave. She shifted from foot to foot due to the cold. Her blue corduroy jacket wasn't warm enough for November temperatures. He opened the door for her and waited while she climbed into the van. She turned the key in the ignition and cranked the heater. "Maybe you should find another lawyer," she said in a manner suggesting boredom over the subject of death and wills. "Remember, he *is* JoAnne's attorney."

"I know," said Russ. "I'll think about it."

But he would never consider anyone other than Jerry. JoAnne would have to be the one to find another lawyer.

Russ closed the door and watched Libby back the van out to the road. He waved goodbye to Olivia. He happened to glance over to one of the kitchen windows of the Lodge and saw JoAnne watching them.

• • •

By the time Russ got to Jerry's office, it was only five o'clock. Jerry said to meet him at five-thirty, so Russ wasn't surprised when the secretary—a short, expensively-dressed woman in her fifties—informed him that Jerry was with a client.

The secretary stopped her work on the computer. "Just have a seat, Mr. Shaw," she said. "Mr. McPherson is with his wife."

Russ settled into a faded tan chair, but he couldn't relax. He kept looking around the room expecting spies lurking about—JoAnne's spies, to be exact. He imagined hidden cameras behind bookshelves and curtains.

As he waited, he noticed that Jerry didn't have much imagination when it came to decorating. Jerry was very frugal, especially with aesthetics; this fact was obvious by the bland colors and the cheap tweed and metal furniture.

Russ picked up a magazine but tossed it back to the table. He studied the square clock behind the secretary's desk. Five-fifteen.

A door opened, and Jerry walked in behind the secretary's desk. He was jumpy and mumbled something to her and then blurted, "Get the file on my accounts right away!"

He was in the throes of a fit, and it apparently had to do with his wife. Her name was Leeann … or Leeanna or Leona. Russ wasn't sure. He suspected that they were squabbling over assets—the numerous lucrative assets of Jerry McPherson.

"Someone's here to see you," the secretary told Jerry. Russ couldn't remember *her* name either.

When Jerry looked over at him, eyes weary behind gold-rimmed glasses, Russ nodded a greeting. Jerry adjusted one side of his glasses and appeared to study and study, as if thinking, *Who the hell are you?*

Jerry wore a white shirt with the sleeves rolled up to his elbows. His pants were black and creaseless. When he walked over to Russ, Russ noticed he smelled of strong cologne and minty hairspray.

Jerry always looked flawless and cool, even in stressful situations. He was more clean-cut and meticulous than Scott Weyman, but his brown hair, silver at the temples, was somewhat untidy and appeared to fluff slightly around his forehead. Too much hairspray and sweat. All in the heat of passion over money.

"Leeann and her selfish shit!" Jerry said, his voice low but his words iced. "We're getting a divorce, and she wants blood. Apparently, every last drop!"

Russ imagined his own *blood* sought after, but he didn't have much by way of money and assets to offer, only a house—no cottage or property as of now. He shook his head. "Speaking of selfish shit," he said. "I've got to talk to you about JoAnne."

"I know," Jerry glanced over his shoulder toward his wife with the big ears and even bigger appetite. Or was that the IRS itself lurking behind the flimsy rayon curtains? "Meet me at O'Grady's downtown. I have to calm Leeann down before I can leave here."

"Well, hurry up!" Russ didn't mean to sound rude, but he was unable, at times, to control his temper and had very little patience for delays. Especially setbacks with ex-wives, mothers, and lovers.

He knew he was chauvinistic; he could admit his faults. Could Jerry McPherson do the same? Russ headed for the door just as Jerry stepped back into his office. "I need you too, Jerry!" he pleaded, not caring who heard him. "Just remember that!"

He had no choice but to wait for Jerry at O'Grady's. He waited an entire five minutes before ordering a beer. He sipped and waited another twenty minutes. No Jerry McPherson. While Russ drank, he compared Jerry's life to his own and realized yes Jerry was in for a battle. Jerry had made big money throughout his career as an attorney, and Leeann would want it all, even the shirt off his back. God help him.

Russ was proud of Jerry's accomplishments, and maybe a little jealous. But Jerry had plans to become an attorney ever since middle school and pursued his dream all the way through high school. He won scholarships to college. He continued his education in Ann Arbor and received his degree several years later than planned, yet he had persisted, and Russ admired him for it.

Now Jerry was a successful attorney in Alpena. Why Alpena, though? He could go anywhere he wanted and earn serious money. And furthermore, why make JoAnne one of his clients? Then there was Leeann. Russ couldn't remember how long Jerry had been married to her. In fact, he didn't really know Leeann at all. A couple of years ago, Russ and Libby went out to dinner with Jerry and Leeann, but they didn't hit it off and didn't socialize again even though he and Jerry had been best friends since grade school. Perhaps Jerry didn't want people to get to know her. She seemed very self-absorbed, Russ recalled, always acting like she would rather be someplace else.

She'd be someplace else soon enough.

He had another beer and made the mistake of switching to bourbon. He left the barstool for a booth near the bathroom. Jerry had forgotten him. It seemed to Russ that he was always waiting for something or someone—for the other shoe to drop, for a raise at work, for Libby to return home and to bed and make love to him at night, or in the morning when he wanted her the most.

Now he was waiting for Jerry McPherson, who never once broke his word to Russ. Jerry was a man who knew exactly what he wanted and went after it.

Presently, a tall figure in a long gray coat moved through the tables and straight for Russ. He slid into the booth; there's never any other way to do it but *slide* into a booth. "I told you *not* to drink," Jerry said as he pushed his briefcase down beside him into a corner, along with a stack of manila envelopes. "You never listen. That's why you're always in trouble!"

"Hey now!" Russ said, insulted. He tried to focus Jerry's eyes behind the glasses; he wanted to see beyond the wind-reddened face and the impeccable white teeth. "I've been waiting for over two hours. What'd you expect? I'm a wreck now! See my hand?" He held out his left hand and was annoyed to find it steady.

"You've been waiting an hour, if that," Jerry corrected, sounding superior with intellect.

When the waitress came, he ordered coffee, extra cream. He took off his coat, positioned it behind his back, and leaned forward onto his elbows. His shirtsleeves, which were rolled up at the office, were now buttoned at the wrists.

"I can't tell you much," he said by way of starting the inevitable conversation of JoAnne and her recent maneuvers. He reached into his pocket and brought forth a pack of cigarettes. "Sorry. I have absolutely no pertinent information."

"That's great," said Russ, shaking his head. "And you'd have to bring cigarettes."

"I know; you quit. You'll just have to be strong."

"Smoking a cigarette is the least of my worries," said Russ. He moved his complaints along by speaking soberly. "She won't give me the deed to my grandfather's land. You remember him? JoAnne's dad?" He paused for Jerry to acknowledge the memory with a nod. "Well, he wanted *me* to have it, plus a trust fund. She found the will he wrote the night before he got sick. Thing is, she doesn't know about the third copy. And I can't find it." Here, Russ leaned over the table as if he were about to put his head down. Pass out in despair.

Jerry watched him and smoked, apparently searching for signs of manipulation. "Just calm down," he said. "Keep trying to find the third copy. Find it, and you've got her."

"If she did have it, she'd tell you about it, wouldn't she?" Russ opened his eyes to detect a reaction from Jerry. After all, he was *her* attorney. "Wouldn't she?" he demanded when Jerry looked away, the cigarette smoke fanning around them.

"I don't know. If she knows about it, she's keeping that card close to her chest. This is the first I've heard about a third copy."

"I need to find it," Russ persisted, his voice cracking. "Tell me what I can do from here."

"I'll have to think about it," said Jerry, his forehead pinched in concentration. But Russ knew he was an excellent poker player, an actor-extraordinaire. "Find that copy!"

"You've got to help me! I can't lose that land. It's all I got left of him!"

"Relax, or you're going to have a heart attack." Jerry became visibly unnerved at Russ's coming apart.

He shifted inside the booth. "Order something to eat," he said in a stern voice, "and have some coffee."

"I don't want anything to eat! I want your word that you'll help me!"

"I'll try!" Jerry's voice lifted enough to be heard over the music and commotion, and yet his forte had always been composure: in the court room, in his office.

And anywhere else, public or private.

"I'm working for JoAnne," Jerry said. "She pays me *very* well. If you were an observant person and not so wrapped up in your own problems, you'd understand that I'm separated from my wife, which means I'm trying to protect my bank account right now. It also means I'm lucky to have JoAnne as a client."

"What exactly does she pay you?"

"More than enough."

"What do you think your wife will get?"

"Everything she knows about. I have some hidden accounts. I anticipated this a long time ago. I don't even know why I married her. Guess it was the explosive sex."

"You'd better get yourself a good lawyer," Russ said, trying not to smirk.

"I *am* my own good lawyer." Jerry paused while the waitress put his coffee down in front of him. She also brought a small pitcher of cream. "Bring him some coffee too," he told her.

After the waitress waddled off to get more coffee, Jerry leaned forward. "Leeann has that bastard David Preece as her attorney. You remember him."

"With the high silver hair?" Russ suggested the height of Preece's hair by placing a hand above his head.

"That back-stabbing son of a bitch who tried to nail you to the wall for having at it with Bishop's daughter?"

Jerry winced at Russ's definition. "Preece is back in town, and his first client is my soon-to-be ex-wife."

"You might as well start digging your own grave, pal. And climb on in while you're at it."

"That's what I'm trying to tell you." Jerry spoke so fast he almost ran out of breath. "Thank God that case never got off the ground. I was acquitted due to lack of evidence. But you know him. Or any good attorney for that matter. We'll probably have to relive the entire shitty episode again, one way or another."

"Why would he do that?"

"For bargaining power. What I plan to do is give her what she wants—within reason. She doesn't know what I *have* anyway. Never tell a woman exactly what you have tucked away. Unless you happen to be married to someone like Libby. Well, don't tell someone like Libby either. Tuck it away; squirrel it. Lie. Deceive. First rule, always: cover your own ass."

Russ accepted the delivered coffee; he stirred sugar and cream into the cup, studied the steaming liquid, and took a sip before adding, "I wonder about Libby. She's acting strange lately. A little too mean. I think JoAnne's going to tell her I'm having an affair just to get back at me. JoAnne threatened to take everything I got."

"Listen here," said Jerry. "She's a lot of talk, your mother. Sure, she's got the deed to the land, and she's added more dirt about this *ongoing* affair—" He grabbed Russ's wrist. "It *is* just exaggerated dirt, right? Loosely based conjured-up fabrication?" But Russ sighed. He was puzzled, lost. "Malarkey?" Jerry attempted. Nothing. He tried again: "Pure bullshit is what I'm asking you, Russ!"

"Yes! She's just trying to stir up trouble! I think it has to do with me blurting out that I saw her push my grandfather down the stairs at the Lodge when he was sick. See, he had been staying with us." It was too much for Russ at this point. He was slightly drunk, and he couldn't control his emotions while talking about his grandfather. "I can't...can't," he stammered, "talk about it right now!"

"Did you actually *see her* do it?" Jerry asked, his expression now proving interest in every word Russ said. "Go on!"

"No, but I was staying there. And I *heard* them arguing. I didn't *see* it happen, but I came around the corner and heard him crashing down the stairs. She was standing at the top of the stairs with her hands on her hips. I should have said something then. I should have reported her. After that, he was bed-ridden. She told everyone it was an accident, but I knew better."

"Did she see *you?*"

"No, I hid—like a coward!"

"Okay, calm down," Jerry said again. He pushed the thermal pitcher of coffee closer to Russ. "Have more coffee and just calm down. I'll see what I can do. I'll look into it as soon as possible."

"I'll kill her," Russ vowed, almost crying now thinking about his grandfather, never mind losing Libby and Olivia. "I don't care that you know it either. I'm going to get her, with or without your help!"

"We'll get her the *legal* way," Jerry said. He paused to open the menu and scanned down the page. "First, I'll buy you dinner; you'll eat something. And you'll drink more coffee before I let you drive home."

"Second?"

"Like I said, I'll see what I can do. But you can't say a word, not even to Libby." Jerry loosened his tie and leaned back into the booth. "I got stuff on her that'd turn your hair white as David Preece's," he promised. "I got stuff on her that will cut her to the quick and make her shrivel up to nothing but dust. Steak or salmon?" he asked. "Don't you worry. We're going to fucking burn that witch at the stake."

Chapter 7

Jerry had trouble sleeping. He drank another cup of coffee with Russ at O'Grady's before they left around seven-thirty. Now he couldn't sleep. He went over and over what they had talked about: school, their jobs, the changes in Alpena, JoAnne.

He hoped Russ was sober enough to drive home. He watched Russ back out onto the main road and turn left toward Grand Lake, but for Jerry, it was a thirty-minute drive to Alpena.

He tossed and turned all night long. He couldn't stop thinking about JoAnne, and Russ's allegations against her. Yes, Jerry knew about the property dilemma. JoAnne had mentioned she needed her father's cottage and land for future investments; she was considering selling the entire package for an exorbitant price. But, she had also mentioned to Jerry that she was playing with the idea of giving the property to Russ for his thirty-fifth birthday. Jerry knew Russ's birthday was in March; if only Russ had kept his mouth shut until then.

Jerry had no choice but to confront JoAnne. He would speak with her the following morning before he headed for his office in Alpena. He needed to meet with her anyway. He promised to bring her some photographs she had asked for weeks ago.

Another thing Jerry decided as he stared up at the ceiling was that JoAnne seemed extremely interested in land parcels up by Thomas Bishop's resort. Jerry knew she would want to discuss the prospect of buying more land from Bishop. She had been buying acreage near the harbor for years. To date, she owned approximately four hundred acres of prime lakeshore land that Bishop wanted—most of the land Aaron's family gave to them when he and JoAnne married. Now Bishop wanted it. JoAnne had her eye on the excess plots he hadn't yet acquired; she wanted Bishop out of business, and he wanted *her* to stay within her league: only running the Birch Hill Lodge.

Jerry lived in Alpena, twenty miles south of Grand Lake on US 23. Rather, he lived in the best neighborhood available in Alpena, near the best restaurants on a street lined with old Victorian houses, some so large, they appeared out of place for a small town.

Alpena was located on the shores of Lake Huron, as was Bishop's resort, which was forty miles north of Alpena, past Grand Lake and even the Birch Hill Lodge. Alpena and Traverse City were the two anchor cities of northern Michigan. The largest employer of Alpena was the Medical Center, and next was a cement plant, LaFarge Corporation, second only to the bigger quarry located fifteen miles south of Grand Lake in Rogers City. Alpena could also boast about the successful Besser Company, a manufacturer of concrete blocks.

Naturally Alpena excelled in tourism since it was conveniently located on the shores of the Thunder Bay Portage of Lake Huron. Six miles north was an enormous boat dock, catering to the wealthy yacht club patrons. There were enough well-to-do people in the area to keep Jerry's practice thriving, not to mention to keep contributing adequate economic stimulation for the city of Alpena itself. Nonetheless, Jerry was considering moving out of the area. After the divorce, he might move to a different state altogether. He was thinking New Mexico, where his elderly parents lived, or Arizona, where his sister and family lived. Every late fall and into winter he thought of warmer climates; he even *dreamed* of warmer climates.

But something other than his career kept him in northern Michigan.

He thought about Leeann at his office earlier that afternoon. She was a puzzle and always had been. Jerry was intrigued by mysterious women, certainly, but not *this* mysterious. Leeann was dangerous—a cunning mind with a moderate dose of stupidity. Jerry hoped he could keep her subdued by offering a certain amount of money up front in the settlement.

If she hadn't hired David Preece, Jerry would have been able to dazzle her with a suitable peace offering. Say, five hundred thousand with maybe the house thrown in. But now that Preece was in the picture, Jerry was forced to produce certain documents, prove assets, and deliver bank account statements.

As Jerry explained to Russ that very evening at O'Grady's, he had hidden accounts other than the main savings account Leann knew about. They also had a joint checking account, an account Jerry avoided making deposits in recently for obvious reasons. If Preece would only keep his nose out of things, everyone would walk away from the table happy. And, if Preece planned on giving Jerry any more trouble, he had better brace himself for a war. Jerry would not let Leeann steal him blind, and so, he had to be extra careful when dealing with JoAnne Shaw.

JoAnne had always been generous with her payments and had even signed some property south of Grand Lake over to him as proof of her appreciation. She promised him some stock as well, after they secured more prime land surrounding Thomas Bishop. Incentive was useful, Jerry realized. It helped her mission along.

But now, he was preoccupied with *helping* Russ, and he sensed the tide had turned.

Jerry got up at six o'clock the next morning. He wandered around inside the apartment he had moved into eight months ago after breaking up with Leeann.

The apartment complex was tucked between two of the larger Victorian houses in the prominent section of town; it was also near the park, which made for a lot of traffic and noise in the summer.

When Jerry got up, he looked out the window above the counter in the kitchen. Although it was still dark, he knew it was going to be a bleak, overcast day. The forecast called for snow, and he already knew it would be cold and windy. Lake Huron was known for stirring up windstorms. Its weather could turn on a dime. She could be mild and soothing, and then within hours, she could turn vicious and perilous. Appropriate, he thought, for his present situation—the women, the scandal, the layers of danger.

He knew the Birch Hill Lodge opened at seven o'clock in the morning. JoAnne reminded him often that the breakfast crowd was "perfectly to the limit" every single morning. She had worked hard to build up a clientele. She was popular with the locals, even respected, because it was a well-known fact that she and Aaron started out with a cottage over twenty years ago, and with that, they had created a lucrative business.

The Lodge had become enormous; it was three stories tall, a plush although "rustic" spectacle. Thirty-one bedrooms for guests—eight suites included. All the rooms complete with a sitting area, double beds, television, phone, and private bathrooms.

The first floor began with a spacious entry, all knotty pine within the extended interior of the lobby. There was a cathedral ceiling veering off into four directions. One toward the long, wide stairway with an ornate wooden landing area, and another turned left toward the first floor of bedrooms.

In the other direction, past the lobby, there was a high ceiling—knotty pine again—and several yards down was a spacious sitting room with a stone fireplace almost the entire length of the west wall. Inside the sitting room were a dozen tables for socializing, drinking coffee or cocktails, playing backgammon, chess, cards; there were several computers.

There was a long screened-in porch in the very back of the Lodge, and one smaller screened in porch on the north side. These were summer porches, closed off during the winter months. But the porches were designed for entertainment and visiting purposes, overlooking Lake Esau, located near the back of the Lodge at the very edge of JoAnne's property line; however, it was a public lake and her visitors were able to swim or fish on the shores of Lake Esau, as well as Grand Lake on the other side, across the road.

JoAnne owned boats for recreational purposes—twelve, in fact, the "fleet" she called them—like fishing and water skiing. The boats were anchored against two long, wide docks in the summer and early fall; during the winter, she stored them in three boathouses on the Grand Lake shoreline and in one larger boathouse on the Lake Esau shoreline.

In the back of her eighty-acre property were nine cabins, favored by duck and deer hunters in autumn. Summer travelers, families mostly, chose the cabins because they were cheaper to rent than a room in the Lodge. These cabins ranged in size. There were five two-room cabins and four one-room cabins. Each cabin had bright knotty pine interiors, log tables and chairs, open living rooms and kitchen areas, baths with tubs and showers, and fireplaces; but the cabins were located on the Lake Esau side of the Lodge, twenty-five feet from water's edge. JoAnne called them the "back lodgings."

Both shorelines were well-maintained, sandy and pristine. The cabins were on the left side of the Lodge, and next in line was a tennis court, volleyball court, and horseshoe pits. Past the games area were three storage sheds, side-by-side for yet another necessary fleet—the lawn mowers, riding mowers, a tractor, and various lawn and shoreline equipment. There was also a huge garage nearby for JoAnne's Cadillac, the maids' cars, the cook's, and other employees. All the buildings' exteriors matched the Lodge, of course.

Everyone knew JoAnne, not Aaron, was the shrewd business person of the pair. What the Birch Hill Lodge didn't have, according to her research in striving for the best of the best, she would eventually add.

And yet, there was a shroud of confusion surrounding her personal history. There had always been *something* questionable about her. Jerry wondered now, thanks to Russ's latest information, if it had anything to do with pushing Russ's grandfather down the stairs. Was JoAnne Shaw, deceiving in business, also a murderer?

When Russ told Jerry that piece of news, it was the first he had heard of such an allegation, and he wondered if maybe Russ imagined JoAnne had pushed her father. JoAnne might have been behind him and had tried to reach out to help him. And the third copy of Grandfather's will? Jerry hadn't heard that one before either. JoAnne did mention that there was a copy, but she said she had gone through the old man's things at his cottage and found all the important papers. No third copy. She even confiscated some envelopes of cash—the total of eight thousand dollars—that the old man had hidden in a bookshelf. He was her father. Everything he had saved, borrowed, and invested in should rightly go to her upon his death.

But even the land and cottage he promised to his grandson?

Jerry knew Russ was lying about the details of his affair. Jerry had been helping JoAnne gather evidence on that very *activity*. He had photos. He had been the one to hire the private detective to take photographs for JoAnne, and he knew she hired a woman who worked for her at the Lodge, an ex-cop from Ohio. They had been girlhood friends, and now, the woman—if one could call her a woman, she was so burly and intimidating—was JoAnne's mole while posing as a maid at the Birch Hill Lodge.

Her name was Marilyn Clayton. Jerry frowned at the mere thought of her as he drove toward Grand Lake. He knew she could become a problem for Russ.

He noticed most of the vibrant autumn leaves were stripped from the trees as he drove along the main road through the Grand Lake community. There used to be more cabins lining the lake as well, log cottages owned by out-of-state, summer people. The cottages of yesterday still accented the trail, but they were tucked back behind the cedars and white birch along the road. Some of the cottages were renovated into homes year-round; one was Russ's house, but Jerry wouldn't pass Russ's house this time. It was located a mile past the library and fire station.

Snow pelted against the windshield, and the ground at the sides of the road and the surface of Lotus Pond were dusted in white. Jerry drove up the hill, past the community post office, until ten miles beyond, he came to the Birch Hill Lodge.

The last three years the Birch Hill Lodge was becoming more of a hot spot for tourists and locals, even more so than Bishop's playground for the rich on Lake Huron. Bishop had the big docks at his disposal. Tourists docked at his harbor restaurant and hotel as they passed by on their yachts and sailboats, or they might be in port during their waterway travels. Nonetheless, JoAnne was getting close to Bishop's circle of prestige. Bishop still had prime land she wanted, property that blocked the expansion of her personal estate.

Now that they were well into November, Jerry counted only twenty-two cars parked in the Birch Hill Lodge parking lot. Her profits were beginning to grow in the fall and winter too, but still not as high as in the summer. JoAnne had even hired better cooks to increase profit. Only the very best recruits from New York, and two chefs who had studied in France. Jerry wanted her to hire locally, but she insisted on the best.

Unfortunately, Marilyn Clayton was the first employee Jerry saw when he walked through the enormous glass and log-lined doors of the Lodge. Marilyn was at the cash register. When she finished up with a man paying his bill, she simply turned to look at Jerry.

Jerry nodded. He couldn't stand the sight of her. Was she really a woman? She had breasts. They were large and round, but they bulged and stretched the material of her green uniform, which was a dress of sorts, the hem landing just below her thick knees.

Her hips were square, not curved as a woman's hips should be. Her hair was a conundrum as well—short and blunt, like a hard hat shoved over her skull. Her hair color was a harsh brown, as if dyed with shoe polish. She wore black eye shadow and dark blue eyeliner. He wondered if her eyebrows had been shaved and penciled back on.

He said, "Hello, Marilyn. Is JoAnne around?"

Oddly enough, her tone and words were in sync with her expression of the moment. For now, showing surprise through the V of her two eyebrows, tight and bowed as if picturing Jerry maimed. "She's around somewhere," Marilyn said absently. "Try her office or the kitchen."

"Thanks." *You ugly gargoyle*, he wanted to add.

JoAnne was speaking to five businessmen who were sitting around a rectangular table in the dining room. She poured them coffee; she bestowed her false smile upon them. Brashly-white dentures, he presumed. Yet another woman who wore too much makeup. Although unlike Marilyn, JoAnne was charismatic and sometimes endearing, and she had an incredibly youthful shape for a woman in her late sixties—other than the curved backbone—and Jerry knew that her physical agility was a result of her passion for the outdoors. She had always been an active woman.

More active than any of us knew, he thought, as he pictured her shoving her father down the stairs.

JoAnne wore shades of purple and red today, a step up from the sinister black and gray that dominated her wardrobe. She wore a light-maroon silk blouse, dark-maroon pants, and an even lighter shade of maroon to accentuate the border of her hip-length pink cashmere sweater. She also wore gold earrings with her usual gold chain necklace. Her hair was black and somewhat gray-streaked. Her hair, short as always, was bunched tightly to the back of her head, pinched and smashed against the middle section.

She pulled out of the conversation gracefully when she saw that Jerry was standing approximately two feet behind her. Jerry knew she could tell he was nearby, as if the prospect of business permeated her very soul upon impact.

She told the three-piece-suited men goodbye and pirouetted to the left, starting to move slowly at first, and then picking up speed. She expected Jerry to follow closely at her heels that were covered with black flat shoes and crashed against the carpeting as if wooden, and afterward, clicked upon the hallway all the way to her office beneath the stairway.

So very foreboding, the Lodge. Most effectively haunting was the long winding stairway that gave one the feeling of *never getting to the end.*

"You're late," she bellowed, sounding strangled. "You were supposed to be here by six o'clock. I wanted to talk to you before we opened!"

Jerry immediately felt a migraine coming on. He stammered, "I had a bad night. I had to—" He stopped there. He knew she couldn't care less about his inability to sleep. JoAnne slept four hours per night. She said too much sleep was a waste of time. She was one of those who also said "I'll sleep when I'm dead."

"Do you have the pictures?" she asked, glaring at him while jerking around the room as if expecting an untimely intrusion. "You had better!"

Jerry lifted the briefcase, bringing attention to the pictures he had inside. "Some of them."

"What do you mean, *some?*"

"Several didn't turn out," he sputtered frantically; he felt like he might throw up. What was it about this woman, who could make a grown man quake. She was only as big as a minute, but a mighty minute at that.

She expanded and dominated an entire room.

The fact was that several of the pictures in his possession revealed without a doubt who Russ was having an affair with, but now Jerry wasn't sure if he wanted JoAnne to have them after having met with Russ.

He decided to keep them. JoAnne fell into the chair behind her desk and positioned her glasses to her pointed, powdered nose. She pushed a hand forward, appeared to be impatient with his progression toward her. "Let me have them," she sneered, trying to keep her voice down. "Hurry up. I have a Lodge to run!"

Jerry wanted to say, *This goes at my pace, old woman! I hold the cards, for now.* Then he recalled the money she paid him and produced the folder of photos, the most damaging ones back at his apartment, locked in a safe.

JoAnne examined the photos; she squinted through her bifocals, scowling. "These are crap!" she declared. "I need clear pictures of her face, not her earlobe or the best of her wide ass! Tell Silcott he'd better come up with something I can use, or he can go back to photographing puppies and babies!"

"Fine," said Jerry, his feet aching, his hair vibrating. "I told him you wouldn't be happy with the results."

"Get better pictures," she shouted again and pulled open a desk drawer to search through its contents, "or you're fired!"

Jerry dropped into the chair beside her desk, pressing the briefcase to his legs. He knew to play her cautiously, but even so, he had to ask: "Are you still giving Russ the property for his birthday?"

JoAnne looked at him as if he were demented. "*Give* it to him? Damn you, never!"

"Well, according to Russ, there's a third copy of the will. Did you know that?"

Jerry wasn't sure which side of the fence his conscience would allow, but for now, he decided to tiptoe his way around JoAnne when her dark eyes narrowed, and her cheekbones twitched. "So, find it, dammit! What do I pay you for?"

"Russ is very upset."

"He should be," JoAnne confirmed. "Not only does he lose out on the property, I'm suing him for mismanaging the docks the summer before last. He asked—no, he *begged* me—to run the Grand Lake docks one summer because he needed the extra money to refinance his vehicle and do some house repairs. So, I broke my own rule of not helping him after he refused to go to college. I'm a good mother, and I give him a job! But he cost me money! I'm suing him for loss of profit! Several customers left because they said he was operating the boats drunk. And one young girl's parents filed a complaint against him. They claimed he tried to molest her!"

"Oh, really," said Jerry, overwhelmed. "Really," he repeated lamely, feeling a vile, bitter taste grow inside his throat. He wondered what else Russ had kept from him.

Jerry started to pick his lip until he realized JoAnne was studying him with keen suspicion. He put his hand down and leaned forward to listen.

"The stupid bastard cost me thousands of dollars!" she elaborated. "I won't allow it!"

"Will this molestation charge go to court?" Jerry sat stunned before her and wondered why she hadn't mentioned the allegation to him before. He was, after all, her attorney. "Did the family contact you?"

"I had to pay them off. Almost one hundred thousand dollars!"

Jerry rocked sideways in the chair. He knew she was bluffing. "I see," he said, and he certainly *did* see the big picture of her lies. "You never mentioned it before."

"I don't have to tell you everything, Jerry. You just worry about the paperwork—the land and the stock holdings. If I need you to know more, I'll tell you!"

Jerry was thinking rapidly; he was now nauseous and recognized, yes, the start of a migraine. "It seems to me that this keeps going in circles," he said. "All Russ really wants is the property. If he finds the other copy, it's his. You really don't need to sell it anyway. You've got so much land already. Why hold onto that piece of land, land that his grandfather actually gave him?"

"I have my reasons. If you must know, I loved my father very much. I loved him more than my mother did, even more than Russ did. I plan to renovate the cottage and turn it into a private hideaway for myself. I grew up in that cottage, and I want it preserved."

Jerry knew JoAnne was lying on this subject too. Barely three weeks ago, she told him a man from Chicago—some fat-cat owner of fast food chains—wanted to buy her father's cottage, and he was willing to pay her close to a half-million dollars. Jerry wondered if she'd forgotten telling him this. Perhaps she was senile, or simply crippled by her wrath.

JoAnne lifted crookedly from her chair. "What I want you to do is blackmail Bishop into leaving town. Tell him I know all about a son—a man in his twenties—who wrote to me recently. I have the letter right here." She held up the letter but wouldn't let Jerry have it for closer inspection. "This man claims to be one of Bishop's illegitimate children. He wants what's coming to him."

"How did you find *him*?" Jerry babbled, woozy from the heat of *her* and the heat of the furnace and way too much information all at once.

"I have a detective, remember? And I'm not talking about Silcott, the one *you* hired."

Marilyn Clayton. "That would be very difficult to prove," he said.

"There are blood tests, which I happen to have the results of. There's DNA. Needless to say, this young man is eager to know he might be able to collect hundreds of thousands of dollars from a wealthy man we can possibly prove is his father. After all, the poor bastard's destitute. Why bother digging up someone well off and happy? No incentive there."

Jerry watched her put the envelope away in the drawer. "So, you want me to tell Tom Bishop about some so-called son crawling out of the woodwork to collect child support?" he said in a restrained manner, like a scared child asking for an allowance. He almost threw up this time, he was so completely unnerved.

"No, you don't *tell* him. You do some work for a change and simply spread the word. Go up there and drink in his lounge like I know you do regularly anyway. Put out the word. Spread some dirt, for God's sake, and then get better pictures of Russ and his whore! Now please leave. I have a business to run; unless, of course, you have more to tell me about my son."

"No, not really." With that, Jerry decided it was time to leave and quickly picked up his briefcase. "One more thing," he said, "Russ is worried about the layoffs at the quarry."

JoAnne secured the glasses, once again, to her mottled face. "Good. Let him squirm. I have a friend who's a foreman there. He's the reason Russ got hired in the first place. I'm going to see what I can do about Russ getting the ax."

"You're going to get him fired?"

"Yes, if he doesn't stop this hideous affair! I'll say it one more time: I promised my dear friend Susan I'd take care of her children. Russ flitting around will kill Libby, the poor girl loves him so much. I can deal with his shortcomings but upsetting Libby I will *not* allow! I want him destroyed if he doesn't stop this affair. The next time you see him, go ahead and tell him I have damaging photos. Libby's only thirty-two years old! She can start over!"

Jerry had the photos of the woman's face as well, but now after learning of JoAnne's plan to get Russ fired, he was positive he would keep them.

Jerry moved toward her desk and put the briefcase down in the middle of it. He opened the case and selected a three-page document. "Here are the papers you asked for on the land parcels at the harbor. I want five hundred for this information. I had a lot of trouble getting it, and it wouldn't look good if I got caught rummaging through the files in the deeds office at the courthouse."

He waited for this to register. She walked back to the desk, unlocked the long middle drawer, and produced her checkbook. "Five hundred," she repeated. "Getting bold, are we?"

Nonetheless, she wrote out and signed the check; she handed it to him with an unreadable expression. "I have to get back to work."

"I need to make a phone call," Jerry said, "if that's okay with you?"

JoAnne closed her desk drawer. "Lock up when you leave," she said.

Jerry waited until he could no longer hear her footsteps. He picked up the phone but put it back. He went to the filing cabinet and couldn't believe it when he found that the drawer he wanted was unlocked. He thumbed through the files. If only he could find the third copy of the will. But, he knew finding it was unlikely. He'd settle for a copy of the tax reports from two years previously and sifted through the files, recalling that she kept some of the damaging paperwork in the bottom drawer.

He opened the drawer. He found sealed folders tucked in the back. One was marked *April*. He knew what it meant because he was the one who handed the very folder to her accountant. He was the one who had instructed the accountant and paid him off per her orders.

He grabbed the folder marked *April*, stuffed it into his briefcase, which was still laying on her desk. He slammed the cabinet drawer shut, picked up the briefcase, and turned back when he noticed he had left his check on the desk by the phone. He folded the check and tucked it into the breast pocket of his shirt beneath his coat.

He walked through the door of her office, locking it behind him as she had instructed him to do. He was grateful that she hadn't destroyed these pages of proof. If she knew he had them, he would be arrested on the spot and sued as well. He knew to cash the five hundred-dollar check as soon as possible, maybe even produce some other documents she wanted and get her to pay him for those—although they would be falsified. He liked the idea. He also liked the idea of the folder marked *April* secured safely inside his briefcase. It was proof that she had cheated on hundreds of acres of property tax. The IRS would certainly be interested in learning that JoAnne Shaw was guilty of tax evasion as well as other crimes.

Chapter 8

JoAnne returned to her office. She thought it was humorous the way Jerry peeked around the corners to make sure no one was watching as he left the premises. She had been discussing the week's menu with the main chef in the kitchen and calculated Jerry's departure. She kept her back to the wall, blending in with the dark logs as she witnessed him slink away.

Jerry had closed the door to her office as she asked him to do. She went inside, flipped on the light, adjusted her glasses, and walked to the filing cabinet. She knew right where to look: the papers in the back of the bottom drawer.

The file marked *April*, as she suspected, was gone.

She was amused that Jerry had taken the bait. The *game*, she decided, was getting more interesting by the day. Now she knew for certain that Jerry McPherson had to go. Or, maybe she should string him along until she gathered more information. The more mistakes he made, the better.

She wondered if he would spread the word about Tom Bishop's so-called illegitimate son—a product of JoAnne's imagination. She wanted to stir Bishop up and make him think she had connections to his inevitable financial collapse and using Jerry to create rumors was a perfect strategy.

But for now, she would wait. Sooner or later, Jerry would call her in a panic, or he'd show up at her office again. She would say she didn't know what he was talking about. She would be polite and thank him for tipping her off to the fact that her father made a third copy of the will.

Yes, it would be impossible for Russ to succeed in finding the last copy, anyway. After she spoke with Marilyn, she would go to her father's cottage and search for this alleged copy. Knowing her father's habits, he probably hid it somewhere obscure, like behind a board of the wall. Maybe he had taped it to the inside of a cabinet door. No matter, if a third copy existed, JoAnne would find it.

Marilyn came into the room and sighed. Her sigh stirred up half the air, or so it seemed. She exhaled toxic fumes: the scent of herself consisting of too much fatty food, not enough deodorant, and sheer rank and deception.

JoAnne wouldn't have hired Marilyn if not for her outstanding detective credentials. She retired from the police force the year before. Her father had been a private detective, and therefore, due to years of his and her experience combined, Marilyn deemed herself qualified for the position, and so did JoAnne. She paid Marilyn well because she was worth it. Jerry McPherson used to be worth it too, but apparently, his views had changed since their last meeting. As soon as Jerry had learned about the affair, he was all for helping JoAnne ruin Russ, but after the meeting JoAnne herself had suggested Jerry arrange with Russ, Jerry had an entirely different attitude.

If only Jerry had left her filing cabinet alone, she would have sailed him along, watching, learning, but using him nevertheless. He had once been Russ's closest friend; he liked Libby and thought of her as a sister, and these two factors had been to JoAnne's advantage. Now she knew Jerry was a traitor.

"Jerry's pictures were not as revealing as I would have liked," JoAnne began the conversation with Marilyn. "Go get me something I can use."

"Silcott's supposed to be the best. Maybe Jerry kept the good shots from you."

JoAnne knew that Marilyn always had suspicions about Jerry McPherson, so she wasn't surprised to hear Marilyn accuse him of keeping the most incriminating photos to himself. JoAnne studied a paper, one of the papers Jerry had given her regarding the courthouse deeds. "Do you think this document looks right?" she asked Marilyn. "Maybe it's a fake."

Marilyn surveyed the page, taking her time. Her small eyes looked like black holes penetrating the snowy skin of her face. She even turned the document sideways, back upright, and re-read it. JoAnne hesitated to rush her with an answer because she knew Marilyn was an expert at identifying forged handwriting and signatures; she could also decipher invalid statistics.

But when Marilyn stuck her tongue out in an irritating manner, JoAnne couldn't take it anymore. "Well?" she inquired, on the verge of rage. "Out with it!"

"It looks okay to me, but I wouldn't trust it completely. I'd contact the realtor and say you're looking into these parcels for a friend."

JoAnne evaluated her, as if for the first time. What an odd creature. They'd used to be good friends, way back. Before she realized Marilyn was so ... damned ugly.

Back when Marilyn's parents used to vacation at Grand Lake, every summer they would meet, and one day, Marilyn vanished. Then about six months ago, she reappeared. She said she had retired from the force in Ohio and wanted to open her own detective agency. She'd told JoAnne, "My dad was a private detective, you know. I think he'd want me to follow in his footsteps."

JoAnne did recall how Marilyn had often bragged about her father. One day over coffee, JoAnne mentioned she needed someone to investigate important personal issues for her—and that's how it all began. Marilyn boarded a room at the Birch Hill Lodge. She posed as a maid. In fact, she happened to enjoy housework and did most of it—or, that is, she supervised JoAnne's other two maids. The arrangement worked out well.

JoAnne sat down at her desk, wondering what exactly this woman was capable of. Yes, she had gathered pertinent information regarding Thomas Bishop and the deal with Jerry McPherson and Bishop's daughter Claudia. How far would she go?

Marilyn convinced JoAnne that if Jerry McPherson happened to turn on her, they would have damaging evidence against him related to the alleged rape of

Claudia Bishop, who now lived in Jacksonville, Florida. Marilyn had discovered that after only two phone calls. Marilyn convinced JoAnne that Claudia Bishop was willing to return to Grand Lake to help them lambaste Jerry McPherson, even though he had been acquitted of the charges. If it didn't hold up in court, at least they would have darkened his name in the community again, causing him to lose clients.

Marilyn was also responsible for uncovering the fact that Russ was having an affair. She heard the rumor from a local furniture shop owner, and from there, she followed Russ right to the woman's house. JoAnne rewarded her with a new Jeep and two thousand dollars. JoAnne also gave her free room and board at the Lodge for as long as she wanted the job. Anything to make Marilyn happy. Who would want such a person to become angry or disillusioned? This creature, Marilyn Clayton, with one chromosome off, must be pampered and encouraged at all costs.

But JoAnne wished Marilyn would let her hair-dresser re-work her thick, skullcap hair so tightly bound around her fat head. And if only she would drop some weight. Although, she was more intimidating stout and homely, and thereby better able to frighten the enemy.

"Get me better pictures," JoAnne repeated. She didn't appreciate the way Marilyn examined her with those tiny dark eyes, and so she added, "Get them by *tomorrow!*"

Marilyn let herself out, closing the door behind her the way JoAnne always insisted the employees do: without sound.

• • •

After Marilyn left, JoAnne drove to the cemetery, located off the main road onto a side road, ten miles south of her father's cottage. She visited the grave of her friend Susan Weyman at least once a week. It had been four weeks, however, since she last "spoke" to Susan.

She brushed away the branches and weeds scattered over the surface of the grave. Libby had been there recently, JoAnne could tell. Even though it was almost winter, Libby always brought fresh flowers twice a month.

JoAnne straightened the vase, for it had tipped due to the wind. Anything out of order irritated her. She crouched down on her knees, thinking about Susan. Never had she known a friend like Susan. Always there for her, always so understanding and ready to share JoAnne's secrets and listen to her dreams, until that one afternoon.

"I'll try to protect Libby and Scott," JoAnne said directly to the headstone, the name Susan Elizabeth Weyman engraved in bold gothic letters. "I always keep my promises."

Then she wiped her eyes with a tissue, pushed herself upright, and walked back to her Cadillac.

• • •

At the cottage, JoAnne went to the bathroom first and turned on the main electrical switch. Luckily, she kept a flashlight right inside the back door of the small closed-in porch near the kitchen.

There was always that musty cedar smell, the same from when she was a child. JoAnne and her parents moved into this cottage when she was nine years old. Before that, they lived in what she could only describe as a two-room shack. The cottage wasn't much better. Her father fixed it up suitably, however, and modernized it to the best of his ability, particularly after JoAnne's mother had died. Her mother, a few years older than her father, died of an overdose of sleeping pills. No one actually came out and said it, but JoAnne knew she took the pills on purpose.

JoAnne's mother was a sad, whimsical woman who wrote music and played the piano, the one extravagant gift her father could afford. JoAnne was the one who found her twenty-one years ago, sprawled out on her bed in the back bedroom dressed in her best skirt and blouse, as if she had pre-planned the *event*. She also had on a beautiful gold chain, the very chain JoAnne wore almost every day. JoAnne removed the chain when she found her mother. There was no way she would let her father sell it.

Every time she walked into the back bedroom, she thought of her mother. Her music. Her depression. Her rage. JoAnne's anger over what happened tore her soul, mostly with an intense anger toward her father for allowing her to waste her life away in a dream world—a dream world where she ultimately went insane and killed herself.

JoAnne thought of the old man with such contempt, her eyes watered up and her heart raced. And yet, he had lived twenty years longer than her mother. How did he have that right? JoAnne's mother didn't want to live at Grand Lake. She had begged her husband to leave. But he loved his cottage, and he loved his job as a boat mechanic.

He loved himself most of all.

"You pathetic old man," JoAnne said, tears colliding inside her eyes until they burned. Her mother wanted to leave but went insane instead.

JoAnne decided when her mother died that she would never compromise the life she wanted. She wouldn't love a man, wouldn't even love her own children if it meant losing herself in the process. No one was worth such sacrifice.

JoAnne used the same tissue she had used earlier at the cemetery to wipe her eyes. She was grateful she was alone. She made it a rule to never let anyone see her cry. She steadied herself and proceeded down a short hallway toward her father's bedroom. At one time, this room had been her mother's music room, but after her mother died, he turned it into his bedroom. There was faded green-and-yellow flowered wallpaper, segments hanging and ripped, an antique mahogany chair and dressing table, her mother's rocking chair, and a bureau, now empty of keepsakes.

JoAnne attacked the bureau first, knowing he hid most of his important papers inside it. Although a week after he died, she searched each drawer inside and out, hoping to find something more of value. Her father was such a hermit. She knew he could have thousands of dollars hidden away. His bank accounts had been plentiful at the end, but he was also the type to stash bills among the dark corners in concealed places, and she knew he would have many secret compartments.

But there was nothing resembling paper hidden in the bureau, and after an hour searching through the entire bedroom, and even standing on a chair to brush her hands along the cobwebbed-lined closet shelves and pressing against the walls for soft spots, JoAnne found absolutely nothing but three grocery receipts and a folded recipe for blueberry cobbler.

She flipped the light switch on near the bedroom door before leaving and almost bumped into a broad-shouldered man. He was tall and sturdy of stature. She jumped backwards, only slightly, for she was not a flighty person by nature. She did, however, push a fist against her trembling chest.

"Russell!" His name spoken by her at that moment sounded more like a statement of regret, as if chastising herself for giving birth to him in the first place. She stopped inside her tracks, shaking her head uncontrollably. "You startled me! You should have called out!"

JoAnne pushed Russ aside and hurried toward the living room. Inside the living room, she faced him beneath the brighter light. She waited for him to explain, but he only glared at her. He looked as if he hadn't slept the night before. He had on the same clothes he wore when he confronted her at the Lodge the afternoon before. His hair was wiry and overlapping, suggesting he hadn't put a comb through it in days.

"Did you go home with Libby yesterday?" she asked. "Why aren't you at the quarry?"

The grim look Russ gave her made her shiver. He said, "None of your goddamned business."

"Are you so tired that you can't stand up straight?" she demanded. "Or are you drunk?"

"I came to visit my grandfather." He looked around the room as if absorbing his grandfather's presence. "And *you* took my keys."

JoAnne occupied herself by straightening one of the torn curtains in the front window facing Grand Lake. She heard a branch tap the roof via the wind, and she felt the wooden floor move. "Why should you have a key? I need to sell the place. When I sell it, I'll give you some of the money. Will that pacify you?"

"I don't want your money!"

"You'll regret trying to scare me, Russell. You'll regret a lot of things!"

"I won't let you sell this place. Do *you hear* me?"

When JoAnne looked him in the eyes—those red, glazed-over eyes—she became frightened of him for the very first time.

But she took a deep breath and elected to feign empathy. "I think you should go home, take a shower, and go to bed."

"Sure, *Mother*," he said. "And I think you should rot in hell."

Russ turned and walked through the kitchen. He slammed the door shut behind him. JoAnne felt a prickly tremor ride up her spine. She had to sit down on the couch, close her eyes, and dream of summer and wild flowers and all the tourists sure to come.

After searching the living room for the will, she went to the table near the door where she always set her purse and keys. She found the purse and her car keys, but the keys to the cottage were gone.

Chapter 9

JoAnne was right about one thing, he should go home, take a shower, and go to bed. He hadn't been home all night, and Libby might have the police out looking for him.

After the meeting with Jerry earlier at O'Grady's, they parted ways. Russ drove around Grand Lake at least twice. He stopped at a tavern he had frequented when he was younger. He also parked at a favorite boat launch near Lake Esau, sat in his vehicle, and fell asleep for about an hour.

There was a twenty-four-hour gas station outside of Alpena and another gas pump at the bait shop on the highway. Russ knew the owner. He was another high school friend, and he let Russ help himself to gasoline.

He drove onward, trying to sort things out in his mind. He decided to drive to his grandfather's cottage in search of the third copy of the will. He should have owned the place by now. He shouldn't have to worry about breaking into it.

He couldn't believe his luck when he found JoAnne's stately Cadillac parked in the yard by the boathouse. Now all he needed to do was walk through the same door she had used, and he wouldn't have to break in after all.

When he found her in the back bedroom, he made sure to create enough friction to throw her off balance. She backed down because she was afraid of him now, he could tell.

And he wanted her to be afraid. He wanted her confused. He wanted her focused on calming *him* down instead of realizing he had taken her key ring with the cottage and boathouse keys and the key to her office.

After leaving Grandfather's cottage, he drove toward Alpena to find a place to make a key. He wondered if Jerry was in his office. It was twelve-thirty. Maybe he was at lunch. Russ was amazed again by his good fortune when he saw Jerry's vehicle parked in front of his office building. Then, as he waited at a red light, Jerry himself came down the sidewalk at a rapid pace.

Jerry motioned for Russ to pull over at the curb. Russ swerved out of the lineup of cars that were waiting for the red light to turn green and parked at an angle behind Jerry's vehicle. Russ rolled down his window. He was anxious to find out why Jerry was so excited. "Where's the fire?" he asked. "You onto something?"

Jerry leaned against the door. "I've got something important to show you," he said. "Meet me at the coffee shop." Then with his long overcoat billowing, Jerry ran up the steps of the post office and disappeared through the doors.

Russ turned off the ignition and stepped into the street. He headed toward the coffee shop, as he was told to do, and found a table near the door. He ordered two coffees and the breakfast special.

He was about to get up and head for the restroom when Jerry bolted through the front door carrying a leather briefcase. He studied the crowd, and once satisfied that they wouldn't be spied on, he sat down at the table and leaned in close to Russ. "You'll be proud of me when you see what I stole from JoAnne," he boasted. "She's not as brilliant as she thinks."

Russ leaned toward Jerry to mock his excitement. "I got something too," he said. "I just saw JoAnne at the cottage and stole her keys right out from under her big nose. No problem though because she left her car keys in the ignition. I checked before I ambushed her. She could at least drive home, is what I am saying."

Jerry slapped the table with his palm. "Good! What you do is make two copies of all the keys. I think the key to her office and her files are on the ring too. Let me see them."

Russ dug inside his jacket pocket and produced the key ring. While Jerry inspected the keys, Russ helped the waitress arrange his breakfast. He was especially interested in the stack of pancakes, although he wished he had ordered a side of bacon and eggs. "Hey, could I get some eggs over-easy?" he asked her. "And maybe some bacon. Toast, whole wheat? You'll help me eat some of this," he told Jerry and served him two pancakes as the waitress walked off to get part two of his order.

Jerry didn't touch the food. He was too busy studying the keys. "Maybe you should let me make the copies. I wouldn't want this screwed up. You've got all the important keys right here. Good job!" he said again.

"When she finds out I have them," Russ said between bites, "she'll probably have the locks changed."

"Then you'd better get on it. Have the copies made as soon as you're done here and maybe we can get our hands on more documents before she makes her next move."

"We?" Russ asked, fork poised. "You're on *my* side?"

"I met with her this morning. I happen to know for a fact that she has a buyer for your grandfather's place. Some hot-shot from Chicago named Robert Weise. He's willing to pay her a half a million for it. Lot and all."

Russ swallowed and said, "Half a million?" Instead of getting angry, he chuckled and cut into the stack of pancakes again.

"Anyway," Jerry continued, leaning back into the booth, "when she left the office, I managed to get into her files. I happen to know she didn't bother to declare at least five hundred acres of property on her taxes a couple years ago. She paid off her accountant, Brett Daniels. You know him." He didn't wait for Russ to acknowledge the name. They all knew "crooked Brett." That is, anyone who needed help at tax time knew him. "You must have met him, unfortunately."

"Yes," said Russ. "I remember the shithead."

Jerry waved off the name-calling and continued, "I had to get the papers of purchase, proof she has these properties to begin with. There are bank statements proving that she bought the parcels, what year, et cetera. I take all this to the IRS. They can get access, but it looks worse if I come up with examples as her former attorney." Jerry whistled, and it wasn't a muffled whistle. But, the racket of people talking mixed with silverware clattering was even louder as the clock kept ticking toward one o'clock. "She's definitely put away with this, or at least sued for back taxes. I think we are talking more than hundreds and into the thousands."

"Well, let's see the papers," said Russ.

Jerry went for the briefcase, explaining as he opened it, "After I met with her, I spent the rest of the morning in court, so I haven't really had a chance to go over these. I recognized the folder when I took it though. I put the papers together myself. She was supposed to destroy this batch, but I'm sure glad she didn't!" He picked through the other folders until he found the one marked *April*. "Why aren't you at work today anyway? You look like you slept in your clothes."

"I didn't go home," Russ confessed. "I called in sick."

"You'd better keep in line," Jerry advised. "You can't go around staying out all night and giving her ammunition. Libby must be frantic."

"I'll go home when we're done here."

"After you copy the keys, drop them off at JoAnne's mailbox. Just do yourself a favor and wise up. Missing time at work isn't smart!"

"I never claimed to be smart," Russ admitted.

Jerry tore the folder marked *April* open and pulled out some pages. But when he discovered that the papers were blank and that there was a note attached to the top one, his grin was replaced with a frown.

Russ waited for the waitress to put down his plate of eggs and leave. "What is it?" he asked, perplexed by Jerry's expression.

"I'll be damned!" said Jerry. He tossed the papers down on the table. "These are blank. Can you believe it? And she's attached a note too. It says, Think I'm stupid enough to trust you *now, Mr. McPherson*? Consider yourself fired and in serious danger for betraying me.'"

Russ stared at the back of the note Jerry had just read out loud. He made a mess of the eggs with the corner of a piece of toast. "Wow," he said, completely dumbfounded and focused on a speck on the wall behind Jerry's head, "that's *almost* brilliant."

• • •

Russ decided that if he had even the slightest chance of saving his marriage and getting his grandfather's property, he needed to clean up his act. He continued with the original plan to drive to Alpena to make copies of the keys. Then, he filled his vehicle with gas and headed back toward the Birch Hill Lodge. Hopefully, he could deposit the key ring in the mailbox without anyone seeing him.

As he drove along the road toward the Lodge, he realized the storm had passed for the time being, and sun rays were spraying through the tree branches of aspen and maple, now absent of their red and orange leaves.

But there was a light powdering of snow blowing through the yards of the cottages and cabins and dusting across fences, gates, and parked vehicles. Now he was in Krakow Township, heading for Presque Isle Township on the verge of Grand Lake. He slowly drove into the parking lot of the Lodge and stopped on the edge toward the front of the building. He drove onward, slowly, slowly, hoping to be invisible, or at least blend in with the customers' vehicles.

Thankfully, the Birch Hill Lodge was lively. Russ could tell by the trucks and Jeeps parked in the parking lot that it was hunting season. The sight reminded him that he hadn't even bought his deer hunting license, and that Thanksgiving Day wasn't far away. After Thanksgiving, of course, came Christmas. He dreaded the possibility of Libby leaving him, taking Olivia, and leaving him all alone for the holidays.

He stopped the Blazer and parked far enough away from the Lodge to remain undetected. He walked up to the wooden mailbox. The mailbox was a small replica of the Lodge; Aaron had made it years ago.

Russ tossed the key ring into the box and slapped the door shut.

The only person he saw was that Marilyn Clayton ogre, that God-awful woman who looked like a man. She was sweeping off the front porch near the right side of the Lodge, but he was sure she didn't see him. He ran back to the Blazer, turned the wheel away from the Lodge, and headed for Grand Lake.

When he arrived home ten minutes later, he knew he was in for a showdown because Scott Weyman's car was parked by the boathouse. He sat in his vehicle for a few minutes, took off his cap, hung it on the gun rack behind his head, and started to comb his thick, matted hair. Using the mirror, he noticed he had gray circles under his eyes. And his coloring was ghostly-white, not normal for him, a man who spent a lot of time outdoors.

Nothing could repair the damage of driving around all night, except for maybe a shower, and a dry, warm bed. Next to Libby.

But since Scott's vehicle was parked in his yard, he knew that sleep wouldn't be possible for a while. There would be questions, accusations, and probably tears—the latter from Libby. He got out of his vehicle and walked down the path to the house. He shook himself alert and opened the kitchen door. Libby was standing at the table, a paper towel pressed to her nose, and Scott was standing next to her, poised at her elbow with his hands on his hips.

When Libby saw Russ, she started to cry and said through the paper towel, "I thought you were dead! They said you didn't show up for work. You didn't call me!" She babbled something about wrecks and heart attacks and ran out of the room.

"Nice job!" said Scott. He moved toward Russ with a menacing expression stretching his lips and eyelids. "Libby calls me hysterical, and what do I say?"

Russ massaged his forehead. "Back off," he warned through clenched teeth. "I don't need your bullshit right now!"

Russ stepped toward the counter, but Scott grabbed his arm and yanked him back to the spot he had just left. "What'd I tell you the other night? Wasn't that enough for you?" He had such a firm grip on Russ's arm, there was no room for movement between them except for a twitch of Scott's right eye.

"If you don't let go, I'll break your neck," Russ said. He had to pull hard to free himself. "Get out of my house. I'm tired, and I don't want you here!"

Scott retrieved his briefcase and folders from one of the chairs. "I've got to go to Toledo for a meeting," he said, "but I'll be back tomorrow night. Let me assure you that I'll be calling Libby the first chance I get. If she's still crying, I'm coming after you."

Russ shrugged as Scott turned and headed for the back door in a blurred frenzy of overcoat and papers, disappearing into the sunny afternoon.

• • •

Libby was sitting at her dressing table by the time Russ went upstairs to their bedroom. She was sewing. She would always pick up some mending and sew away at a fast clip whenever she was distressed. She didn't even look up when he walked into the room.

"Where's Olivia?" he asked as he sat down on the edge of the bed to pull off his boots. "At my *Mother's?*"

"She's at a friend's house. I'm supposed to pick her up in an hour. Good of you to come home." The last part was laden with bitterness.

"It's this nonsense about my grandfather's place," Russ said, his voice faltering. He knew if he could manage to sound desperate, she might offer him a bit of sympathy. "I contacted a couple of other lawyers. I've got to find the third copy of his will because it's the only proof of what he wanted."

Russ saw her look at him through the mirror of the dressing table, but she kept on stitching. She was that good of a seamstress, that good at reading him. "I don't know what to say," she whispered. "But you could have called. If I'd stayed out all night during a storm, wouldn't you picture me dead in a ditch alongside the road?"

"Sorry. It's the will! I'm all confused. I met Jerry for dinner last night, then I drove around. I fell asleep in my truck. Out at the boat launch where you and I used to go swimming. Remember? In the moonlight?"

He hoped to get her full attention with the memory. He wanted to catch her lovely green eyes blinking at him through the mirror, but she kept on sewing and cut a thread with her teeth. "We should go back there this summer," he added. "We haven't been there in a long time."

"I called JoAnne," said Libby. "She said she saw you this morning. She said you tried to break into your grandfather's cabin!"

Russ pulled off his shirt. Once the shirt was off, he stepped out of his pants. "She's a liar. She was there, so I stopped. I only wanted to talk to her."

"But you stole her keys!" Libby clarified. "*Stole* her keys, Russ!"

Russ rolled his eyes toward the ceiling and then looked in the mirror where this time, Libby was watching him dead on. "I gave them back to her," he said. "She took mine a few weeks ago. I just wanted to make another key of the cottage."

"That's all wrong. You need to let it go!"

Libby's hair was pulled back into a ponytail. It was very long, even longer than Russ had realized, past the middle of her back and auburn in color, streaked with blond and even some red. He wanted to touch her.

She wore jeans and a pink and black flannel shirt. Her feet were bare. Although the floor was cold, she never wore shoes inside the house unless she had to. Russ decided it was time to plead with her. "I need your help, Libby," he said, trying not to look directly into her eyes. "Please stay on my side, like you said the other night. Try to understand how much the cottage means to me." Libby lowered the sewing bundle to her lap. "You have the dressing table that was your mom's," he continued. "I have nothing but the cottage. Since I was a kid, my grandfather said it would be mine. And, I'll tell you something else, something I suspect—" He walked over to where she sat and put his arm around her. "I really do think she tried to kill him. She pushed him down the stairs. She probably drugged him too."

He didn't expect Libby to take him seriously. Simply shaking the animosity from her eyes would do. But she smiled at him through the mirror. "Some imagination," she said. "You sure *do* think big. You should have called me though," she said again. "I was worried."

"I told you, honey. I fell asleep. It's better than falling asleep at the wheel and crashing into a tree. It won't happen again."

Russ lured her onto the bed. "I love you," he said. "Don't leave until I fall asleep."

Chapter 10

When Libby got home from picking up Olivia, she expected to find Russ at the kitchen table, or at least as far as the shower, but he was still in bed. She covered him up, thinking he probably had another horrible nightmare. He had one leg over the side of the bed and his face was damp. She decided to let him sleep longer. Maybe he was coming down with the flu.

She went back downstairs to attend to medical bills—the stack of bills from her recent gynecology and fertility specialist sessions. Three more had arrived yesterday in the mail.

Meanwhile, Olivia was trying to clamp the leash onto Pat's collar. "I'm taking Pat for a walk," she told her mother, her hand on one hip, reminding Libby of herself.

Libby knelt next to Olivia, made sure the clamp was on securely, and rubbed behind Pat's ear. "Be careful," she said. "And don't go by the road."

Libby looked at her daughter's face, the miniature features that, yes, looked more like Russ's than her own. Libby marveled at Olivia's large blue eyes—exactly like his—and her hair was the same light-brown shade as his.

Before she became sentimental thinking about Olivia as a baby, and how she would never be able to have more children, Libby pushed herself up to her feet and watched Olivia direct the aging Labrador around the yard. Pat, always agreeable to almost any plan, would make sure nothing happened to Olivia.

Libby went back to the stack of bills on the kitchen table. Russ dealt with the finances every other week after he got his paycheck. She was too busy with the household chores, and since he was exceptional at math, she had no objections to him managing the bills.

But she needed to go into his study and find out the exact identification number of the medical insurance Russ had through the quarry. The insurance numbers had to be written out clearly on her forms. She needed to determine the yearly deductible, and she could never remember what it was, as the number changed from year to year.

Oddly, she felt like an invader among his personal things, even though she was after something they shared—an insurance number, an invoice, anything to provide her with the appropriate documentation and numbers.

She found his bottle of Scotch first and thought nothing of it because during their marriage, she had only seen him drunk twice if that. She noticed an envelope of pictures and couldn't resist looking inside. She found several pictures of herself and Olivia.

Next Libby pulled out some files. She was impressed, as always, with his organized system. One would never think of Russ Shaw as "tidy" in any way, but he was when it came to invoices and the checkbook; each file was marked and in alphabetical order.

She opened the file with the word INSURANCE in bold lettering. It wasn't difficult to find the information she needed, which she wrote down on her pad of paper. She put the paper back, then discovered a file marked CHECK STUBS and decided, why not make sure his wages added up to what he'd claimed all these years.

Of course, he received raises and mentioned them to her. But she had a feeling he made more than he told her; she had a feeling he used extra for his hunting and fishing projects. After determining what they needed for groceries, miscellaneous expenses, and monthly bills, he always gave her money for clothes and other items, but still, she sensed he wasn't telling her everything.

According to the statements, Russ made three hundred dollars more a month than he had claimed. She pecked at the calculator on his desk. No, make that almost four hundred. He used some of it for gas, lunches, hunting and fishing paraphernalia, and going out with his friends, but she wondered where almost three hundred dollars more was going per month.

She put the papers back exactly where she found them, now wishing she hadn't even looked. It bothered her to think there was a secret, particularly regarding money, between them. All she could do was ask him about it later. In the past, if something bothered her, she knew to just ask him.

Somehow, this felt different.

She closed the drawers, turned off the desk lamp, and returned to the kitchen with the medical insurance information. She put on the kettle of water to boil for tea and sat back down at the table to finish filling out the insurance forms and pay the difference for the bloodwork she'd had done recently for a viral infection.

When the water had boiled, she fixed a cup of green tea with one spoonful of sugar and listened to the one-sided conversation of her five-year-old daughter outside the front door. She saw Olivia lead Pat up and down the pebbled path, back and forth, the dog patient, as was the nature of the breed.

Soon there were footsteps descending the stairs, and Russ stood in the kitchen doorway, wearing only blue shorts, his hair tousled. "I'm sick," he announced morosely.

This was nothing new, but he normally started out by saying, "God, I'm tired" or "I can't get moving" or something just as obvious. He was not one to awaken easily; Libby had spent many mornings coaxing him to get up for work. But this time, she could see that he was truly under the weather. He had dark circles beneath his eyes, his shoulders sagged, and his face was splotched-red.

"I'll make you some tea," she offered.

"No, I'm going back to bed. I've got to get up in an hour."

Libby moved past him to the stove. "Tea will help. I was going through the files in your desk—" She selected a tea bag and placed it into a mug. She wanted to find out what he thought of her going through his files, and she had to know now.

He propped himself against the frame of the door-way and blinked a few times, but otherwise appeared unaffected by her snooping. "And?" he asked. "What did you find?"

Libby poured steaming-hot water into the mug and dunked the tea bag. "I found that three hundred dollars go out every month to—well, something or someone. You don't have to tell me if you don't want to."

He pressed on the wooden structure of the doorway, saying nothing at first. "Just curious," she added when she determined he was taking too long to provide an answer.

"I've been helping Andy for a year or so now," he admitted. "I didn't want to tell you. She and that jerk-off Edwin Mayfield are in over their heads in debt. She called me and asked for my help. Anything else you want to know?"

Now he was irritated, she could tell. She said, "Okay, I see," and started to rummage inside the cupboard for Olivia's cereal. "I'm glad you help her out."

Libby knew Andrea was not exactly self-sufficient and resourceful. Russ's younger sister, lived in Petoskey. Although Petoskey was one hundred miles away, they only saw her twice a year, over a holiday. Usually Christmas and the Fourth of July. No one knew the real reason Andrea and her husband Edwin left years ago.

"She's my sister," Russ added. Before he turned to go back toward the stairs, he asked, "Where's Olivia?"

"Outside with Pat."

"Make her come in. It's cold out." He was already in the shadows of the living room. "Like I said, get me up in an hour!"

Libby couldn't imagine what kind of errand would be so important to override flu symptoms, but it didn't matter. She didn't want to know anyway.

• • •

She talked Olivia back inside by telling her, "We're going to the Lodge. I have to talk to Grandma."

"But can we take Pat?" Olivia asked. She didn't like leaving Pat home alone.

"Yes," said Libby. "Of course, we'll take her."

"Will Grandma make me lunch? I'm hungry."

Libby wanted to get moving and talk to JoAnne now that her mind was made up. "Yes, we'll eat there. Let's go."

Olivia had some difficulty rousting Pat up again and directing her out the front door. Then Olivia had to wait for Libby to get her jacket and purse. She held the door open for Libby and watched her turn to shut the door.

"What about Dad?" Olivia asked, her expression gloomy at the very idea of Russ trying to make his own dinner. "Dad can't cook."

"Daddy's tired," Libby explained. "We'll leave him here for a nice, quiet rest and take care of him when we get back."

It was a chore to get Olivia and Pat into the van and off to the Birch Hill Lodge. Libby noticed that evening was falling fast, and to her, it looked like another storm was stirring in the corners of the gray, swirling sky. Snow might be good, a substantial amount, and not the slight powdering they'd had so far.

Snow might put her in a holiday mood. Thanksgiving was coming. Maybe it would even help cheer everyone up.

• • •

Libby doubted that Russ would deer hunt this year, and as far as she knew, he never missed a season. She turned into the parking lot of the Lodge and parked in her usual spot, close to the side door—the entrance reserved for family. She helped Olivia and Pat out of the van and waited as Olivia instructed Pat around the grounds by the leash. But it was getting colder, and the sky was turning cloudy and blending purple with the faded light of day.

A northern wind began to stir.

Olivia walked Pat over to the fence, the swing-set, and back to the pavement. "Honey, let's go inside," Libby said. "It's time for dinner."

"But we can't leave Pat out here."

JoAnne would not allow pets, not even Pat, inside the Lodge except for emergencies, but she might agree to let Pat on the screened-in back porch. "We'll put her on the back porch. If she's quiet, Grandma will never know."

Libby and Olivia went into the Birch Hill Lodge through the back porch and down a wooden tunnel of sorts. Libby asked the head cook to fix a hamburger dinner for Olivia, and she asked one of the waitresses to look after her. "I'll be right back, Olivia," Libby said. "Eat your dinner when it comes."

Libby searched for JoAnne. She checked JoAnne's office, but the door was locked. She made the long trek through the first floor, up the stairway to the second, and finally recognized JoAnne's voice on the third floor. The best bedrooms of the Lodge, the larger suites, were on the third floor. JoAnne was inside one of the rooms speaking in a low voice with the door ajar. Libby was about to knock but she heard Scott's name mentioned and backed up to listen.

"He needs to know," JoAnne said. "We must tip him off."

The other voice was lower than JoAnne's. After only a minute of listening in, Libby recognized the voice of Marilyn Clayton. Marilyn muttered, "I'll see what I can do."

"Make sure he gets there in time."

Then came the rustling of sheets. Libby didn't feel comfortable eavesdropping, so she pushed the door open and entered the room. "JoAnne, I need to talk to you," she said, trying to compete with the sound of snapping sheets. "Right now, if you don't mind."

Libby could see that Marilyn was helping JoAnne change the sheets on the antique, four-poster bed. At first JoAnne was startled—more so than Marilyn—who resumed the task at hand. JoAnne patted the sides of her tightly curled hair and flipped her beige cotton blouse down over the waistband of her black pants. "You scared me, dear," she said, laughing like a choked seal; she shot Marilyn a concerned glance. "What can I do for you? Marilyn and I were just talking about you working here for a few hours every day. I need a good bookkeeper. You could work while Olivia's in school. And you could make your own hours."

JoAnne smiled at Libby, causing her caked-on makeup to crack. She continued to smooth her blouse down with her arthritic hands that were crisscrossed on the surface with blue and purple veins. Her smile didn't recede for four or five seconds. Her expression, stuck temporarily, created doubt in Libby's mind. Could she trust anything JoAnne said? Was Russ right about her?

JoAnne had mentioned an opening for a bookkeeper to Libby over a month ago. Recently, with Olivia in school, Libby found herself wandering through the house or outside in the yard, and she was seriously thinking about going back to work part-time. Working at the Lodge might be the answer. She needed something to fill the void, but work for JoAnne? Russ would go into hysterics.

"I haven't asked Russ yet. But I think—"

She knew JoAnne would cut her off: "Ask Russ?" she quipped with a pulsating smirk; she looked over at Marilyn and shook her head. "My dear, why would you *need* to ask Russ? He's off at work, or doing God knows what. Why worry about what *he* thinks? That's absurd! You need more time out of the house. Like I said, I'll pay you fifteen dollars an hour to start. I need a trustworthy bookkeeper. Especially now that I had to fire Jerry McPherson. David Preece is now my attorney as of last week."

Libby had trouble believing this news about Jerry McPherson, and furthermore, she wondered if Russ had anything to do with JoAnne firing him. She said, "Jerry's no longer your attorney? What happened?"

"Never mind," JoAnne said briskly; she moved to the far-left corner of the bed and helped straighten the blanket Marilyn attempted to lay over the sheet. "It's not for you to worry about."

Libby knew that the comment "not for you to worry about" meant the end of JoAnne discussing Jerry and their parting of ways. Whenever JoAnne became vexed and ready to end a conversation, she would say, "It's not for *you* to worry about."

"Maybe I'll start next week," said Libby, "and see how it works out."

JoAnne looked at her with a sly grin, as if she'd won a round. Of course, she expected to win *every* round. "Excellent," she said, the very notion of victory tumbling off her tongue. "It will do you a lot of good. You'll see!"

Libby, however, intended to get to the point of her visit. "I'd like to talk to you in private about something. That is, if you have the time." She looked over at Marilyn, who took the hint, picked up the dirty sheets, and backed out of the bedroom, closing the door behind her.

JoAnne was involved with pillow shams, her jagged back to Libby.

"Do you know if Russ sends Andrea money every month?" Libby asked her straight-away. "He told me he does. He said Andrea and Edwin are destitute."

JoAnne halted the process of stuffing a pillow into a pillow sham; she tossed it to the side, sat down on the edge of the bed, and placed her face in her hands while moaning. Libby thought she was crying and regretted bringing the whole subject up, but suddenly, JoAnne lifted her head to reveal that she hadn't been crying. She'd been laughing until she cried.

JoAnne pulled a tissue from her blouse pocket. "Oh my," she said, trying to control her speech. "Russ wouldn't give Andrea a penny, if we're talking about the same duo here."

"Yes, Russ. Your son," said Libby. "You know who I mean."

"Well, he might be my son, but believe me, he doesn't send Andrea money. *I* send her money. I have since they left. A thousand dollars per week, to be exact, and if that's not enough to keep the sorry two afloat, God pity their useless souls."

"Russ says he sends them about three hundred a month," added Libby, unable to contain the information.

"Oh, he did, eh?" JoAnne chortled, her tone mocking. "Leave it to *him* to stretch the truth out of proportion."

"Yes, he did," Libby insisted, standing back from the heat of her. "And so, if you send them money, why does she ask Russ for money?"

"I'm sure she doesn't ask him, dear," JoAnne clarified with a sigh. "I pay for their food and their rent besides. It's the reason they're coming home for the holidays. Neither one can make a go of it. Andrea's so-called job amounts to pushing French fries at a fast-food joint, and Edwin apparently doesn't know how to walk. He sits on the couch all day long and watches cable. A service I've paid for, no doubt. I told her not to marry that scrawny hillbilly with the brain capacity of a flea, but she wouldn't listen. All he knows how to do is push the buttons of the remote and fondle himself."

"What?" cried Libby, wondering about this fondling.

"Never mind, dear."

JoAnne turned away to finish the ordeal of dressing the pillows.

But Libby persisted. "What are you saying? Are you implying Russ is lying to me?"

"Oh, goodness," JoAnne said. "Of *course,* he's lying."

"Russ is *lying* to me," Libby repeated, her fingers touching her lips. She had to sit down on the cedar chest beneath the window to consider the possibility.

JoAnne turned to her, feigning sympathy, but not quite. "I talked to Andrea a few days ago," she said, her voice falling weary. "Andrea said that Russ hasn't contacted her since last Christmas."

Libby looked down at her shoes. Damn Russ for lying. He could do anything he wanted if he didn't lie to her.

JoAnne brought tears to Libby's eyes by saying in a conspiratorial tone, "All men are like that. They lie so much they don't even know when or why they're doing it. And besides, Russ lying to you about money is the least of your problems. If you like, I'll set up a meeting for you with David Preece. I have a feeling you're going to need a good attorney."

"But doesn't he specialize in divorces?" asked Libby, her mind racing. "He's a divorce lawyer, and Russ and I aren't getting a divorce." She said the word *divorce* in a whisper, searching JoAnne's pretending-to-pity expression.

JoAnne put her arm around Libby and smoothed her hair with a gnarled hand. "Yes, he does, dear. He specializes in separations and divorce, and he knows how to beat his opponent to a bloody, withering pulp." She saw the shock in Libby's eyes, the horror, if you will, of beating people into pulps—bloody, withered, or otherwise. "Now, now," cooed JoAnne, her smile falsely wise. "I'll be right there with you and help you every step of the way, my dear. It's not for *you* to worry about."

Chapter 11

Russ decided to get dressed and leave before Libby returned from her errand. He assumed she had gone on an errand. She had taken Olivia with her, and even Pat. He needed to take care of something without delay. Especially now that Libby had discovered he was making monthly payments. He would just tell her he had to meet Jerry McPherson about important legal matters they needed to discuss.

Dusk had quickly fallen. He turned on his headlights and watched the sides of the road for the glowing eyes of deer. He didn't need to hit a deer, or any other varmint, for that matter. Consequently, it took him twenty minutes to get to his destination.

He remembered Scott would be out of town on business, providing the perfect opportunity to stop by for a visit. Beverly's vehicle was in the driveway, and Scott's was nowhere to be seen.

He was out of town.

Russ parked a few blocks down the street and walked up to the house. To him it was a house, yes, but it wasn't a home. Beverly's *house* was boldly modern, not the rustic structure Russ had always preferred. Then again, it wasn't *his* house. It was Beverly's—and

Scott's—and the house reflected Scott's personality. A meticulous, well-kept yard, a tidy square of white fencing around the house and garage, and bushes lined up in a straight, calculated pattern. Everything exact. Materials wooden and brick. The garage matching the exterior of the house with shades of white and green trim. There were houses on both sides. Russ didn't like the idea of neighbors anywhere near his home, and so, he didn't have them. Not where he lived on Grand Lake. On Grand Lake, the houses and cottages were built on larger lots. There was plenty of room to breathe. There was adequate privacy, and Russ *required* privacy.

The lights were on in the kitchen. There were three bedrooms, a large basement, the kitchen, and an L-shaped living room. She also had a sewing room, and Scott had a den.

Beverly worked four days a week at a gift shop in Alpena. He could tell by the way her vehicle was parked that she had been out and about that day. Sometimes at the quarry, he would imagine what she was doing—if she were at home or driving around or maybe out with a friend.

He knocked twice before hearing her footsteps. She opened the door, wearing only a red velour robe. Her hair was damp because she had just washed it. She appeared self-conscious at the intrusion and pulled the door to partially hide herself. "Can I come in?" he asked.

He watched her closely. She was glowing, her skin pulsating light. He felt heat coming from her. Whatever made her glow and burn, he wanted every part of her.

She opened the door and moved over to the kitchen counter where she made coffee. He sat down at the table, watching her. He wanted to touch her, but first, he would have coffee and tell her the latest information.

"Libby found out about the money," he said. He leaned back into the chair and pushed the heels of his boots against the orange squares of the tiles. "She knows."

"What did you tell her?" Beverly asked in a gentle voice. She was busy at the counter, putting oatmeal cookies on a plate. "How did you explain it?"

"I told her I'm sending money to my sister. Like I said before, I'll keep doing what I can. But Libby doesn't need to know about it."

"Frankly, I'm tired of hearing about Libby. Libby this and that. Oh no, can't let *Libby* find out! I don't want Libby to *leave* me!" Her calm nature gone, she chastised him, and at that moment, he realized how beautiful she was without makeup. If only she knew. If only he had the courage to tell her, "Do you know how beautiful you are without makeup?"

She said, "You keep forgetting about us. Why *is* that?"

He knew that the "us" didn't include him. He took off his ball cap and put it on the table. He crossed his legs and leaned back to examine the ceiling. "How could I forget?" he asked. "I give you money. If I didn't care, would I take on the responsibility?"

"You give me money because you know I'll take the matter to court if you don't!"

"Oh, sure," he muttered. "Off to court! I know!"

"She needs things," Beverly said, forgetting about the coffee and the cookies, forgetting that she loved him.

"She *needs* things," Beverly repeated. "And so do I!"

"I might lose my job," Russ confessed, weighing the pros and cons of her. "Things are slowing down at the quarry. JoAnne's giving me a hassle about the land and property my grandfather left me. I need more time."

"You don't *have* time if Libby knows about the money!"

He gestured toward the coffee maker, which had stopped gurgling. "Coffee, please?"

She selected a white mug from the cupboard and poured him a cup of coffee. He liked sugar and cream, so she moved items around in the refrigerator until she found the liquid creamer. She reached for the sugar bowl in the cupboard above the stove. He watched her prepare the coffee the way he liked it. That impressed him—women doing things, from coffee to love-making, the way he liked it.

She walked over to him and put the mug down on the table. She was about to turn back to the counter, but he clamped his hands around her waist.

"You're so beautiful," he said.

But then, so was Libby. Libby, a natural beauty. Soapy-smelling skin. If Libby wore makeup, it was barely noticeable, enhancing her features rather than covering them up. She smelled like vanilla soap compared to Beverly, who smelled of lavender.

She wore the lavender scent because she expected him to show up.

Scott is out of town.

Russ pulled her onto his lap and slipped his hand inside her robe. He moved his fingers across her breasts. She would never stop him from touching her anywhere he wanted; she was that way. She let it happen. She would not stiffen at his touch the way Libby sometimes did.

Their "meetings" weren't inspired by a bond of physical means alone, although that was strong enough. They came together by the necessity to speak with their emotions. Russ appreciated this talking without saying a word. If he had a choice, no one would ever *talk*. People would gesture, touch, maybe write short notes to each other.

He tasted her lips. She was good at kissing; she slid her tongue deep into his mouth and kept it there, then moved her tongue, slowly, over his lips and back into his mouth. He put a hand between her legs. She was ready for him before he even started.

He pulled off her robe. The kitchen was chilly. He felt tiny bumps lift across her skin, like Braille all over her body everywhere he touched her—down her leg, across her back. She unbuttoned his shirt and scratched his chest lightly to make him shiver. She put her hand down lower, unzipped his pants and touched him, still slowly. It was their usual process; it just happened this way between them. She always knew what to do and exactly how to do it, letting him kiss her on the mouth, their tongues pushing and pressing. He liked putting his hand between her legs and touching her without her flinching or pulling away from him. Like Libby did.

She lifted upward. He moved his tongue over her breasts again. She worked herself into a straddling position on his lap, facing him, her hand holding his. He pressed his other hand against her back, and then, there was a crash down the hallway.

Next, they heard only the tick of the clock above the stove. A second later, the coffee maker sputtered. Russ knew what was happening even before he turned and saw Scott standing there. Scott was in a suit. His work clothes. Scott pointed the .38 he showed Russ not too long ago, his hand shaking.

Beverly stayed straddled on Russ's lap, her hands falling from his chest. "Who talks first?" Russ asked.

Scott said, "Don't move. I want to look at this a while. And remember it."

A mere two inches apart, Russ noticed Beverly's thick eyelashes; he noticed tiny freckles on her nose and that her breath was congested with peppermint. They were close enough for her to press against his chest. Looking at her intensely was the only thing left to do. He knew she was going to cry seconds before she did. One tear after another slid down her blanched face. She closed her eyes and opened them again, raising them to the spinning ceiling fan above.

"Ah," said Scott, unable to steady the hand pointing the pistol. "Don't cry, honey. I should have knocked first. Oh wait, this is *my* house!"

"Put the gun down," Russ said. "We'll talk about this."

"Talk about what, you fucking my wife? Maybe you're going to sit there—my wife naked on your lap—and *lie* about it?"

"I don't want to die tonight is all I'm saying."

"You should have thought about *that* before you came here."

Russ knew if he kept him talking, Scott might not pull the trigger. Besides, Scott could only shoot one of them at a time if he could shoot anything at all. "Thought you were out of town," Russ said. "Downstate somewhere."

"And I thought my wife was loyal," Scott replied. "That makes us both look like idiots, don't you think?"

"I already know *I'm* an idiot. But I sure as hell wouldn't shoot anyone. Not over sex. And not with a goddamned shaking hand! You're going to do it? Do it right. Shoot me, not her, and shoot me between the eyes. I don't like the idea of becoming a vegetable just because you've had too much to drink."

"Shut up!" Scott yelled. He pointed the gun at Beverly. "Get off him, bitch. And get dressed!"

When Beverly climbed off Russ's lap and bent over to pick up her robe from the floor, Scott pointed the gun at Russ. "Seems you've been caught with your pants down, brother."

"Don't call me brother! You know I hate that!"

"Here's my *brother-in-law* sitting at my kitchen table with *my wife*, half-naked, and about to do it. Zip up before I shoot it off!"

"Well, that wouldn't be good!" Russ admitted, zipping up quickly.

Again, Scott pointed the gun at Beverly. "I knew you were screwing around, but I had no idea you preferred hillbilly white trash like him. All this time, I wondered *who*, and here it was *him*!" Scott winced and smiled at the same time. He clicked his tongue against his teeth, feigning surprise in regard to the facts. "My sister's hillbilly slob of a husband. I guess you prefer his stench. Maybe you like the fact that he doesn't brush his teeth."

"I brush my teeth," Russ said defensively. He chuckled, despite his obvious predicament. "And I wash behind my ears too."

Scott pointed the gun back at him; he cocked the hammer, and they all heard it. If there'd been people sitting in the next room, they would have heard the click too, just as loud and twice as deadly. "I want to blow your demented head off!" he said.

"So, *do* it," Russ said, both hands out.

Beverly cowered at the counter. She lowered her eyes when Scott mentioned blowing Russ's head off: "I'll leave, and you'll never have to deal with me again," she shouted. "You can have the house. Everything. Don't shoot him!"

"Don't shoot him?" Scott pretended he hadn't heard her and repeated, "Don't *shoot* him?"

Russ turned in the chair in time to witness the melting of Scott. His face as he perspired, his shirt and the jacket of his suit stained by his leaking body. Russ couldn't speak. There was nothing more to say. If Scott wanted to shoot him, and of course it appeared that he did, he should just go ahead and pull the trigger.

Russ looked at Beverly. Her crying stopped, but she was paralyzed at the counter, her sensual vitality long gone. Scott put the pistol to his head. When Beverly saw this, she screamed and covered her eyes with her hands, but within seconds, he shot at the floor, then aimed the gun behind his left ear.

Russ stood up. He knew if he did anything important in this life, he had to keep Scott Weyman from shooting himself. If Libby found out about his affair with Beverly, she might get over it in time, but if her only brother shot himself because of catching them in the act, Libby would hate Russ for the rest of her life.

He was going to knock the gun out of Scott's hand, or at least try to tip it out of his grip, but Scott backed up and yelled, "Don't follow me!"

He turned and walked back down the dark hallway.

Beverly looked over at Russ. She said through the fingers at her mouth, "He'll go off somewhere and shoot himself. You have to stop him!"

Chapter 12

JoAnne was drinking a gin and tonic and discussing the latest information about Russ and Beverly with Marilyn Clayton. Marilyn didn't drink alcohol. She was sipping a soda.

"And so?" JoAnne prodded, feeling light-headed because she was on her third drink. They had just closed the restaurant, and every evening JoAnne summoned Marilyn to her living quarters upstairs to get the lowdown on her most recent discoveries. "What do you have for me tonight?"

Marilyn rolled her oblong body among the pillows of JoAnne's mauve-colored couch. She arranged her papers in order before speaking. When her eyebrows arched a half-inch into an expression of shock, JoAnne knew she had something exceptional to report. Marilyn said, "Russ and Beverly have a child."

JoAnne's lower lip dropped. She fiddled with the gold chain around her neck. "Go on," she said, suddenly dizzy.

"A baby girl. Remember when Beverly supposedly lost a baby about a year ago? Not so. She took the baby to live with a friend, somewhere outside of Standish. She visits the baby every other week."

JoAnne was speechless, but only for a second. She continued to study the walls, as if she wasn't quite sure it was the same room she had lived in for the past twenty-two years. She swallowed the rest of her drink and wished she had another.

Marilyn jostled the papers before going on. "I checked with a woman I know at the post office. Russ buys money orders for three hundred dollars a month. He does this without fail and has done it for about a year now. Beverly is making him accountable for child support."

JoAnne murmured, "I see," and again played with the gold chain around her neck. "Even Beverly would probably be able to supply the proper proof. But, of course, Russ is so gullible, it could be that she's lying, and he doesn't realize it."

"I don't know. I just got back from Beverly's house and Russ was there, doing his thing. I couldn't get a good picture of them. Scott showed up, like we planned."

"Excellent!"

"I'm not sure about that. Scott had a gun. I could see most of what happened through the window. I thought he was going to shoot them both, then himself. In fact, he had the gun to his head, but apparently, he thought better of it and left the house. He didn't see me though. I hid in the bushes."

"Scott needs to know about this child," said JoAnne. "The poor dear. Here he thought his beloved wife lost their child. He let her go to Standish alone to mourn. And didn't mind her going there every other week afterwards. No doubt he thought she was visiting the baby's grave. Aren't people muddled-up idiots?" JoAnne said this last part adamantly. She was generally unable to control her stalwart views on human ignorance to begin with.

Marilyn concurred by saying, "Yes, for the most part." She shook her massive head of hair, which was stuck, plastered and stiff like a cumbersome helmet. "Terribly gullible *and* blind."

"That's excellent work, Marilyn," said JoAnne. She was elated and even awed, not a common reaction for her when judging the effort of others. "We have to find out more about this friend taking care of the baby." She adjusted her bony hips against the couch, her eyes darting about as she plotted. "Get her address and inform David Preece about this new turn of events."

"I'll get on it. First, I need another drink."

When Marilyn stood up to get another soda, a knock on the door interrupted her last step. She went to the door and opened it. The hostess from the downstairs dining room delivered a message, "Scott Weyman's in the kitchen. He wants to talk to JoAnne. I think she'd better see him."

JoAnne was already standing and had smoothed her outfit down her bent body. "Tell him to come up," she told the girl sharply and turned to Marilyn with wide eyes. "If he wants to grill me about Russ, I'm telling him the truth!"

Marilyn mumbled, "Fine with me." She held the door open for Scott. She watched him stumble toward JoAnne, and then left the scene. Scott had been drinking, that much was clear. He smelled of alcohol, enough to impair his movements and speech. He was still dressed in his work clothes—a suit and tie, black trousers, all of it wrinkled against his haggard body.

JoAnne had always been fond of Scott. She had genuinely loved him and Libby's mother, Susan. She even remembered how happy Susan was when Scott was born. Now he was in agony. And JoAnne knew why.

"Sweetheart," JoAnne began. "Come in. You look ill!"

Scott put a hand over his eyes and leaned forward. "JoAnne, help me," he said.

JoAnne took his arm and led him into her living room area. She led him across the brown carpeting and deposited him upon the couch. When Scott slouched forward, JoAnne pushed him back against the couch. She could see that he had been crying. She smoothed his hair down with the tips of her fingers. "Now there, what *is* it?"

"Russ and Beverly," Scott said. He slurred his words like his tongue was thick inside his mouth. "They've been together all this time."

"Russ and Beverly," JoAnne echoed. "Go on. What about them?"

"I caught them. Did you know Russ was seeing my wife?" His eyes sought hers, suggesting that she had known all along and didn't bother to tell him. "I saw your friend, Marilyn, leave my house when I did. She was watching them for you?"

JoAnne sighed and bit her bottom lip, pretending dread over revealing what she knew. She put her hand to the back of Scott's neck, trying to console him. "Yes," she said. "I'm so, so sorry. I figured they'd get caught sooner or later. I'm sorry you had to be the one to catch them at it, dear. But then, isn't it better to know?"

Scott peered through the fog of disillusionment. "What, to know?" he stammered. "I suppose, but I'm not sure!"

JoAnne persisted. "Take my word for it. It's better to know the truth than look like a blazing fool. Soon the whole town will know. Affairs are never kept secret for long. Believe me, I know. My husband had an affair. I found out from the woman who runs the bait and tackle shop on route twenty-three. It was hideous, I tell you!"

JoAnne's eyes narrowed at the memory. "He'd been having an affair for over three years, and it took some old woman with a goiter and bad eyesight to wake me up to the truth. But I didn't really care," JoAnne concluded piously, still rubbing the back of Scott's neck. "Most men *do* require a variety."

"Aaron had an affair?" Scott asked, stuck on that piece of news.

"Yes, and I wasn't surprised when I heard about it. Don't dwell on that right now, dear. You've bigger fish to fry."

"Bigger fish?"

"The woman you saw at the house, Marilyn Clayton, is a good friend of mine. She's also a private detective. For personal reasons, I've been having Russ followed. You see, he's trying to cheat me out of some property that belonged to my father. Anyway, I'm afraid you're up for another dose of truth. I'll simply have to tell you what I know."

"Another dose of the *truth*?" Scott echoed, closing his eyes. "I don't know if I want to hear it."

JoAnne waited for him to look at her again. "Be a man, dear. You need to know. We can't have you looking completely daft. We can't allow strangers to fill you in on your wife's unsavory activities, now can we?"

He said, "I suppose not."

"Good. Now before I tell you, I want you to promise you'll stay the night in one of my guest rooms here at the Lodge."

JoAnne squeezed his arm until he nodded yes. "I have proof that Russ and Beverly have a child," JoAnne continued. "She told you the baby that she gave birth to about a year ago, I believe, died as an infant? Afraid not. This baby is alive and living with Beverly's friend."

JoAnne waited for the first part to register in Scott's mind. She knew it had when he ran his index finger over his lower lip, trying to keep it from drooping. JoAnne proceeded. "We have proof that this child is Russ's," she lied. "Obviously, Beverly made up the death story to hide the facts. I suppose Beverly thinks Russ is going to leave Libby and marry her."

Still touching his lip, Scott whimpered, "D-does Libby know?"

"Not yet. You see, Russ pays Beverly child support. And I do know for a fact that Libby discovered another piece of the puzzle recently. She found out he's been spending three hundred dollars a month, but she doesn't know why. Russ told her he's sending money to Andrea every month. Libby asked me about it. I had to tell her Russ is lying. If anyone's sending money to

Andrea, it's me. I've been supporting that freak of nature for twenty-seven years now."

"My God," Scott whispered, horrified. He leaned back, and this time, JoAnne didn't bother to pull him forward.

"You need some sleep," she advised. "I'll have someone open up my best guest bedroom. You stay here tonight where I can keep an eye on you. I'll help you all I can. We'll help each other."

"Get me a drink," Scott said, his tone harsh. "Whatever you have handy!"

JoAnne went to the counter to fix him a gin and tonic and another one for herself. She felt a ripple of exhilaration roll up her rickety spine. The cat, as they said, was out of the bag.

She soothed Scott while he drank and then escorted him to the guest bedroom herself. She even tucked him in bed, just as she knew his mother, Susan, would have done. Once she was satisfied he was asleep, JoAnne went back to her own bedroom.

• • •

Russ left Beverly's house, but before going home, he parked at the harbor. The lights overhead illuminated the docks and shoreline. There were several sailboats and two yachts docked at Bishop's Resort.

He wanted a cigarette, but he didn't give in. He knew he had to be strong with all aspects of his life, now more than ever. He also knew that Libby finding out about his affair with Beverly should come from him. Libby was upstairs in bed by the time he got home. First, he checked on Olivia. She was sound asleep, as he knew she would be. Her faithful companion, Pat, was curled up on the bed by her feet.

Russ walked into the master bedroom, detecting a blend of vanilla and cinnamon. Libby's bath gel and lotion. He made it all the way over to the bed and sat down on the edge before she even heard him.

Suddenly, she sat up. Her hair hung down, long and silky. She wore a thin cotton nightgown that was too big for her. She looked at him, as if wondering why he was there. "You had already left when I got up earlier," he explained. "I had an errand to run."

"I went to see your mother," she said, even though she was still half asleep.

"Why the hell did you do *that*?" He knew that Libby spending time with JoAnne, for any reason, was *not* good. "Tell me, Libby!"

"She says you're not giving money to Andrea."

Russ reached out for her as she slipped from the bed. He couldn't let her leave before telling her everything, but for now, he would omit the part about giving Beverly money to support their one-year-old daughter. The only thing out in the open was the affair itself. Since Scott knew, other people would find out soon enough.

If Russ could get over the fear of what Libby might do, he would know how to deal with Beverly blackmailing him for more child support. He wasn't even sure the child was his but knew that she very well could be. He had been seeing Beverly for over five years.

That part Libby didn't need to know about either.

"What else did JoAnne tell you?" he asked.

to be haunted. In the new lighthouse, for example, it was said that the ghost of a woman in her thirties had died during the early 1900's and was trapped there. She lost her mind during one long brutal winter, and thus she haunted the grounds forever.

Russ recalled Scott talking about this particular ghost, as if in awe of her. There was another lighthouse ghost Scott frequently mentioned, that of the keeper who would not leave his post, and during storms on February nights only, he would continue to light his light. Knowing that Scott was fascinated with local history, particularly that of the two lighthouses and their residential ghosts, Russ thought maybe he might stop at one of these locations to think things through.

Scott also enjoyed looking at the boats and watching the whitecaps on Lake Huron and the freighters on the way to port carrying cargo. Like Russ, Scott always said that the Great Lakes were the reason he lived in northern lower Michigan, near Lake Huron—for the spectacular scenery, the sandy shores, and the deep blue water. Lake Huron was the second largest of the Great Lakes and the third largest freshwater lake on the face of the Earth. Lake Huron, named Lac de Huron—Lake of the Huron—by the French, was on the same waterway and level as Lake Michigan, separated by the Straits of Mackinac. A spectacular scene, Russ admitted. A sign, truly, of longevity.

Yet there was no sign of Scott Weyman.

Russ drove in the opposite direction, the northeastern direction on Lake Huron, toward Rogers City. Also called the nautical city, Rogers City was where Russ worked. The open pit Limestone and Chemical

Company, essential in steel making was one of the world's largest, and it felt like it too. It was backbreaking labor, day after day.

He checked into a motel that was close to the quarry. Jerry was right. The last thing he needed was to lose his job. If Libby sued for a divorce, or if she even obtained a legal separation, he would end up paying child support. And God knows what would come after that. Libby might follow JoAnne's advice, and the two of them would conspire to rob him blind.

He tried to push these thoughts away as he drove onward. He scanned the streets of Rogers City, driving past the Hoeft State Park on US 23 North. This threehundred-acre park was another old stomping ground for Russ, Jerry, and Scott, back when they were kids. He wondered if Scott might be hiding among the cedar and birch.

He continued to drive along the outskirts of the city limits. Once he was satisfied that Scott wasn't in the vicinity, he checked into the cheapest motel he could find. It was called Magic Moon. He ate dinner— a chicken sandwich and fries—and settled into the double bed but could not fall asleep until two in the morning, the television still on and sputtering static.

• • •

He forced himself to go to work at the quarry the next morning. He even signed up for overtime. He had no family to go home to and nothing to do after his shift ended. And, he could use the extra money. Maybe, the physical work would exhaust him enough so that he could sleep at night. He was used to the rhythm of

Libby's breathing, of Libby lying next to him. Basically, it was a matter of shrugging off old habits and trying something new, and besides, it was freedom. A vacation into the unknown. No Libby. No schedules to adhere to. No chores. Nothing expected of him other than waking up on time.

He woke up late the first morning with only ten minutes to shower and dress. Even though the quarry was twelve miles from the motel, Russ found himself needing the extra time to simply navigate. He had forgotten to pack his toothpaste and toothbrush. He barely remembered his keychain and wallet. He wanted to drive across the street to the same restaurant where he bought takeout the night before, but he didn't have time. He worried that he wouldn't be able to wake up in the morning without Libby's help. He would never get anywhere on time. He would not be able to adapt to a life without her.

By the time he got to work, spoke to the foreman about his absence the day before, asked about more overtime, and reported that he had moved to the Magic Moon in town, he looked like he had worked a full shift, although it had just begun. All day long, operating the forklift and the front-end loader, transporting from one deck to another, Russ looked over his shoulder. He couldn't help but sense conflict forthcoming.

For the first time ever, in fifteen years of working at the quarry, he didn't trust his skills and reflexes. It was an industrial-manufacturing environment, and the workers, including Russ, were exposed to explosives and unpredictable outdoor elements and faulty conditions.

There was the risk of radiation poisoning, and there was a constant vibration of high-tech equipment coming from every direction, loud clanking and banging noises despite ear plugs. He endured because Jerry was right, if he lost this job, he could kiss his life goodbye.

Instead of going home that afternoon—he remembered he didn't have a *home* to go to anymore—and instead of going back to the drab and depressing motel room with no cable or room service, he decided to drive past Beverly's house to see if Scott's car was in the driveway. Beverly's car was gone, and so was Scott's.

He wondered if Beverly had left for Standish already, or maybe she'd left Michigan altogether, seeking a place to hide until things settled down. What if he couldn't find her? What if she took a bottle of pills, drank while taking them, and went over the edge? What would happen to the baby?

He was about to pull into the driveway and inspect the situation—perhaps Beverly was there, but her car was in the garage—when he noticed a dark green Jeep behind him. He couldn't swear to it, but the driver looked a lot like that ugly friend of JoAnne's. That obese gargoyle, Marilyn Clayton.

He came to an abrupt stop and jumped out of the vehicle so quickly, he didn't realize he was pounding on Marilyn's window until his fist throbbed. "Open up!" he shouted. "Why are you following me?'

He kept pounding until she rolled the window down. "You'd better not break my window," she said. "I've been looking all over for you. There's been a tragedy!"

"What do you mean a tragedy?" Russ was so worked up over Marilyn Clayton following him, he had trouble translating her words. "What is it?" he insisted. "Tell me!"

Marilyn was visibly shaken. "JoAnne told me this afternoon," she shouted back. "I've been trying to find you. Some realtor called JoAnne. He said Scott Weyman was found inside a house—the house that was for sale near Otter's Landing. Scott was interested in buying it."

"What do you mean *found?*" Russ insisted.

"He had a key to some house and was going to buy it for Beverly. But, he shot himself. He's dead!"

"Libby?" he asked. "*Where's Libby?*"

"She—she's out of her mind. That's why JoAnne sent me to find you. JoAnne went to your place to tell Libby what happened, and Libby broke down. JoAnne took her to the Lodge. She called a doctor. But Libby wants you."

"And my daughter?"

"She's at the Lodge too. JoAnne wants you to come and get her. She doesn't want the child to hear about her uncle."

Russ didn't stand around for more talk. He ran back to his vehicle and drove off toward the Birch Hill Lodge.

• • •

When Russ arrived, he found JoAnne standing inside the doorway to the restaurant of the Lodge; she had watched him run across the parking lot. The restaurant had been closed early, but JoAnne couldn't very well shut down the bedrooms she had already rented out. She couldn't very well tell her guests they had to leave because there had been a death—a suicide, rather—in the family.

JoAnne held the door open for him. Her creased expression was the same as when she informed Russ that his grandfather had died, slack-eyed and grimacing. And it was the same when she told him Aaron had died of a heart attack. It was her *we have a tragedy but I'm not to blame* look.

JoAnne played with the gold chain around her neck as she was prone to do in a crisis. Suddenly, she grabbed Russ's arm, gave him a sly nod, and said conspiratorially, "Let's try to get along for Libby's sake."

Russ didn't care what JoAnne felt, or how she wanted things handled. "Where *is* she?" he asked, thinking that Libby should be the one standing by the door waiting for him, not JoAnne.

"She wanted to be alone," JoAnne said. "I left her on the back porch. See if you can talk her into coming inside; it's *terribly* cold out there!"

Russ pushed past JoAnne and went straight for the back porch. As a boy, he would hide there from JoAnne and her list of chores. He was responsible for taking care of the rich, ignorant tourists, pruning JoAnne's damned bushes and apple trees, weeding her flower beds, scrubbing floors, hauling in firewood, the endless shoveling in the winter, and tracking down his sister, before she took off with her wayward friends.

"Go find your sister," JoAnne always demanded. "You'd better look after that stupid sister of yours or I'll send her away!"

JoAnne stopped Russ in his tracks. "Listen to me," she said. "Libby's not well. She asked me what happened, and I told her. Scott came here last night, and we talked. He had been drinking. I wanted him to stay the night, and I thought I had convinced him to sleep it off, but he left. Even after I got him settled in one of the rooms, he *left!* I want you to know he was out of his mind drunk! This unfortunate *accident* had nothing to do with *me!*"

$$\bullet \ \bullet \ \bullet$$

Russ knew she wasn't telling him everything. There had to be more. Why would Scott shoot himself? Over finding his wife in the arms of another man? Who happened to be *him*. He had to admit such a scene would make him crazy for a while, but push him to suicide? Hardly. "What else did you tell him?" Russ asked her. He wanted the lowdown quickly. "Tell me all of it!"

"There's nothing more to tell. I only wanted Scott to sleep off the alcohol. He asked if I knew about you and Beverly. I told him I did. But then, half the town knows!"

"Fuck half the town," Russ said, turning toward the back porch.

"Oh! I'm sure you have!" JoAnne shouted after him. Fortunately, Russ didn't hear her.

He was focused on Libby.

The storm windows were in place, but it was a summer porch, and there was a sharp chill throughout the entire room. A layer of frost covered the card tables, flowered vinyl chairs, and matching couches.

141

Libby was curled up on one of the couches—the brown and blue flowered one. She wore black jeans, a red sweater, and black boots. She sat up when she saw Russ and worked a wad of tissue around inside her hand. "When we were children," she began, "Scott and I played back here. Our mothers were good friends."

"I remember," Russ said. He hesitated, wondering if he should touch her.

What he remembered most vividly was that Libby's mother always reminded him of a fragile paper doll, and yet, abnormally quiet and composed. She was a dainty wildflower, fluttering in a breeze. Somehow, he knew that her death was more than a slip off a break wall and losing her footing and falling down a cement structure on a windy afternoon.

When he reached out to take Libby's hand, she pulled away from him. "I don't want to see Beverly!" she said, her hands now clamped together. "Keep her away from here! Away from my family!"

"I will," Russ promised. "I won't let her near you!"

Truthfully, the fact that he was the cause of this tragedy hadn't registered in his mind until now. If Scott hadn't found him and Beverly in his kitchen, Scott would still be alive. He didn't really like Scott, but he had talked with him on a weekly basis. Scott was at all the family celebrations—birthday parties, holidays. The memory of him, even his irritating, scratchy voice, made Russ feel shaken. Responsible.

He said, "I *am* sorry, Libby." But then his mind changed direction. "Where's Olivia?"

"She's upstairs. We're going to stay here for a while."

"I think we need to be together." He knew it was the wrong thing to say when Libby lifted her head and acted as if she didn't even know him; as if she didn't *want* to know him and wished he would just go away and invade some other woman's life.

"Together?" she asked. She combed two fingers through her reddish-golden hair. Her hair was—long and straight and incredibly shiny.

"Libby, listen to me. There will be a funeral. Olivia will ask a lot of questions. And there are things we need to take care of."

"Take care of?" Libby laughed uncontrollably. "Why should *you* worry about taking care of me *now*? I needed you yesterday. I needed you the day before yesterday. You were off with her." She shook her head, angry again. "I can't even say her name!"

"Forget her, for Christ's sake! I'm here for *you*."

"Olivia and I will live here for a while. You can move back to the house until we decide what to do. Later, we'll sell the house and split the money."

"Dammit, Libby!" he yelled. "Don't try to make decisions right now! You're in shock. We've got to deal with *that* problem first."

"Never mind what I deal with first; never mind what I deal with at all! You go back to the house. I left Pat in the kitchen. Tomorrow I'll get her and some of our things."

Russ decided it would be best to let her have her way for now. If she wanted to stay at the Lodge, he wouldn't argue with her. He didn't think JoAnne was cruel enough to tamper with Libby's emotions while she was distracted by Scott's suicide. "I'm not sure that's a

143

good idea," he said, thinking of all the ways JoAnne could brainwash her. "I've got a room in Rogers City. You take the house."

Russ moved forward to touch her, but she stood up and turned away from him. "Libby," he said. "I love you. I love Olivia. Please come home so I can take care of you."

"I'm tired, Russ. I'm going up to bed."

She had one hand on the door knob. When she opened the door to the Lodge, Russ could feel the heat from the fireplaces. So terribly, uncommonly hot.

As he watched Libby leave, he knew it would be a struggle to see Olivia tomorrow, or any other day thereafter. Libby looked back at him before walking through the door, and there was a strange, trance-like void of recognition inside her sea-green eyes.

Russ knew JoAnne had drugged her, and it would be a very long time before he got her back.

Chapter 14

The day of Scott Weyman's memorial service, David Preece had an unexpected visit from JoAnne. His office was on the second floor of an ornate brick and marble building on the south end of Alpena. Several professional businesses paid rent in this building as well. Two doctors, three accountants, and two other attorneys. The scrollwork frame on the sign outside proved that Preece was worthy of JoAnne and other local socialites.

"Are you coming to the service?" JoAnne asked him, even before closing the door behind her and selecting a chair by the window. "It would look good if you did."

"Of course, I'll come."

Preece had just finished a phone conversation with another client and was scribbling notes on a pad. What he intended to do with the notes would have to wait; JoAnne Shaw had arrived, and the fact that she paid him more than he demanded meant she came before anyone else on his client list.

Preece was a moderately tall man with a lean body, and he carried himself without curvature of muscle or bone. He was athletic and well-dressed, perfectly manicured and groomed. He noticed JoAnne made a big production out of situating herself on the suede, high-backed gray chair. Her slim body gyrated in various angles and points; her black dress—a yarn material—looked like a stocking for her entire body, from below her knobby knees to the turtleneck wrapped tightly around her ribbed throat.

JoAnne had complained to Preece not too long ago about her arthritic legs and a painful throb in her backbone due to a car accident years before. She claimed that the car injury had returned to haunt her; it caused her to walk with rigid motion; made her pause for breaks she had never considered taking before. Breaks, she insisted, were for slackers.

"Can't you afford comfortable chairs, David?" she asked with a slap of arrogance. "I'd much rather sit on a rock—" She turned, looked downward, as if to see beneath herself. "Oh, it *is* a rock. A cushion made of cement perhaps." She steered her dark eyes toward the mahogany-framed clock above Preece's head.

"It's affordable," Preece said, gambling that he might be able to determine if she was joking. He decided she *was* and added, "That way my clients don't stay too long and bore me with their endless prattle and detailed instructions."

He glanced over the rim of his bifocals to add hastily, "That doesn't include you, of course. You're never a bore, my dear."

"Cut the crap," JoAnne cackled. "And don't ever call me *your dear* again! I'll *bore* you with this: Have you contacted that spineless Brett Daniels, my apparently former accountant?"

146

"No, it seems he's left town."

"The bastard!" JoAnne grumbled. "Find him! For all I know, the son of a bitch made copies of my, shall we say, questionable little sidetracks with the government. Nothing major, mind you," she said, "but enough for Jerry and Russ to distract me... temporarily."

"How much was this?" Preece asked, daringly. He had put the tablets away and sat back inside his leather chair to concentrate completely on JoAnne.

She never failed to pique his curiosity. He studied her, mesmerized by her drive and her taut bronze complexion, which carved brittle around her lips. "You need to be honest with me, JoAnne," he said, although he realized by the ripple crossing her face that she was not about to divulge this information. He said childishly, "Thought I'd give it a shot."

"Well, don't do it again! Here's the thing. Find Daniels and pay him off. Put the heat under Thomas Bishop. I want to buy most of his land as soon as possible. It's crucial to my plan. He's jerking my chain. *No one* jerks my chain! Get a price, and I'll pay it! Better yet, tell him I found his secret bastard child, who I'm certain will make big trouble if he doesn't do as I say."

"A secret bastard child?" Preece repeated, somehow keeping a straight face. He felt, however, as if he were composing, wall by wall, a mental vault to store her words when in fact, he was merely rubbing his neck because it ached, and he picked at his silver hair as it drifted lopsided upon his skull.

"And Claudia Bishop," JoAnne continued, as if reading down her list of supporters, "find that little

147

whore in Florida and convince her we need her to come home for a visit. Tell her Auntie JoAnne will pay her grandly for her *efforts*—the details about her encounter with Jerry McPherson."

"I believe McPherson was acquitted due to lack of evidence," Preece said, wanting JoAnne to know he would not participate in the resurrection of an alleged molestation case. If nothing else, McPherson was a fellow-lawyer and Preece might need him for a favor someday.

"Acquitted?" JoAnne sneered, leaning forward, her frail arms exposed. "I'm certainly not implying that there could ever be another trial; I know he was acquitted! I'm saying this Claudia-slut can come back to town and start the horrid rumors up again. If you can't follow what I'm saying, perhaps I'll need to find a lawyer who can."

JoAnne's lips relaxed. "I like that diamond ring you're wearing, David," she felt provoked to mention. "You want to keep it?"

Preece puffed inside his chair. "Of course, and I *will* keep it!" He examined the diamond respectfully, as if it were a spark of fire. He looked at JoAnne. Who was she to bring up his jewelry? Next, she'll go for his sexual preference and she had another thing coming if she thought she'd get *that* information.

It was as if JoAnne could read his mind, most explicitly. "Did one of your boyfriends give it to you? Perhaps the *boy* I saw you with the other day at Hambert's restaurant?"

Preece snorted and wheezed; his chair sucked him downward when JoAnne smiled with such deliberate force her bronze makeup split around her papery eyelids. "I have my ways," she said. "We wouldn't want it to get out that you're bedding young boys, now would we? This isn't the big city. This is Grand Lake, northern Michigan—in the woods, mind you. Stick with women for show. Like Leeann McPherson. Keep sleeping with *her* and take *her* out in public. Not your ass-buddy whore!"

Preece was so unnerved by her last comment, he almost retched. He tugged at his silver curls and jerked forward, hoping to brace himself to set things straight. Was he losing his hearing? Did she say what he thought she had said? "My *what*?" he inquired, babbling as he proceeded to pull his striped tie. "And... how do you know about Leeann McPherson?"

"Dear God, what do you take me for? Do you think I make threats for the hell of it? Do you think I make things up as I go?" JoAnne lifted her purse from the floor and pressed at the stiff cushion beneath her with a bony knuckle. "Perhaps this is all too much for you, David," she said again. "Perhaps we need to make some changes."

"Perhaps you can pay me an extra two hundred dollars an hour, goddamn it, if you expect me to partake in your schemes and digest your verbal abuse!"

"Digest this, *Davy*. McPherson's divorce is only pending at this point. You ought to know that. You're Leeann's attorney. Jerry could nail your faggot-ass to the wall with adultery charges. We all know about adultery, don't we now? That little extracurricular activity no one around here can refrain from?"

"You mean, like your husband, Aaron?" Preece said with reckless descent. He promptly regretted the comment as he watched JoAnne's face fall in hanging loops before springing into a mask of glee.

"I'm afraid you just made a monumental mistake," she said, clicking her tongue against the roof of her mouth. Nonetheless, she folded herself up and away into a sinister calm. Even her quaking chin was still.

She jingled the gold chain and flipped the gauzy scarf around her neck.

She waited for Preece to attempt reconciliation. "I'm s-sorry," he stuttered. "I had to go for it. You're hurling insults at me right and left. I'm just repeating a rumor I heard years ago when I used to live here. I didn't believe it at the time, but I can see by your expression that it's true. Now I know why you're so adamant to get Russ. In your eyes he's a womanizer like his father. I'm correct, aren't I, JoAnne? It seems—"

JoAnne bounced forward and cut off his words as if she'd sliced his throat with a straight razor. "Stick with what you're paid to do! You know nothing about my husband. Nothing of my marriage. If I were you, I'd play mute until I tell you to speak! I'll pay you the extra two hundred, you greedy-ass bastard, but by God, you'd better do everything I say. Dream about it in your sleep if you have to. Learn to read my mind! Do we understand each other so far?"

"More money *helps* me understand," Preece admitted dryly, and adjusted his tie when she pinched her scarf again. "Yes, yes," he droned on pathetically. "It certainly helps me understand!"

"*That* I already know," she shrieked. "Here's what *you* need to do. First." She pulled a manila envelope from her enormous purse, which had been balanced upon her knees. She unfolded herself and delivered the envelope to Preece's desk. "These are pictures of Russ and Beverly *in the act.*" She pulled a smaller envelope from her purse; it was white and quite fat. "Here are addresses you'll need, the address of Beverly's friend, for one. She's the woman who's taking care of Beverly's child. Find out how much Russ is paying her. I think around five hundred a month, not three. *You* get her to talk."

"The child is Russ's? How do—"

Again, JoAnne felt it necessary to cut off his words: "The second thing you need to know is that my daughter, Andrea, will be arriving this afternoon for Scott's memorial service. She's bringing that idiot husband of hers, that putrid, sickly-looking knave with the rotten teeth."

Preece simply nodded and plucked his earlobe. "Check him out too," she ordered curtly. "His name is Edwin Mayfield. I know he's got a record. We might need him later."

JoAnne shifted before Preece's desk, then sat back down and shifted some more, implying again that the cushion was uncomfortable even for her, a woman who could sit on a throne of spikes and still spin a viable web of deceit.

She proceeded to rummage inside her purse, which made Preece wonder if there was a number four to come, or number five, or six. Her perplexed expression made him think she could imagine him entwined with one of his lovers.

"Keep an eye on Andrea," JoAnne blurted out. "She's not quite right in the head."

"Imagine that," Preece said, lifting his tired eyes toward the ceiling.

"She's retarded, I'm afraid," JoAnne emphasized precisely. "I shouldn't have water skied so much when I was pregnant with her. I shouldn't have smoked and worked all day and night at the Lodge either. The strain cut off the oxygen to her brain. I'm surprised she can walk and talk at the same time."

Preece produced a paper napkin from his suit-jacket pocket and dabbed his chin with it. He couldn't help but stare at JoAnne. He tried one more time to cast a fixed stare over her shoulder, but to no avail.

JoAnne said, "Are you shocked that I'm not exactly fond or proud of my children, David?"

"Well, it *is* a bit odd."

"I never wanted children. I told my husband that, but he wouldn't listen. Now he's dead. If only people would listen to me the first time around!"

JoAnne stood up again, and this time, gripping her purse strap inside her curled hand, she prepared for the door. "As I've told you before, and hopefully, for the *last* time, David, I don't make a habit of repeating myself. Not for you, not for anyone. Now, you've got the photos. Guard them with your life. You can use them as evidence against Russ in court."

"Court?" Preece stood up, hoping to match her height. Although he was several inches taller than she was, she seemed taller. "Court? Evidence?" he said again, awed, worried, even terrified at the prospect of butting heads again with McPherson.

"That's right. You're my attorney and Libby's as well. I'm close to talking her into filing for a divorce. We tackle Russ so forcefully with the news, he drinks too much, misses a lot of work, and then I talk my friend at the quarry into firing him. It's really quite simple."

Preece watched JoAnne move toward the door. The arthritis jerked her joints and stunted her stride, but her fierce determination pushed her beyond all physical afflictions.

"Fire your own son?" Preece asked, completely dismayed. "But if it goes to court, how will he pay for child support and other expenses?"

JoAnne grabbed the doorknob with a purplish hand and tilted her head "Are you up for this or not, David? If you aren't I can find another attorney."

Preece knew JoAnne loved to play mental poker, but even so, he couldn't merge enough courage to match her ability. "I'm up for it," he said urgently, lest she think him incapable. "You can count on me, JoAnne."

"What a perfectly gentlemanly compliment," JoAnne said. "Go on, David. You want more money, I suppose."

"Yes! At least five thousand more as a retainer. I'm sorry, but this situation is out of the ordinary, not to mention illegal."

JoAnne chuckled so hard, her chain chimed. "Illegal? I've heard you are the king of illegal. That's why I hired you! All right, *sweetheart*—" He knew she was stroking him emotionally. "Here's what we'll do. You find the third copy of my father's will before Russ does, and I'll pay you an extra ten thousand dollars. How does that sound? Inviting?"

Preece tapped a slender foot. "I've been looking long and hard for that copy, JoAnne. Have you considered the possibility that Russ might be bluffing about this so-called third copy?"

"Russ isn't smart enough to bluff," JoAnne said, her impatience showing. "It's just like something my father would do. Father really wanted Russ to have the place, but what can I do? Russ would let it fall to ruin. What we'll do is rip the place down, board by board if we have to. The man wanting to buy it will tear it down and rebuild anyway. You find the will first, David, and the ten grand is yours. Then we go after Bishop. He knew I wanted that harbor property at Lake Huron and went behind my back and bought it himself. I want his balls, so arrange it!"

"Dear God!"

"You do what I ask, David, and not only will I pay you handsomely for the rest of your life, I'll give you all the photos I have of you and Leeann McPherson."

Preece went for the napkin again and wiped his forehead. "Photos, you say?"

"Yes, of you and Leeann, all caught up in a vivid entanglement of flesh."

"Vivid?" Preece wondered, staring past her again.

"So vivid I now know you have quite an unusual deformity. Well, I won't go into detail on that. I'm sure you know what I mean. See you at the service." JoAnne was halfway out the door. "Don't forget, four-thirty at the Grand Lake Chapel. Be there."

"A deformity?" Preece babbled, trying to recall the worst of his physical traits. He knew of three.

"Oh, my goodness, am I going to have to *repeat* myself?" JoAnne asked, her eyesight wavering and her head swooning. "You *know how* I *hate* that!"

Preece's expression went from shock to rage. He took a step forward but checked himself in time. He realized that JoAnne had more to say. Consequently, it was obvious the game was just beginning.

JoAnne touched her lip with a gnarled fingertip. "Oh David, by the way, I also have pictures of you and your little friend. What's his name? Kevin-something-or-other? Really now, David, he's so hairless and pink, like a—well, never mind. I'll explain to you what the video reveals later."

She winked at him.

Then she turned and left him with his eyes wide with bewilderment. He spent a long time thinking about this deformity. Did he have one *that* unique now captured on film? Where, exactly? And which one was she referring to?

He concluded that he'd have to get a hold of these pictures and the video and see for himself.

Chapter 15

After sending Olivia off to school the next morning, Libby had coffee with JoAnne. She sat in a stupor as JoAnne attempted to console her about Scott, and then she drove to the house to get Pat and other necessities. Only one day and night had passed, and the kitchen was a mess of dirty dishes, suspicious greasy odors, and papers and clothes scattered about.

Libby rubbed behind Pat's ear. "Sorry I didn't come for you last night," she told her. "You poor thing, you had to stay here in this mess!"

Libby was exhausted and wanted to lay down on the couch before going upstairs to access the damage there, but she knew it was important to keep moving. Keep moving. If she stopped to rest, she might have second thoughts about leaving.

That very morning, JoAnne ordered, "Get your things at the house and come back right away. The school knows to drop Olivia off here for the next few weeks. So, do your errands and come straight home!" But this, the house she had shared with Russ for the past seven years, *was* her home.

Libby studied the pictures on the walls, the knick-knacks, the furniture, and even the braided rugs with a sense of accomplishment. She was the one who put it all together, or at least, she had orchestrated the construction of the interior with Russ's help. They bought the house several years ago and saved up to remodel. At first, there were only two bedrooms, and now there were three. The two original bedrooms were upstairs. Later they added the third bedroom downstairs next to Russ's office. The third bedroom was used as a guest bedroom, although Libby stored clothes inside it and fixed up a sewing area in one corner. The front porch had been repaired four times. In fact, they had some work done to it the previous summer. They'd put in new storm windows, the kind with sliding glass, and all the windows were identical along the front and sides.

In the living room there was an old map of Grand Lake, framed and hung on the wall near the porch door. She looked it over for the first time in a long time. Grand Lake was approximately seven miles in length and one point five miles in width, located between Presque Isle Township to the east and Krakow Township to the west, fifteen miles north of Alpena. The map, dingy due to the wood smoke from the fireplace, had belonged to Russ's father's parents.

Libby opened the heavy oak door and walked into the chilled porch. Outside before her, Grand Lake quivered beneath a partially iced surface. A little early for snow, but she could see sparkling ice crystals floating along the surface. She heard a shotgun blast—duck hunters from one of the islands, probably Brown Island.

She knew they were in for another long winter, which would mean astronomical heating bills, and she wondered if she would be able to afford the cost by herself. She stood on the closed-in knotty-pine paneled porch and opened one of the six windows. She wanted to feel the impact of the cold air drifting off the lake. She waited and listened as the breeze pushed the cedar and balsam branches.

The air revived her. She closed her eyes. She thought about JoAnne and how they had their coffee together every morning. This morning, in fact, JoAnne told the cook to bring in a special breakfast that Libby barely touched. Libby remembered drinking some type of grape juice with a bitter taste. The omelet tasted bitter, too. She drank three cups of coffee, and yet, she still had trouble waking up. She dressed hastily into jeans and a tan sweater. She couldn't remember much else. She *did* remember that the night before—she and JoAnne—went to Alpena to make sure things were arranged for Scott's funeral.

They approved the casket and decided on the time of the service and the burial at the Grand Lake Cemetery, near the Chapel. The funeral home, Thorgenson's, was located in the new section of Alpena near the park and marina, a half mile from the relatively modern building complex of Jerry McPherson's office.

Libby knew she had to find peace with Scott's act of taking his own life, a decision he made under the influence of alcohol and sleep deprivation. "Oh yes," JoAnne told her on the way to the funeral home, "Scott came to see me that very night. He was distraught over Beverly and Russ. I tried to calm him down, dear. I even put him to bed in one of the guest rooms. He took off right after I left, apparently. He was *so* drunk; I'm sorry to say it, but he was. He can rest in peace now."

"Rest?" Libby cried. "What would you know about it? My brother wasn't the type to kill himself over an affair! He didn't love Beverly *that* much!"

JoAnne kept her eyes on the highway before them; she was a good driver and wouldn't let Libby distract her. She said, "Not to worry," and listened to Libby cry next to her in the front seat.

JoAnne had waited for Libby in Thorgenson's office. It was heart-breaking for Libby to see Scott lying there. He was only thirty-seven years old. Libby touched his forehead, noticing they had patched him up quite well. Even though the right side of his head had been blown off, they managed to cover the torn areas of the skull with his hair and thick makeup. Her mother was dead and now her brother.

• • •

The sound of the wind through the trees brought Libby back to the present, standing on the front porch of the house she shared with Russ. She closed the window, left the porch, and went upstairs to collect her clothes and Olivia's. Pat followed her everywhere she went in the house. At least Pat never argued with her or insulted her. Pat would never take off to be with another family.

Libby walked around the room to pick up Russ's clothes before she could decide on what to pack. There was an empty wine bottle on the nightstand. He had brought that bitch to her bed. And because of the pictures invading her thoughts, she grabbed the few things she would need immediately and would pick up

159

the rest later. The house had secrets. The house knew what had gone on when Libby wasn't there. Everywhere she looked, she expected to find evidence. A tissue on the bed stand. A trace of lipstick on the pillowcase. The lingering mist... of her.

Libby packed the van with two suitcases of her own and one of Olivia's, and then went back to the house to get Pat's things, a bag of dog food, two bowls, a brush, a leash. Like it or not, JoAnne would have to put up with the dog. There was no way Libby would leave Pat with Russ. Pat went wherever Libby went. That was the way it would always be. She locked the house door behind her and ran to the van, Pat at her heels. She opened the front passenger door and waited for Pat to jump up onto the seat. Pat rested her large head upon Libby's leg while Libby backed the van out of the driveway and turned off the lake road toward the Birch Hill Lodge.

• • •

Jerry stood at the counter rubbing his palms together. He unbuttoned his heavy wool coat. Underneath he wore a blue suit. It was cold outside, probably thirty-two degrees and had started to snow in subtle airy shafts, but inside Beverly's house, the waves of heat overwhelmed him.

"Dear God," he said. "It's too hot in here!"

Beverly had collapsed into a chair at the kitchen table. She was not dressed. She still wore the yellow nightgown and robe she had on when Scott caught her with Russ. She put her head against the cool surface of the table, and from this angle she watched Jerry fight his own discomfort, mostly the heat, but also his conscience. She could tell.

The makeup she wore earlier had been washed away by her crying fits, and her hair, normally styled and glossy, hung limp around her face and neck. Jerry knew she had been drinking. He also knew she spent the night before with Russ. He could tell by the illumination of her skin.

She had that look of having just slept with Russ.

Jerry went to the sink, picked out a glass, and helped himself to water from the faucet. "JoAnne had that Marilyn Clayton broad set it all up, I'll bet." He drained the glass and went for another.

He went on. "She's been paying Marilyn to take pictures. I *told* you to be careful."

"I can't refuse Russ," Beverly said in a forced voice.

Jerry straightened his posture, tall and confident. "Well now," he said, trying to sound unaffected. "There will *definitely* be fireworks. You need to pull yourself together!"

"Thanks for helping me arrange things with Thorgensen's," Beverly said pleasantly. "And everything else too."

"I'm your friend," Jerry reminded her. He wanted to add *and then some* but refrained. He wanted to ask her where she would be without him. Where would she get the extra money when she needed it? Who would help her with the stock market and investments? Who would keep all her secrets?

He walked over to the table and smoothed her hair down with the palm of his hand. "You should leave," he said. "Go to Standish and be with Christine for a while."

"And back off on seeing Russ too," he added, trying to sound like he was giving her legal advice rather than personal. "Back away from *him*."

"I can't! I love him. I know he loves me—deep down. I *know* it!"

"He's married to Libby."

"He comes to *me*, not her. He loves *me*!"

"Have some coffee, make a good impression at the service, and leave for Standish tonight."

She lifted her head and wiped her tears away with her finger. "Will you help me sell the house? I have to get rid of some stock and sell the house. I want to put it on the market right away!"

"I'll take care of it," Jerry promised. "You just get dressed for the service."

As he moved toward the door, Beverly pushed herself up from the table. She took his arm and brushed her lips against the side of his neck. "Please look after Russ," she said. "Make sure JoAnne and Libby don't destroy him."

"You just watch your own back when it comes to JoAnne. If I know her, *and believe me I do*, she's not finished with you. She probably knows about Christine by now. When you get to Standish, it might be a good idea for you to find another place to live."

"I'll have to tell Russ I need more money. Or borrow it from you until I can sell the house and find a good job."

"I'll see what I can do."

Jerry pulled away from her. He wanted rid of her spell, her inability to *hear* him. But he had known Beverly even longer than Russ had known her. What mattered now was selling her house and liquidating all Scott's investments. Thank God, Scott was smart enough to sign everything over to her before his death.

Jerry knew he would need to give her more money to help her set up a new life. He just hoped it was farther away than Standish. At least someplace where he would not have to see her very often or get pulled in by her hypnotic force without warning.

He knew he had to be cautious, let her play the game of trying to possess a man who didn't love her. After all, Beverly was just another woman Jerry couldn't have, thanks to Russ Shaw.

Chapter 16

On Tuesday, Libby took a drive up to the Harbor Resort area to clear her mind. Her eyesight was blurred, and her reactions were impaired. She drove past the Lodge, but she had to come to a full stop in front of Lotus Pond. She closed her eyes to clear her vision.

She wondered if all the stress of late had caused her to develop anxiety attacks, a series of sharp hallucinations, and a warped sense of place and time. She forced herself to concentrate. This was Tuesday. Yes, and Thanksgiving was two days away; it will be on a Thursday. Always a Thursday. Scott's memorial service is this afternoon at four-thirty. It will be held at the Grand Lake Chapel.

Libby knew through JoAnne that Beverly wasn't going to pay for an elaborate service, although she would let certain people—Scott's closest friends and relatives—to sit in the church and pay their last respects. JoAnne reported that Beverly instructed Thorgenson's to transport Scott's body to the cemetery in the woods near the chapel where all the local people had been buried since the early 1800s.

The gathering at the church, under the guise of a memorial service, was Beverly's way of proving that she cared about Scott, or at least, she was fully aware that *other people* cared about him.

But now, Libby wasn't sure she could get through the service or attend the gravesite ceremony afterwards. She wanted to go to drive all the way to Alpena, but instead, she turned around and drove back to the Lodge. She almost missed the turn into the parking lot. She turned in a circle to the back area and parked by the porch. There were several other vehicles parked in the back as well, vehicles Libby didn't recognize—two trucks and three cars that weren't there when she left earlier.

To distort her vision even more, it started to snow again. The snow was more like a mist, a cross between snowflakes and ice crystals. Libby wore a jacket, but it was too thin for an abrupt change of weather, and she knew she should be cold. She didn't expect to find a strange man standing inside the doorway. She didn't expect to see her sister-in-law, Andrea, standing beside him either. It had been three years since she had last seen her. "Andrea?" she asked, trying to jolt her memory of the poorly-postured, anemic-looking young woman. "Is that you?"

Andrea murmured a greeting and touched Libby's arm, or maybe Libby thought there had been contact between Andrea's pale finger and Libby's sleeve. Libby peered at Andrea. Her skin was opaque and she had unfocused, fluid-filled eyes. She was moving her lips, but nothing audible was developing; or maybe her words had formed but couldn't fall from her mouth. Then Libby recalled that JoAnne had said Andrea was so distraught by the news of Scott's death she insisted on coming for the service. She was going to stay through the holidays.

Libby imagined a beautiful, festive table, but also screams and insults, blood spraying from tall trees. She felt faint, and realized she was held upright by Andrea's husband, or was he her boyfriend? She knew the face—skin of an adolescent, blotchy and acne-covered across the cheeks and forehead, scattered upon his chin. He had thick black hair draped from one ear over the top of his head to the other. He was stout across the shoulders but spindly everywhere else.

When he spoke, he had a southern accent. "Hey there, Libby. Maybe you need to sit down." At least, she thought he said something along those lines.

"No, I'm fine," Libby insisted. "Where's my dog! I shouldn't have left her here!"

She let Andrea's husband—she remembered now that his name was Edwin—help her stand, but when she didn't see Pat, she fell apart. "My dog!" she shouted down the hallway, creating an echo, *"Where's my dog?"*

"She's right here!" Andrea's lips were nearly twisted. "See, Libby. She's right here. Don't worry."

"I hate Thanksgiving," Libby yelled. "I'm not doing it! Do you all *hear* me?" She stared at Andrea and then over at Edwin. "You hear me?"

"You'd better lie down," Andrea suggested.

Edwin seemed to enjoy Libby's outburst. He told her once that in his family, outbursts were common… and that he always thought Thanksgiving was a waste of time too. Libby pulled her arm away from his grip. "My dog!" she said again. "Where is she!" When Andrea snapped her fingers, Pat appeared. Pat stood by Libby so that Libby could at least touch the top of her soft black head. "She stays with me!" Libby insisted.

"Okay, okay!" said Andrea. It didn't matter to her one way or another. She looked over at Edwin, and it annoyed Libby that they were exchanging eye signals to imply that *she* was losing *her* mind.

JoAnne said, "Andrea, dear, take Libby upstairs. And Edward, or whatever your name is, go help Marilyn. Pronto!"

JoAnne's shrill voice caused Edwin to automatically pass Libby's elbow over to Andrea, who directed her toward the stairway. Libby wondered where JoAnne had disappeared to, but then when she reappeared, her shoes hitting against the wooden floor, *click, snap, bang*, Libby wanted to run. JoAnne was a mass of purple. A purple dress with a purple scarf around her neck to conceal her wrinkles. She wore purple-tinted nylons and a purple-beaded necklace. Her hair could have been purple for all Libby knew. It had hair-spray all over the top and sides and it looked like a glittering net.

JoAnne managed a smile for Libby's sake. "You go rest before the service," she said. "We'll take care of things." She handed Andrea a tall glass. "Andrea, take Libby upstairs and make her drink this," she added, nodding her head.

"I don't want anything to drink," Libby yelled, struggling against Andrea's fierce hold on her. "Where's my dog!"

JoAnne grabbed Libby's arm and squeezed. "Simmer down, dear," she said with rigid lips. "Go on upstairs and rest. Drink this. It will help you relax."

She pushed Libby up another step and then pushed Andrea behind Libby, as if directing a parade of mindless sheep. Andrea helped Libby all the way up the stairway and steered her to the largest guest bedroom, which had been fixed up by one of the maids. "Calm down, Libby," she said. "And drink this."

Libby drank the glass of water; it was bitter-tasting. She walked a few steps to the bed and fell across it. "Andrea?" Libby heard Andrea moving around the room. She heard her pull the drapes shut, blocking the only light left in Libby's life. "Andrea!"

Libby's eyes teared up. She was stiff and frozen and full of fear. "JoAnne will kill Pat," she said. Andrea came over to the bed and sat down beside her. "She'll kill Pat!" Libby insisted. "Find Russ and bring him to me!"

Chapter 17

Jerry couldn't find Russ. He drove out to the house, but no one was around. He drove to the quarry. The foreman in Russ's section said that Russ had left early for a funeral. Jerry decided to head out to the Grand Lake Chapel. The service was to start at four-thirty, and he didn't want to be late. He was hoping Russ might be there early too, but he didn't see any other cars parked in the tree-shaded lot except for JoAnne's Cadillac, and he knew it was best to avoid her for now.

Jerry had tracked down Brett Daniels, who had apparently moved to the Detroit area nine months ago. Jerry was able to convince Brett to send him copies of JoAnne's dirty deeds regarding tax evasion. Thank God, Brett's instincts had warned him to save the papers. He explained to Jerry that he knew the papers would come in handy one day. Jerry couldn't believe this stroke of good luck. Now they had evidence to use against JoAnne. Of course, Jerry had to pay Brett Daniels off to the total of eight hundred dollars, but Jerry knew the payoff would be well worth it. He paid Brett half now and would pay him the other half when he received the papers, which Brett promised to send priority mail. Jerry made it clear he also wanted the originals.

Jerry was anxious to relay this information to Russ. JoAnne's indiscretions provided leverage, and therefore, Russ could relax. If JoAnne got rough with them, as Jerry knew she would, they had the income-tax-evasion card to play.

Jerry waited in his car beneath a canopy of snow-laced pine trees. The radio weather report announced that the partly sunny sky would cloud up and there would be two more inches of snow by late evening. He held his breath when he saw Leeann's car approach—that damnable blue Mercedes she insisted *he* buy her two years ago. He shuddered at the thought of being in the same room with her, let alone a church, of all places, but he knew she had been fond of Scott Weyman, and he really wasn't surprised to see she was going to be at his memorial service.

When Leeann stepped out of her vehicle, dressed from head to toe in some fake-fur garment—a gaudy, mismatched outfit—with her blondish-brown hair teased up into a frizzy ball stuck to the back of her head, Jerry couldn't help but study her. She nodded and smiled at him as she walked by. The smile, if anything, revealed her cunning mind. A bow of her forehead all but said *see you in court, dumbass!*

Jerry watched her step along the gravel, which was slick due to a layer of snowfall, in her four-inch high heels. He didn't understand how she could walk in those shoes, but then again, there were many mysteries he couldn't figure out about Leeann. He *did* get the picture about one thing after six years together: she married him for his money.

He had just received a letter from her attorney, David Preece, regarding a meeting over the divorce settlement. Apparently, Preece refused to approve Jerry's proposal of a hefty monetary settlement and he even offered Leeann the house. Rather, the house Jerry bought six years ago. No, Preece would not agree to the very things Leeann herself had suggested to Jerry.

Now things had changed. Preece had his hooks into Leeann. He had convinced her to hold out for more money and assets, and around and around they would all go for God knew how long, until someone got impatient and resorted to vicious threats or violence. Jerry knew how these things could go. If Preece decided to play hardball, Jerry might lose most of what he had, or worse, he might lose his composure. He knew from the tug-of-war experience over the alleged molestation of Claudia Bishop that Preece was ruthless. Jerry had believed Claudia was of age at the time, and he knew he could find ways to prove she was, despite her altered birth records.

As Jerry reminisced about Preece's tactics, Preece pulled into the parking lot in his silver BMW. Jerry thought about slinking beneath view, maybe folding himself under the steering wheel until Preece passed by. Then he came to his senses. Why should he hide from him? Preece was the transplant from parts unknown. He was the one who had the right to set up a law practice in this neck of the woods. He was born and raised here.

Jerry hated the mere sight of David Preece. He even hated his hair that matched his silver vehicle. He hated Preece's straight-as-a-pole posture, although Preece had to push his chest out to achieve such an exaggerated visual effect. He wasn't even six-feet tall, Jerry wagered. He only *appeared* tall in those pumps, or rather, high-heeled black cowboy boots that accentuated his charcoal-black suit and tie. He hoped Preece would slip on the gravel, go sprawling face first onto the hard ground below. Or maybe when he hit the pavement at the side entrance of the church, he would fall flat onto his big square ass.

It didn't happen.

Preece inched his way under the trees across the graveled parking lot, over the cement sidewalk that surrounded the white brick building, and toward the door, where Jerry witnessed something quite interesting. Leeann had been waiting for him inside the arched doorway. She stepped forward and kissed Preece on the cheek.

After ten minutes went by, more vehicles appeared in the parking lot. People Jerry recognized but didn't know stepped out of shiny, expensive cars. He watched them walk across the gravel and enter the church. Then, thankfully, Russ's Blazer turned the corner and came to an abrupt stop next to Jerry's car. Jerry turned the radio off, turned down the heat, and unlocked the passenger door for Russ so they could talk in private before going into the church.

He was surprised to see Russ dressed up in a suit and tie. His hair was cut and gelled, and he'd even shaved off his whiskers. Jerry squinted to be sure the man beside him was actually Russ Shaw. He knew for sure when Russ spoke—high-pitched and rattled—in contrast to the toneless inflection he was known for.

"Goddamn it," Russ muttered. "I thought I was going to be late!"

"You shaved," Jerry noted. "An interesting look for you."

"You're observant," Russ said. "At least *that's* to my advantage." He wanted to leave the premises and not deal with the death of Scott Weyman. "Just give me the lowdown before we go in there."

But before Jerry got the chance to speak, Russ started to fidget. He wiped his perspiring forehead with the sleeve of his suit; he coughed and cleared his throat. Jerry waited for several seconds and finally, Russ closed his eyes and took a deep breath as Jerry proceeded to tell him about Brett Daniels. Then he brought up Libby. "Have you talked to Libby lately?"

Russ looked sickly pale. "No, but she was at the house this morning to get the dog and some things. She cleaned up a bit too. You know how she is with the cleaning. Last time I saw her, she looked distracted, and well, out of it! I'm worried JoAnne's drugging her!"

"Really?"

"Yeah, she looked right through me. I mean, sure she's upset about Scott and what I did, but she acted really strange, even for her." Russ started to perspire. "I got to go inside, right? I got to be there for Libby, even though she won't talk to me, and even though Beverly will be there. And shit, who knows what'll happen? What do *you* think might happen? I mean, with Libby and Beverly in the same room? Maybe I should just go back to the quarry. I didn't really like Scott anyway. It's kind of hypocritical for me to be here when I didn't even like him. Oh, I don't know! Damn it! I don't know!"

"Under the circumstances, you *have* to be here. Besides, it will look like you're more aboveboard than everyone thinks. Of course," Jerry said, chewing on his lip, mulling the options over, "I'm sure the whole town knows about the affair by now."

"Jesus! You think the whole town knows?"

"I'm sure JoAnne had that Marilyn Clayton creature spread the word, probably as you were doing it. They might have set Scott up; I wouldn't be surprised. Believe me, if they did, we'll find out. They could be responsible for Scott's suicide."

Mentally, Jerry went to work on that particular angle and was about to elaborate when he realized that Russ had turned all the way around to watch an approaching figure. "It's that goddamn David Preece coming right at us," Russ yelled. "What the hell does *he* want?"

Jerry rolled down the window to find out.

Preece gave him two envelopes. "I wanted to deliver these in person," he said. "It's very convenient that you happen to be sitting out here with your client. The papers are in regards to him, of course."

Jerry shifted inside the seat, straightened his glasses upon his nose, and opened one of the envelopes. It was a copy notifying them that JoAnne Shaw had filed a lawsuit against Russ for his actions three summers previously. The suit alleged that Russ cost the Birch Hill Lodge eleven thousand dollars of profit due to his questionable antics. Jerry laughed and opened the other envelope. "I like getting mail," he told Preece. "Are you taking a break from banging my wife to play mailman?"

Preece managed to keep a poker face, but his left eyebrow twitched ever so slightly. The twitch didn't escape Jerry's keen eye. Preece said happily, "Read on. I think you'll really like the next part."

Jerry read the paper. It was a restraining order keeping Russ away from his grandfather's property, which for now, JoAnne owned. "Oh, no!" Jerry said, pretending anxiety. "What'll we do? Run for the hills?"

Jerry handed the papers to Russ for his inspection, and he wasn't surprised when Russ began to mutter obscenities. But, before Russ could shout threats to Preece, Jerry put a hand up to warn him, "Don't talk," he said in a searing voice he had never used on Russ before. "Just *don't*."

But the stern warning had been for nothing. Russ started to hyperventilate. "This is bullshit!" he screamed at Preece. "I never cost her a dime, and not only that, I'll go wherever the hell I want!"

Jerry tried to justify Russ's outburst. "He gets overly excited, I'm afraid. And, so do I. So, listen carefully. Tell JoAnne to back off. Tell her Russ will stay away from the cottage—" Here he had to put a hand up again to silence Russ from interrupting. "I'll make *sure* he stays away, but this little lawsuit, if that's what you want to call it, won't fly. Tell her we'll need proof."

"It doesn't matter what *you* need," Preece said, his nose pointed upward, his gold and pearl cufflinks twinkling in the sunlight. "The suit's been filed. I just wanted to give you the papers. Believe me, this is only the beginning. JoAnne asked me to tell you that. See you all inside."

Preece turned on his boot heel to leave but backed up to add, "By the way, Claudia Bishop's been summoned. You *do* remember *her*?"

Jerry shrugged and rolled his eyes toward the car ceiling. He kept his stare on the beige fabric overhead until he was certain that Preece had left. He wondered what Preece had meant by the remark about Claudia. She had been raised in the area, so she was probably in town to confer with her father about his resort. After all, Thomas Bishop was in his late seventies and hadn't looked well the last time Jerry saw him.

Claudia was his only heir.

"What do I do now?" Russ yelled. "You'd better think of something fast!"

Jerry pulled the key out of the ignition and opened the door to the chilly late afternoon. "Well," he said, "it's four-thirty. What you'll do *now* is go on in the church and act like nothing's happened except a suicide."

Jerry waited for Russ to get out of the car. He waited for Russ to straighten his tie and smooth down his hair, and as they walked toward the church, he couldn't help but wonder what David Preece had up his sleeve. Once inside the foyer, Jerry noticed that JoAnne was running the show as she stood crooked and snug inside a black dress.

Russ staggered as he walked. Jerry had to direct him to a chair, where he ordered him to sit down. "Where's Libby?" Russ babbled, sounding drunk and desperate. "I don't see her!"

And he was right. Libby wasn't in the room. This fact worried Jerry as much as it worried Russ. Why wasn't Libby visible for all these people—mostly friends of the family—to console? Jerry looked over at JoAnne. What a display she was putting on. JoAnne kept dabbing at her eyes with a tissue, her facial expression suggesting to-the-bone grief. She was talking to three middle-aged women. But Jerry looked away from this sedate little group and turned in time to see Leeann step up to the photo of Scott on a table next to several wreaths of roses. She blew her nose into a lacy handkerchief. She closed her eyes and shook her head. She was a heavy-duty crier, Jerry knew for a fact. She could turn the tears on quickly and turn them off even quicker.

But today, Jerry knew she was genuinely in mourning. He knew that she liked Scott Weyman. She liked his mother too. One of these days, Jerry would question her and find out exactly what she remembered about Susan Weyman's death.

Jerry couldn't believe it when Thomas Bishop swaggered into the church, supported by a gold-handled cane. He was dressed to the hilt in a black and gray three-piece suit, quite appropriate and stately. Bishop went right up to JoAnne, accepted her gloved hand, and shook it as if they were relatives, or even friends. Jerry inched closer to listen, hoping words would be exchanged. Consequently, he found himself crouched behind a large palm plant, snagging his suit jacket in the process.

JoAnne murmured, "Well, hello, Tom. Good of you to come."

Tom grunted before responding, "I'm very sorry to hear about Scott. Where's his wife, Beverly?"

"Good question, dear. She's wandered off somewhere, I suppose. Perhaps she's in the rest room, chugging down a flask."

Jerry knew sparks were about to fly. He could tell by JoAnne's sneering tone and because she had called Bishop "dear."

Tom Bishop leaned against the cane. Jerry could see through the ferns of the plant that it was a struggle for him to stand still, let alone conjure up a conversation with his top adversary. He said, "You wouldn't have anything to do with my daughter's sudden arrival to Grand Lake would you now, JoAnne?"

"Goodness sakes, why think such a thing? Claudia's such a devoted daughter."

"And hasn't been back here for five years," Bishop added, his raspy voice running low on fuel. "Yet suddenly she's quite interested in my holdings."

"I imagine she ought to be," JoAnne said, her best play at innocence put forth. "After all, her father's quite the entrepreneur. She stands to gain a lot—providing she remains your only heir."

"She certainly does, unless, of course, there are children I don't know about." Bishop laughed nervously, his cleft chin pointed toward the tiled floor.

"Well said!" JoAnne shouted with child-like animation. "We never know what surprises lurk around the corner, do we?"

Bishop caught on, despite his physical deterioration. "Don't you bother her about that damned seventy-five-acre parcel you want of mine, JoAnne! It *won't* happen!"

JoAnne tittered, a vibrating sound that made Jerry's spine tingle. "It'll happen," she promised. "Claudia and I have an understanding."

"Stay away from my daughter," Bishop said again, now red in the face. His thick white eyebrows began to pump, and consequently, he leaned against the organ for leverage near the minister, who was shuffling papers at the podium. "You have enough of the prime land locked up around here," he wheezed as a last resort. "You greedy bitch of a woman, *damn* you!"

"The next funeral we attend will be yours, I'm thinking," JoAnne said happily; she followed along to badger him as he shuffled, cane clinking, toward the front of the room. "It looks as if your legs are giving out on you, dear."

"Sounds like your common sense and manners have given out on you... *dear,*" Bishop snapped. "And I'll wager *you're* next for the box!"

Jerry stepped away from the plant when he noticed two men were watching him, and then they, and several other people, focused directly to the right. At the front of the room near Scott's memorial shrine, consisting of a large photo and a display of garish bouquets of flowers, was Beverly, in a bright blue suit, huddled with the minister, fighting back tears as he consoled her.

Jerry watched her closely. He knew she had been fond of Scott; she had even confessed to loving him years ago, but Jerry also knew her tears were fake. She could hardly stand up, somewhat like Bishop, who meandered toward her. Jerry knew that her disability, however, came from too much to drink, whereas Bishop's was simply from too much living. He staggered and sighed; he just about collapsed at Beverly's feet. He took her hand, leaned close to her and spoke into her diamond-studded ear. To the left of them, JoAnne slithered into view, no doubt hoping to listen in on their conversation.

Jerry searched the room for Russ, who was sitting rigid, exactly where Jerry had left him. Russ's eyes were glassy, and his left shoe tapped against the tile. As he stared and tapped, Andrea and her husband, Edwin, or so Jerry had recalled that might be his name, walked over to Russ and filled the two chairs next to him.

Andrea looked as if she had just stepped out of bed. Her hair, greasy and stringy as always, hung past her shoulders to her elbows. She looked older than twenty-seven. Her skin was indented, especially around her eyes and mouth. There were freckles splashed across her forehead and scattered down her thin arms, which, Jerry noticed, were quite pale and puckered.

She wore a short-sleeved dress. The dress was too long, a bell-shaped style from the seventies that was blue and white checkered. She wore a necklace of metallic material, not a cross. It looked more like a smiley face. She shed not a tear and didn't even blink. She glanced over at Russ a few times, maybe even looked at Edwin once, but mostly she was obsessed with the wall behind the reverend's podium, directly in front of the brass organ pipes.

The organist, a rotund woman in her mid-sixties—Jerry couldn't recall her name either, although she had played the organ in this church for what seemed like centuries—pounded the keys with her short fat fingers.

Her strained expression and her gray-cropped hair accented the grim mood of the hymn.

Jerry turned to watch Russ, who was watching Beverly. After speaking with the reverend—Reverend Stover, Jerry finally recalled his name—Beverly chose a chair in the front row between JoAnne and a cousin of Scott's. There was a lot of nose-blowing and sniffling, and even JoAnne participated. In fact, she had started it. She lifted her gaze toward the ceiling and dabbed at the corners of her eyes with a tissue. Twice she sighed loud enough to be heard by all and muttered, "Oh, my. *Oh* my!" trembling and gasping.

Russ lowered his head when Beverly sat down. After that, Jerry didn't have a clear view of her anymore. The reverend took his place. He asked for everyone's attention; it wasn't difficult to do because no one was talking, only blowing into handkerchiefs and tissues. The reverend droned on and on about Scott as a boy, Scott as an adolescent, Scott in college, Scott as a husband, uncle, brother, and abruptly, the accolades faded.

Jerry looked at Russ again, and then over at Andrea and Edwin Mayfield, who was sitting- slumped beside her. Jerry assessed him, and immediately thought Edwin was dangerous and would no doubt cause problems. Jerry knew that Edwin's family owned a liquor store; eight years ago they were cited for selling to minors. They were questionable characters, at best. The father a drunkard, the mother out of her mind with some rare muscle disease that affected her ability to rationalize and function. The story goes that Mrs. Mayfield sat in a rocking chair in the kitchen all day long and rocked back and forth, although occasionally she would scoot the chair over to the stove and cook. Rumor has it that she had worked for JoAnne as a cook in the kitchen of the Birch Hill Lodge.

Obviously, Edwin met Andrea through her.

Edwin kept picking at the skin on his arms. Quite consistently he picked, raised the skin, and watched it fall back into place at the bone. He appeared to enjoy the sight of his white skin lifting and returning to place. He scanned the entire room with narrowed eyes, and his square mouth jutted outward as he contemplated the crowd.

Edwin wore blue pants that were much too tight for his short, stocky frame. And although his fingers were in proportion to the rest of his body, his head was not, which was understandable, Jerry decided, considering his family tree. There was possibly some inbreeding going on—several cousins scattered about the county, half of them fathered by their grandfathers. As an attorney, Jerry had seen and heard it all.

When Edwin yawned loudly, JoAnne turned inside her chair. She stared him down, and Edwin had the audacity to wink at her before going back to the skin picking; this time, he concentrated on his pink neck. Picking at his neck brought Jerry's attention to the stiff collar of his shirt. The shirt was a high-quality cotton material, but the design itself was a faded blue and white stripe. He wore black boots that left imprints from the damp grass outside on the carpet. His thin, greasy hair was spread unevenly across his oddly triangular skull.

Russ was looking down at his shoes. When he suddenly stood up, Jerry felt a tremor of anxiety. Russ moved behind Andrea, who was next to him in the row of chairs and knelt next to Jerry. He whispered, "I'm going to go look for Libby. I don't see her anywhere. Something's wrong. And where's Olivia? What the hell's going on here?"

"Olivia's in the restaurant with a babysitter," said Andrea. "JoAnne didn't think it was a good idea for her to be here. You can see her after the service at the get-together at the Lodge."

Beverly was speaking from the podium. All eyes were on her. Every heart, clearly, ached for her. Poor Beverly. Her infant daughter dying a few months after birth, and now her husband committed suicide. Poor, poor Beverly. Jerry knew her "speech" would be as long-winded as the reverend's, and he noticed that the threat of more monotone monologues didn't escape Edwin Mayfield's attention. Edwin moved inside his chair, making it clatter against the floor.

Edwin looked over at Jerry and cleared his throat with such vigor, Jerry swore that his milky-brown eyes had crossed in the process. "I'm hungry," Edwin told Andrea; but his eyes remained stuck on Jerry. "I can't sit here no more in this hard chair!"

"I'm going to go look for Libby," Russ said again. This time he meant it. He stood and slid sideways, past the row of poised mourners.

Beverly reminisced about Scott and the fact that they were married "in this very church" by none other than Reverend Stover. Stover bowed and signaled Beverly to continue her gibberish about the beautiful

Grand Lake Chapel and grounds, praising the community in general, but her voice stopped mid-sentence. Jerry turned to see what she was looking at and saw Libby walking toward the front of the room.

Libby was wearing corduroy overalls, of all things, with a yellow shirt beneath it. There was a black sweater draped over her shoulders. Her left hand gripped the sweater tightly, and somehow, she overpowered Russ when he reached out to grab her. She also escaped JoAnne's gnarled hand, even though JoAnne had actually stood up and lunged forward as she went by. Everyone watched Libby move in slow motion to the front of the room, and once she got there, her finger traced along the edge of Scott's photograph.

She didn't say a word; she didn't even cry.

Russ walked up behind her and waited. If she should run, he would go after her. If she happened to faint, he would be there to catch her. She blinked, put a hand to her mouth, and stepped back from the podium. She looked over at Beverly and fell backwards into Russ's arms.

"Can we go now?" Edwin whined. "My head's pounding. I gotta eat!"

Jerry envisioned Edwin pulling out a switchblade and sticking it into his ribs, over and over until he—Jerry—was covered with blood, dead on the cold church floor. Right then, Jerry knew Edwin Mayfield would try and kill him.

For now, he helped Russ carry Libby out of the church. Figuring out what to do about an evil interference like Edwin Mayfield would have to wait.

Chapter 18

Russ helped Libby out of the sanctuary, down the hallway, and into a small room at the back of the building. He tried to carry her, but she revived just as he attempted to pick her up, and so he propped her up all the way to the small back room where the congregation held meetings and dinners and bridesmaids and brides prepared for weddings.

But the room was too cold; apparently, the heating system had been turned off. He helped her settle into the only chair he could find. She leaned her head back and closed her eyes. Seconds later, she opened them again and yelled, "What do you want from me, Russ!"

"Are you taking drugs?"

"Never mind what I'm taking. Did you see your lover? She could barely stand. And all that talk about my brother. That woman! She killed him! *You* killed him. Why even be here? Take her away. I don't want to look at her or you!"

"You need a doctor."

"Who are *you* to tell *me* what I need?" Libby pushed herself up from the chair. "I want you out of my life. I don't want you to come to the cemetery, you hypocrite! Don't come here pretending to feel bad over what happened!"

Clearly, she had trouble standing; she leaned sideways and put a hand to the back of the chair for support. He said, "I came here for *you*. Don't you understand?"

She pushed past him and made it all the way to the door but toppled over again. This time, she fell to the floor with a *thump* and laid there rigid, both hands to her face. Thankfully, whenever Russ needed Jerry, he showed up. Russ told him to help pull Libby to her feet.

Behind Jerry, however, JoAnne's bent body entered the frozen room. "What have you done to her?" Russ asked, causing her to put up a hand and shake her head convulsively. "Tell me, goddamn it!"

It was clear that JoAnne had developed the early stages of palsy, but it was difficult to determine how much shaking was a result of aging and how much was anxiety. "Oh, she's just exhausted!" JoAnne said, her voice spitting and snapping. "She won't eat! She's just fainted!"

Jerry helped Russ pull Libby to her feet, and as Russ instructed, with hand signals and such, they carried her back over to the chair. A man stepped into the room. Russ wasn't sure, but he looked a lot like Doctor Burlow, the local doctor who had retired ten years ago. The old doctor, who had diminished in size over the years, shoved his way past the gathering at the door and even ordered the minister, standing next to JoAnne, to move aside.

He shouted, "Outta the way, eh!" and continued to push people aside, starting with Russ and Jerry. He proceeded to examine Libby, while muttering, "Hmm," and finally, he took a deep breath and exhaled with a hearty "Hah!"

"What does *that* mean, Doc?" Russ asked. He noticed the old man's face was full of creases; his jacket was tweed, his pants a dull brown.

Russ remembered that Doctor Burlow came to the Lodge several times to check on Grandfather. He also remembered the old doc bought a hundred dollars of candy bars from him when he was selling them for little league. Russ touched the doctor's arm, "And so?" he asked. "What do you *think*, Doc?"

"This woman is suffering from acute exhaustion," Doctor Burlow diagnosed, his eyelids twitching. "Get her to bed, goddamn it. And then leave her *alone*, you bunch of loons!"

Doctor Burlow took a deep breath, heaved himself back up onto his legs, and walked toward the door. He glanced around and snickered, his skinny lips pinched together, and his eyes slanted in disgust. "Jesus, what a shame, a damn shame!" He stalked out the door, as if he couldn't breathe in company of such lunatics.

Thereby, JoAnne grabbed a handful of Russ's hair and yanked so hard, she almost ripped half of it out of his skull. "You're taking her back to the Lodge!" she screamed, twisting his hair with her bony hand. "Have you forgotten that she left *you*? Have you forgotten *why*? You have no business making decisions for her right now. Can't you see she's semi-conscious and not in any condition to go back to that hovel on the lake!"

JoAnne, back bent and hands trembling, released Russ's hair, but then she grabbed his suit jacket at the shoulder and jerked so hard he was surprised the material didn't rip. "I said leave her be!" JoAnne screamed, shaking from head to toe and simultaneously wheezing. "Haven't you caused enough trouble already?"

She managed to collect a flock of helpers, starting with Edwin and David Preece, who she was able to summon with the flick of her wrist, ordering them to pick up Libby and take her toward the door.

"Get your hands off her!" Russ yelled. He grabbed Edwin's striped shirt and lunged for David Preece's lapel. "Hands off my wife, you sons of bitches! My attorney's here. Tell them Jerry! Tell them to leave her alone!"

Jerry stood directly behind Russ. He couldn't think of what to do except grab Edwin's hands as Edwin clawed at Russ's neck. Jerry yelled, "Get your hands off him, or we'll press assault charges! I *said* get your hands off him!"

"*You'll* press assault charges?" Preece scoffed, his face and neck bright with rage. He was all worked up and ready for an old-fashioned fistfight. He instinctively clenched both fists, adding, "Libby is staying at the Lodge by choice. She's petitioned for a separation, and the next step is divorce, pal! *You* get your hands off *her*!"

"I'm calling the authorities if this doesn't stop now!" yelled the reverend. "Maybe I should remind you that we're in the middle of a memorial service! We're in the house of God!"

Meanwhile, Edwin Mayfield kept trying to pick up Libby, but he wasn't strong enough to get her away from Russ. Russ was twice Edwin's size, and when angered to such proportions, he didn't know his own strength. Thereby, Jerry had a firm grip on Russ' arm. He pulled and tugged until Russ's rage eased off.

Jerry said in a determined tone, "We'll let them help you take Libby back to the Lodge, Russ. She can rest there, *hear* me?"

"But I can't let them *take* her," Russ protested. He had calmed down with Jerry's help, but still, he didn't trust the other people around him, his own mother least of all.

He knew Jerry was right; he knew things would only get worse if he tried to take Libby back to the house. If nothing else, Libby would despise him for making such a move against her will.

"Let her decide where she wants to be," Jerry repeated until Russ finally let go of her. "There you go; it'll be all right."

But Russ turned to JoAnne and told her in no uncertain terms, "I'm coming along. I want to make sure she is settled…do *you* hear me?"

JoAnne stood in the doorway, preparing to lead them all back to the Birch Hill Lodge, "Whatever you say, Russell," she said through her clenched teeth. "But some of us need to go to the cemetery. There's still the matter of burying Scott!"

She instructed Edwin and David Preece to help Russ carry Libby out of the room and to the car. Libby stirred a couple of times as they moved her. She whispered something about Scott and started to cry.

• • •

The Birch Hill Lodge was closed due to the memorial service. The sign on the front door said *Closed until the day after Thanksgiving.* Russ carried Libby up the stairs to the bedroom and put her on the large, four-poster bed. He covered her with a red and green quilt.

Olivia came into the room, followed by Pat. Olivia was happy to see Russ, but she was worried about her mother. "Dad, what's wrong with her?" she asked him quietly. "Is she sleeping again?" She sat down on the edge of the bed, and Pat sat down on the floor next to her.

"Yes, she's sleeping," said Russ. Olivia was dressed up in a skirt and purple satin blouse. She wore black patent leather shoes—a rarity—and her short brown hair was tucked behind her ears and curled. Russ pulled her to his lap. "Has she been sleeping a lot?" he asked her.

"Yes, all the time. Grandma says she's sad about Uncle Scott. Did they bury him?"

"They're doing that now," Russ said. "Mom didn't feel well. She fainted, so I brought her here."

When Pat started to whine, Russ looked over at her. She moved over to the dresser, whined at it, and pushed at the bottom drawer with her nose. Russ knew from previous events that Pat was a very intelligent dog. A year or so ago, Libby left the stove burner on, and Pat led her to the kitchen and barked at the stove until Libby realized the burner was bright red. Another time Olivia had wandered down to the dock. She was only three years old and had wandered out the back door. Pat was with her but came back to the house and whined at Libby and Russ until they followed her down to the dock where they found Olivia, sitting on the bottom step, about to start walking.

Russ got up from the bed and walked over to the dresser. He opened the bottom drawer—the drawer Pat was looking at—and beneath a stack of sweaters, he found a vial of pills. "Mom takes those," said Olivia, moving in to stand beside Russ and Pat. "Grandma gives them to her. Grandma tells her it will help her sleep."

Russ noticed on the label that the doctor who had prescribed the pills was none other than the retired Doctor Burlow. He had prescribed them to JoAnne, and the date was for a month earlier. There were seven pills left, seven Valium. Russ put the bottle into his jacket pocket. He turned to look at Olivia. "I want you to tell me if you see Mom take anymore pills."

"Grandma put those pills in the dresser," Olivia stated forthright. "She keeps them in the dresser so they will be handy. Sometimes she sneaks them in Mom's food and drinks when Mom doesn't know it."

"Well, you tell me if you find more pills around, okay?"

"Okay," Olivia agreed. She sat down on the floor to be near the dog; she moved her small hand along Pat's soft fur. "Pat showed you where to find the pills," she said. "She's always following Grandma. Always watching Grandma."

• • •

An hour later, there was a wake for Scott Weymann held at the Birch Hill Lodge. Russ and Olivia went down the stairway, turned the corner, and entered the dining area. Jerry was there to meet them. He was drinking coffee. He told Russ he didn't think it was wise for him to go inside where everyone was chattering and eating. He said, "I'm keeping a distance, as you can see. You should do the same."

Russ told Olivia to take Pat outside. He showed Jerry the bottle of Valium. "The old bitch is putting drugs in Libby's food and drinks. I could kill her. I'm going to find her right now and tell her I'm onto her!"

Jerry took the bottle from Russ and inspected it. With his other hand, he placed the coffee cup down on the telephone table. "Now we know why Libby is so groggy. But we can't prove JoAnne has been making her take them or slipping them to her either."

"I tell you, JoAnne's been drugging her, so she doesn't know which end is up. Olivia saw her do it! That way Libby does what JoAnne wants. I say we call her on it, right now!"

Jerry studied the bottle a bit longer and shoved it into his suit-jacket pocket. "We'll keep it for evidence. I think you should go talk to your sister. She probably knows what's going on."

"She won't help me," Russ said. "We had a falling out a long time ago. I accused her of helping JoAnne destroy my grandfather."

"Andrea was here when your grandfather was living here?"

"Yes, she lived here until she met that Edwin idiot and moved out. I think JoAnne paid her to leave, just to get rid of her."

Jerry picked the coffee cup up again. He looked at it for a second or two and put it back on the table. He whispered to Russ, "Maybe she *saw* JoAnne push your grandfather down the steps. Ever think of that?"

Russ rubbed his chin, thinking hard. "Okay, I'll go look for her."

"By the way," Jerry said, knowing they didn't have time for delays, "I know you've been seeing Beverly. You have to be honest with me from now on. With *everything*, understand?"

"I don't think you need all the details," Russ said. He already knew Jerry had picked up on the fact that he had been seeing Beverly, but he wasn't ready to tell him more. "There are some things you don't need to know!"

"This is going to get rough, "Jerry stated firmly. "If JoAnne talks Libby into filing for a divorce, a lot will be at stake. They'll get you for adultery, among other things. So, you have to tell me the truth from now on!"

"Maybe we'll talk about it later. I'm going to go find Andrea."

And he wanted to talk to Beverly before she packed up for Standish. He knew she was going to sell the house, quit her job at the gift shop, and move to Standish. He also knew Jerry was right. Things were going to get rough, and not only with JoAnne, but also with Libby and Beverly. He was not making enough at the quarry to battle both women for child support. He was drifting among these visions of despair when Jerry interrupted with another important question.

"What do you know about Edwin Mayfield, other than the general rumors?"

"I know he's bad news," said Russ. "He was arrested for breaking into a carryout store in Oscoda. Not sure exactly when that happened. I remember JoAnne ranting about it."

"I'm going to run a check on him," Jerry said. "I think there's more to Mr. Mayfield than just breaking into a carryout store. I think he might have had something to do with the death of that old woman. Remember, Sadie something or other, a summer vacationer. She was found dead in her cottage by the pond several years ago."

Russ nodded. "Yes, I remember," he said. "She was stabbed thirteen times in the neck and chest. I remember JoAnne hired extra security for the Lodge. Everyone thought the murderer would strike again."

"Maybe JoAnne suspected it was Eddie-boy. Maybe she's blackmailing him. I just have a really bad feeling about him, and I think she called him back here for a reason."

"It wouldn't surprise me," Russ admitted, sounding amazed, but not necessarily sad. "My own mother a murderer or associating with a murderer. Look slowly to your right. That she-bitch Marilyn Clayton is hiding behind the stairs. She's been watching us and trying to listen in!"

"I'd be careful from now on," Jerry suggested. "And find out what Andrea knows. Don't try to contact Beverly."

As Russ strolled down the hallway, he said into the shadows at the stairway, "I'm leaving now, Marilyn" and laughed, making fun of her, as he walked out of the Birch Hill Lodge.

Chapter 19

Even though Jerry advised against it, after Russ felt confident he had lost Marilyn, he drove off toward Beverly's house. He knew Beverly would be home. She would be storing items that she wanted to leave behind and packing her suitcases.

She left after the service, not taking part in the post-service festivities.

She answered the door right away, wearing what Russ considered *traveling clothes*. She had changed out of the navy-blue blouse and suit she wore for the memorial service into casual clothes for the road. Unfortunately, she had been drinking for the road too.

When she saw it was Russ, she stepped back to invite him in, but a wave of remorse swept over him, and he couldn't move from the doorway. "So, you're leaving tonight?" he asked. "Leaving for Standish?"

"Yes," she said. "I need to be with my daughter."

Russ leaned against the wall. He was nervous around her now, and oddly enough, he couldn't stop thinking about Libby staying at the Lodge. "Libby's exhausted," he said, surprised he had even mentioned her, realizing, probably too late, that she was the only person who really mattered. "I don't know what will happen next. I guess she'll file for a separation."

Beverly looked at him with damp eyes. She found a chair and fell into it. She put two fingers to her brow as her chin transformed into a landslide of convulsing skin. And he knew what she was going to say next. She would bring up money. *Our child*, she would say, *needs money.*

"I hate to tell you this," she said, "but three hundred a month isn't going to cut it."

"Oh, really?" He knew if he threatened to stop paying her, she would fall apart. "How much *will* cut it?"

"I need another four hundred a month, at least. There are expenses, you know. Medical bills, food, supplies. I'll be staying with a friend for a while, and then I will have to find a place for us to live. For Christine and me. A place away from here."

Christine? Oh yes, that's what she calls his other daughter. He hadn't seen her for two months. She *was* beautiful, his daughter, and he claimed her because she was, like Olivia, his flesh and blood. His daughter. He held her closely, possessively, when he found out Libby couldn't have any more children.

"I want to see her," he said. "Maybe over the holidays. I'll probably be going to court soon," he added. "My mother will try to hang me out to dry, and Libby's staying at the Lodge with Olivia. I should probably tell Jerry about Christine. I have a feeling it will come out soon anyway."

"Probably," she agreed. "It will have to be out in the open, but a judge will demand you pay me more!"

"A judge would want blood tests to *prove* I'm the father," Russ said, feeling pressured now more than ever. "You can count on *that*."

"Leave Libby and come with me now," she said, echoing the many times she had asked him to leave Libby in the past. He knew that her dream, her hope was of him leaving Libby.

"I'm not going to leave her. I already told you that!"

Instead of looking tired and drained, she sprang out of the chair. Her eyes, seductive seconds ago, now brimmed with rage. She reached out and tried to grab his jacket, but the alcohol had impaired her reflexes, and she missed by inches.

Russ steadied her. "Get a hold of yourself!" he said. "If you're going to turn into a goddamned drunk, maybe I should take Christine!"

Beverly pushed away from him and raised a fist. He thought for sure she was going to take a swing at him, so he braced himself and waited. He could handle her easily. She was just drunk. She had no muscle, physical or mental, behind her threats. "Go ahead and hit me," he urged. "Take your best shot!"

When she lowered her fist, her eyes filled up with tears. "I love you," she said. "I've always loved you."

He shook his head at her words. He wanted to tell her to sober up. Hadn't Jerry suggested the same thing to him, hours ago? Her stint mourning Scott had been so brief that the thought alone made Russ angry. Not even two hours after the memorial service and she was packed up and ready to leave town. How pathetic. He wondered if Libby would mourn him if he died suddenly. Would she give a damn, or would she take the money and freedom and run?

"I think you should leave in the morning," he said. "Get some rest."

And he knew if he stayed with her, he might sleep with her again.

He turned away from the clouding up of Beverly's eyes and walked through the front door. He heard her scream. He knew she had selected some sort of weapon—probably a vase—he was always getting the vase pitched at him, mere inches from his head. He heard her say something like, "You'll regret ever knowing me, you son of a bitch!"

He regretted that already.

• • •

When he got home, the phone was ringing. It was Jerry, advising him to sit tight; there was a court hearing scheduled for the following week.

"A court hearing already?" Russ yelled, shocked at Jerry's words. He had barely stepped through the kitchen door before the phone rang. Nothing unnerved him more.

He had hoped it was Libby and had rushed to answer it, only to find Jerry McPherson with more trouble, on the other end.

"It's just a preliminary hearing," Jerry said calmly, as was his professional way. "Don't panic. Libby has already filed for a separation. I know it's bizarre, but JoAnne seems to know, or rather David Preece knows, all the right people. We'll appear, and you'll agree to the terms if they're reasonable."

FOR ANOTHER WOMAN

"Agree to the terms? Why should I do that? And *what* terms? I don't understand how it could happen this fast."

"Listen, I can't talk right now. I've got my own court hearing coming up soon. Apparently, a judge decides who gets what in my divorce. I'd like to keep things simple in yours."

"There isn't going to be a divorce!" Russ shouted into the phone. "When Libby feels better, I'll go talk to her. She'll listen to me! How can there be a hearing when the woman's half out of her mind on drugs? I want you to postpone this goddamned hearing. Libby isn't well, and there's no point in haggling over support payments and visitation rights. You get a hold of that damned Preece today and tell him we'll meet when Libby's coherent. I know JoAnne's behind all this anyway!"

"I'll see what I can do," Jerry promised. "But don't hold your breath."

"And get that accountant, Brett what's his name, on standby in case we need him. I want his testimony if this goes to court. I'm beating the bitch over the head with that one! Meanwhile, I'm going back to the cottage to find the copy of the will."

Now it was Jerry's turn to shout into the phone. "You stay away from the cabin! We've got the court order keeping you away from that property! You want to get arrested? I think not!"

"*I think* let the bastards try and arrest me for stepping onto my own grandfather's land! I'm finding that copy. I know he hid it there!"

With that remark, Russ slammed the phone down. He sat at the table awhile, hoping to build his energy. Instead of going straight to the cottage, he called the Birch Hill Lodge and asked Andrea to meet him at the harbor restaurant.

The Marina at Lake Huron was a hot spot for servicing boaters. It housed twenty slips for anchor at the docks. The boats were able to hook up to electricity, gasoline, and entertainment to suit their individual needs. The DNR Harbor Master was always on hand, complete with crew.

Russ waited at the bar at the far right of the elegant restaurant and waited for his sister to appear. He was surprised she actually showed up a half hour later. They couldn't very well talk in the restaurant area of Tom Bishop's harbor resort, so they decided to sit at the bar.

Andrea came toward him with a sluggish gait. He saw that she was dressed in shabbier clothes than earlier that day at the service. She had on blue jeans, a tattered yellow sweater, tennis shoes, and a blue wool coat.

He said, "What took you so long? I've been waiting for a half hour."

"Mom suspected something," Andrea said, out of breath. "She kept trying to distract me. I told her I had to meet a friend." Andrea pulled a pack of cigarettes out from her coat pocket and lit one with a silver-plated lighter.

"How's Edwardo?" Russ asked, thinking he should break the ice and maybe even order a drink. He didn't know Andrea smoked. There were a lot of things he didn't know about her, he realized as he watched her inhale, exhale.

"He's fine, and his name's Edwin. Why would you care anyway?"

"Just being polite," Russ admitted, "or at least I'm *trying* to be polite. JoAnne wants to ruin me," he said, omitting further small talk. "I was wondering what you know about the subject."

"Not much, I just got back." She watched the smoke from her cigarette drift throughout the dark room. "We came for the holidays. Edwin lost his job, and we ran out of money."

"Big surprise," Russ said, but he refrained from chuckling. "Good ole-Edwardo, the loser."

"If you have a point to make, get to it!" Andrea said. He knew she meant it when she looked him square in the eye.

"I want to know what's going on at the Lodge," Russ said. "I need you to watch things and let me know, particularly about Libby and Olivia."

"I'm upset about Thanksgiving," he droned on, knowing he was losing her attention when her sleepy eyes started to wander. "I've never been apart from Libby on a holiday."

Andrea shook her head and put her cigarette out in the ashtray. "Well, don't you think your affair with Beverly has something to do with *that*?" she asked sullenly. "Mom told me everything. Why did you do that if you're so in love with Libby?"

"Don't criticize me," Russ said. "You married that moron Edwin Mayfield, the ex-con!"

Andrea blinked and sighed. "Oh, you know Edwin's been in prison?"

"Yes, heard a rumor he had something to do with that old woman being stabbed to death a few years back."

Andrea summoned the bartender for a drink. "I don't know exactly, but I guess I'll help you get information on Libby."

"Good. And we never had this conversation," Russ said. He was not going to drink with her. He was going home. "Don't drink too much, little sister," he said, getting up from the bar stool. "We don't want anything to happen to you."

"Sure," Andrea said haughtily. "Thanks for your concern. I have my own issues to settle with Mother." She turned on the stool and watched him leave.

Chapter 20

JoAnne had a feeling that something was going on with Andrea. The following Thursday Thanksgiving dinner proved to be useful in sorting out personality disorders. No one was safe.

JoAnne sat at the head of the table, her vision rotating now and then in order to analyze her dinner guests. She had an excellent view of Libby, who sat straight and staring in a drug-induced state. She watched Edwin fidget in his chair, refilling his wine glass as soon as he emptied it, and Andrea, dressed in a bulky red knit skirt and sweater ensemble, downed her wine much too quickly as well.

JoAnne knew Edwin would prove to be useful thanks to his questionable past. He was a criminal at heart, a deviant, helpful to her quest of destroying Russ.

But Andrea held her attention the most, with her wandering eyes and her continuous adjustment of clothing.

She was up to something, JoAnne decided.

JoAnne tried to steady her own hand as she sipped wine and attempted to butter a roll. She smiled and buttered, although her entire body ached. No surprise, her arthritis and osteoporosis problem of late. Her grandmother and great grandmother had acquired the same afflictions.

What worried JoAnne even more than the physical impairments was the fact that they both had suffered from an aggressive form of dementia.

Why would this happen to me now? JoAnne thought, scanning the bodies positioned around the long dining room table. *I have important things left to do.*

JoAnne watched Andrea lift a fork to her crusty mouth and eat what appeared to be dressing. *She eats like a damned bird.* An observation not exactly new. Ever since Andrea was a baby, she had no appetite to speak of.

JoAnne recalled taking Andrea to the doctor often between the ages of ten and fifteen. She asked the doctor what was wrong with her, but the doctor said nothing, that she just "has a quirky way about her." JoAnne was not a fan of "quirky ways." Not with children, and most certainly not with adults. Therefore, despite Aaron's protests, JoAnne took Andrea to psychiatrists and neurosurgeons and anyone else related to the business of the brain.

Now as she watched Andrea, fully grown but still childlike, she wondered if Andrea knew what the operation had really been about. JoAnne herself flinched at the memory. She recalled having to bribe the doctor into performing the drastic operation, and no one else knew about it.

Even Aaron never found out what JoAnne paid to have done to their daughter. He was a bit slow anyway and favored looking the other way when he thought

JoAnne was up to no good. He was not the best of fathers, in that respect.

As JoAnne recalled the memory of Andrea's operation, Andrea suddenly looked over at her, as if she could read her mind. Poor child. JoAnne put down her roll. She'd done her a favor, really. Besides, she married a man with the mentality of a slug. What could she expect to produce genetically?

Yes, JoAnne did her a favor. She did them all a favor.

When Andrea turned seventeen and was able to seek her own medical care, JoAnne explained to her that as a child she had had a rare malfunction of the uterus which unfortunately made her sterile. At the time, Andrea accepted the explanation. After all, she barely had periods. "Just think, dear," JoAnne told her. "You'll never have to worry about getting pregnant."

And thank God, the doctor who performed the operation was long since dead by the time Andrea found out she couldn't have children. Although Doc Barlow had assisted, he was too feeble now to give a damn.

JoAnne turned her stiff neck toward Olivia, who was dressed in a green skirt and blouse and sitting near a huge stone fireplace by the picture window, petting Pat. JoAnne made a face at the very idea of the dog laying by the fireplace, on one of her best Oriental rugs, no less. She believed pets belonged outside, but for now, she knew she had to go along with Libby on the issue of Pat. Libby made it clear in the beginning that if Pat couldn't stay in the Lodge—at least confined to

Libby's bedroom and the back rooms—she would take Olivia and Pat and find someplace else to live.

"Sweetheart, come back to the table for dessert," JoAnne said to Olivia, trying to get her attention. It appeared that JoAnne wore a neck brace by the way she struggled in the effort of turning. Gesturing with a stilted nod was a chore as well. However, she wore a high-neck brown velvet dress for concealment. She added, "Let Pat take a nice nap."

Perhaps she'd put a little something into Pat's dinner to make her "nap" forever.

Once JoAnne was satisfied that Olivia was on her way to the table, she turned to Andrea and said, "Andrea, why don't you take Edwin outside for some...air."

It was obvious she wanted to speak with Libby and Olivia alone. Andrea shrugged and motioned for Edwin to follow her outside. Actually, they would go to the kitchen and see about getting some pumpkin pie, but dessert in the kitchen was what JoAnne had in mind for Olivia. She wanted to be alone with Libby.

Olivia looked over at JoAnne, pursed her small lips, wrinkled her brow, and shouted, "I want my dad, damn it!"

Libby, wearing an orange dress with lacey trim and large pearl earrings, tried to sit up straight in the chair. She blinked. "What did you say?" she asked Olivia.

"I *said*— I want my dad!"

"And added a 'damn it'," JoAnne put in, clicking her tongue against the roof of her mouth and shaking her head. Was it palsy or aggravation? She said, "Perhaps the little angel would like to go into the kitchen and ask Auntie Marilyn for a nice ice cream sundae. Tell her Grandma said you could have one, all the flavors you want."

"Grandma, that fat warthog *isn't* my aunt," Olivia stated.

Libby merely blinked. But Olivia elaborated, "Dad told me to stay away from that Marilyn cow." However, she turned to Libby for confirmation, "Can I ask the cook for a sundae, Mom?"

JoAnne's head started to shake, and her crooked finger tapped the table. "We won't have that talk in Grandmother's Lodge," she said. "I insist you have some respect for Marilyn and everyone else working here."

Olivia got out of her chair and stood with her arms crossed. "My dad said Marilyn is a spy. I don't like her!"

The white bow in her short light-brown hair quivered. She gritted her teeth and stared directly at JoAnne. "Go to the kitchen!" JoAnne told her, her own face just as hard, if not harder, due to all the years of practice. "Your mother and I need to talk!"

Olivia lifted her chin to report further, "And after I have dessert, my dad's coming to get me. I'm spending the night with *him*."

She stomped off toward the kitchen, never mind Libby's approval. Libby was sunk in a daze anyway. She had that blank expression and a shortness of breath that Olivia was getting used to. This sort of behavior she was supposed to report to her father. And she would tonight.

Libby smiled slightly while turning toward JoAnne. "I'm tired," she said. "I told you the first night I stayed here I wanted a sleeping pill. Why is it that I still feel tired?"

"Oh, honey," JoAnne put forth her best sympathetic expression, yet it fell as flat as the mashed potatoes on her plate. "It's the stress; the separating from Russ." JoAnne slid forward, her elbows moving across the tablecloth. Presently, her skinny eyebrows lifted. "The *affair*," she added, her lips clamped, pretending she shouldn't have said it.

She had to keep reminding Libby about the affair, saying it repeatedly, if necessary. Whenever she mentioned it, Libby's eyes flashed. She knew Libby had to stay angry, even hateful, toward Russ. The best way to keep her sad and enraged was to mention Scott's death and Russ's affair. If possible, both in the same sentence. And when the time was right, she'd tell Libby about Russ's other daughter.

JoAnne felt the need to add, "Your body's just reacting to all the stress. That's why you're so tired. When David gets here, we're going to have a private talk in my office. Then you should go upstairs and lie down."

"A chat with David?" Libby asked, thinking JoAnne's brown dress had sparkled.

"Yes, he's coming for dessert, then a much-needed conference. You should be happy I retained him as your lawyer. He can get things rolling before Russ gets a chance to think things through. You'll see. Russ will lose everything."

Libby drank some water. She pushed at her hair, pinned to the back of her head. She tried to tuck in the tendrils that fell at the sides of her peach-colored cheeks. She had a flawless face, but she was low on spunk. "What if I don't want Russ to lose everything," she said to JoAnne. "What if I need more time to think?"

"No thinking involved! That's what we have David for. You need to strike while the iron's hot. Have you forgotten, Libby dear, that he *slept* with—or rather—has been having a lengthy *affair* with your brother's wife? And right under your nose! Oh, come now, this is no time for you to turn weak and forgiving. After what he's done to you and your daughter? Your *brother?*"

"Yes, Scott found them together," said Libby. "I remember."

"Yes, and that's why he shot himself," JoAnne continued, edging her on. JoAnne began to tremble, uncontrollably, at the image of Aaron behind the boathouse, kissing her best friend Susan Weyman.

JoAnne stood up as if shot out of her chair. She bent over and pounded the table with her fists. For a second, she thought Libby was Susan, but somehow, JoAnne managed to brace herself, steady her trembling head and hands.

She heard herself yell, "I finally caught you, you bastard!"

Libby was shocked by the vibration of JoAnne's voice, never mind the power behind her words. JoAnne held herself upright by pushing on the tabletop, thereby making a glass topple over and fall to the carpet with a muffled crash.

Libby could only stare at JoAnne, her eyes wide as JoAnne almost fell over from the impact of her own shaking. She closed her eyes, seeing it all again, her husband and that woman behind the boathouse. They'd thought she was still away visiting a friend, but she had returned early.

Libby was able to register JoAnne's outburst, even though she was still stuck within the storm of drugs. JoAnne smoothed down the front of her dress. "Oh, look. Perfect timing. It's Mr. David Preece. Sit down David," she said amicably. "Have some coffee and a piece of pie."

She lifted her finger for the maid, but Preece said, "No thank you. No time for refreshments." He cleared his throat. "Shall we just get down to business?"

"Fine, but we shall get down the hallway to *conduct* it," JoAnne said, moving away from the table with her dress, hose, and jewelry, everything about her now flat and fallen-askew upon her body.

She started walking, jaggedly, toward the hallway.

And they moved, single file, all three trance-like, all looking as old as JoAnne felt.

When JoAnne passed the huge, rectangular picture window past the fireplace, she noticed the yard was powdered with snow. She saw Olivia, yes, good, wearing a coat and walking Pat. She saw Andrea sitting on a swing; there was no Edwin to be found. They finally reached the office. JoAnne snapped on the lights and said to David, "I want you to keep an eye on that imbecile, Edwin Mayfield."

She went over to Libby, "Now, Libby, we have important things to discuss. Why don't you find a comfortable chair?"

"I'll stand," Libby said, although she was barely able to.

JoAnne shrugged as if to say *suit yourself*, found the leather chair behind her desk, and deflated down into it. She motioned for David to take the other chair across from her. "Libby," JoAnne went on, thinking it was best to take care of matters while Libby was still semi-coherent. "Listen to me carefully. Russ is out of the picture when it comes to inheriting my estate. And believe me, it's substantial. Am I right, David?"

"Substantial *is* a good word for it," David agreed, sweating.

"Unfortunately, Andrea's incapable of running a lodge or maneuvering stocks and properties, which I find so very sad." JoAnne paused here, pretending to think over the lack of savvy in her only daughter, her flesh and blood, the apple of her eye. She sighed, her chest rattling. "So, there's no one else but you. You're the only one I trust with my estate."

Libby looked over at JoAnne. JoAnne thought she was going to say something, maybe even perk up at the surprise, but she simply stared and pressed her slender hands together as if to steady them.

"It's all yours, Libby," JoAnne droned on. "Yours and Olivia's. All I ask of you is this: divorce Russ; put the house on Grand Lake up for sale, and don't let Russ have custody of Olivia."

"I'll have to think about it," Libby said, startling JoAnne with a voice of authority.

"Think about what? Your brother's suicide? And all because he found out your husband was *sleeping* with his wife?"

"I'll consider it," Libby said, leaning against the bookshelf, "if you give Russ his grandfather's land."

David jostled slightly in the chair, looking seasick. He resumed the twisting of his diamond ring. And he waited.

JoAnne's eyes became black glass. "*That* will never happen! Take my offer. My children have disgraced me, and I'm getting old. Not only that, but I'm sick. Who knows how long I have left to live. I want things settled!"

"I don't know," Libby said again. Although, to JoAnne, it appeared that her wheels were turning and the mist was gathering.

Then suddenly JoAnne stood up and put a hand to her hip. Her legs pulsated with pain, and her neck felt like a rope was tied around it, tugging and pulling, but she steadied herself successfully, thinking of strokes. Thinking how she would rather have a heart attack than a stroke.

She knew people who had suffered from strokes, and they could not speak or move. They became immobile, stuck in a bed, completely dependent on others. JoAnne would shoot herself before irreversible paralysis would happen to her. Before she would trust her life, her every breath and movement, to another human being.

"Now you listen to me, Libby," she said. "Russ has a daughter in Lansing." Here she noticed David Preece gawked at her. It was Standish, but JoAnne had reasons for not revealing the exact location.

She looked at Libby for a reaction, but Libby had already turned away, touching one of the books on the bookshelf.

When an electrical current of pain climbed up JoAnne's spine, she leaned forward and bit her lip. Still, she was able to say, "The child's Beverly's too. You know, the baby everyone thought was dead? No, indeed. Beverly took her to Lansing and is there with her now. A little girl, mind you. Beverly and *Russ's* baby daughter."

David Preece took a deep breath.

JoAnne said, "David has the court date arranged, don't you David? It's all set. The papers, your motion for divorce. God knows you have grounds, Libby."

"Well McPherson managed to delay the hearing," Preece piped in, his sentence ending in a stammer. When he saw JoAnne's rippled skin stretch tightly, unnaturally, he added, "But just for a couple days; it's nothing for you ladies to worry about."

JoAnne placed a hand to her hollow chest, sensing her lungs regress to mesh-netting, all raspy and wet. She wished she hadn't smoked so much when she was younger. "It's important to go with your instincts," she told Libby. "And face the truth. Russ has another family. He has for years. Think of the shame that puts on poor Olivia. Not to mention you. Not to mention the Birch Hill Lodge."

"Yes, the Lodge," Libby said, the wheels turning so slowly now. Only JoAnne felt the breeze. "Where do I sign?"

Chapter 21

The weekend after Thanksgiving, Jerry drove fifty miles to Standish to talk with Beverly. He left early Sunday morning. He hoped Russ didn't know where she was living yet; he wanted to see her first, talk her into letting him take care of her and the child.

Beverly had moved out of her friend's house in town and rented a farmhouse, twenty-five miles away. A two-story, drafty old house with a front porch and rows of pines and cedars in the front yard and a five-mile-wide field in the back.

Jerry had precise directions. He had asked her to call him as soon as she relocated, to give him her new phone number along with the details of how to get to her house. As he turned off a rural road and onto another dirt road toward the long driveway of Beverly's property, he thought about how he would never be able to live in the country. He had always been a Grand Lake resident. He had lived in the city when he went to the university, but he didn't consider Grand Lake rural or country. It was more of a resort community and close enough, he rationalized, to Rogers City and Alpena.

When he arrived, Beverly was in the kitchen unpacking cookware. Christine was taking a nap on a plush pink couch in the living room. Beverly looked as beautiful as ever to him. When he took off his hat and walked into the kitchen, he wanted to kiss her but knew, as he'd always known, that she didn't feel the same way about him. He was just a friend to her, nothing more.

He said, "I wanted to be sure you and Christine are getting along okay."

But she didn't respond right away.

She wore tight black pants and a striped cotton blouse. He noticed her hair was professionally styled, so he assumed that she had enough money for extras like hair maintenance, and nails. Her fingernails were well-manicured and painted red.

The house was nicely-furnished. All antiques, he could tell, and the appliances were brand new, top of the line. She had plenty of money, apparently. This was a disappointment in a way. He had hoped that if she needed money, he would be able to help her and be with her more often.

He asked her straight out, "Have you seen Russ?"

"No," she said. "He doesn't know where we are. In fact, he made it clear to me before we left that he wanted to stay with Libby. We'll see. I haven't given up on him, and I never will."

She turned to straighten out a drawer of potholders and dishtowels. As she concentrated on folding items, Jerry became puzzled by her obsession with Russ rather than the ability to show sorrow over Scott's suicide. He didn't know what to make of her, really. So, he decided to fan the fire about Russ.

He reiterated in a stark voice, "Russ loves Libby. And that'll never change." Then he slapped a folder of papers on the kitchen table, getting down to the purpose of his visit. The papers were in regard to Scott's estate—the insurance on their house, some dividends on stocks Scott had bought a few years ago. "I brought documents for you to sign."

Beverly simply shrugged. And even though he was happy just by being near her, his hand started to shake. He added, "I have something else for you." He pulled a small box from his jacket pocket and put it on the table, next to the folders.

But she ignored him. She seemed more interested in folding her laundry. For a second, after he put the box down and realized she was not going to acknowledge it, he wanted to take it back. He said, "I *have* something for you," as if she hadn't heard him the first time. "Open it."

She turned to look at him. He knew she knew what it was, what it had to be, and she smiled at him as if he were a child with an adult idea. "Jerry," she said, going back to the potholders.

"It's a diamond ring," he told her in a tone too eager, he knew. "I want you to marry me after I get my divorce and you get things straightened out. I want to be a father to Christine. I want to help you."

"It won't work, Jerry," she said, trying to let him down easy. "I'm going to make a new life here. And I'm waiting for Russ."

"Damn it, that's foolish!" He didn't mean to shout at her, but her obstinate way of believing Russ loved her enough to leave Libby astonished him.

He said, "Russ will stop at nothing to get Libby back. He'll love her until he dies. You have to get that through your head."

When she refused to speak, he continued, "The court will insist on blood tests. Maybe the baby's Scott's. Or maybe she's—well, God knows whose!"

The insinuation of paternity got Beverly's attention. "What does *that* mean? Christine's Russ's daughter. I know it; he knows it! And Scott was hardly ever home. I didn't sleep with him around that time. We had separate bedrooms."

"If you say so," Jerry relented, looking at her suspiciously. "The court will want proof. That's how it's done these days in paternity cases if you want to collect child support and *make* him help take care of Christine."

She ignored him, rushing now to straighten piles of dishcloths she had already stacked twice. "You could at least look at the ring," he said.

She shook her head as he stood watching her. Because he knew he didn't have a chance with her, he asked if he could see Christine. She nodded toward the living room. He went into the living room where he found the baby asleep on the couch. There were pillows arranged around her to keep her from falling off onto the hardwood floor. Inside the living room was the couch, a rocking chair, a wood box, and a fireplace. There were no drapes over the large front window, and the morning sunbeams fell over the baby—the one-year-old child—

sleeping in a cotton nightgown, a tiny hand against her curly dark hair.

What a beautiful baby. But her hair was darker than Russ's.

He pulled the quilt over her and tucked it beneath her small shoulders. She moved slightly but did not awaken. And he knew then he had to try and get Russ to let him adopt her. Maybe he could talk Russ into switching blood samples so that he could be her legal parent. First, he would consider all options of the law, all methods of adjustments, as he was trained to do. With this plan in mind, he told Beverly goodbye and took the ring from the kitchen table.

• • •

When Jerry returned to his condo later that night, there were two messages on his answering machine. One from Brett Daniels, and the other from David Preece. He waited until the next day, Monday afternoon, to return the calls. Brett Daniels only wanted to report that JoAnne had "hunted him down and tried to buy him off." Brett told Jerry she was willing to pay twice what Jerry paid him, and so he agreed to lie to her and tell her she could have all the copies.

Brett continued, "She asked if you had contacted me yet, and I told her yes, but that I didn't want to deal with you. I made it sound like I was holding out for her call, waiting and knowing that she would offer a better bargain. She wired one thousand dollars to me, even before receiving the papers. I call that stupid, but here I am, eighteen-hundred dollars richer, thanks to both of you."

Jerry asked urgently, "But you're on our side, right? And you'll testify against her in court about the tax evasion?"

"Yes, I have the money. Proof that she tried to buy me off. I have several copies of her tax schemes too, plus the copies I sent to you."

"Good," said Jerry, "then we're one up on her. She'll snap when she finds out she paid you before getting the proof. This just goes to show she's starting to slip."

"Well, it was her lawyer, Preece, who negotiated the deal. Maybe he's trying to trip her up. Who knows? He called me after she did."

Jerry told Daniels that he would verify everything they had just discussed and call him back later. This turn of events was in their favor. JoAnne would be arrested, at least heavily fined, and her antics would become documented when the tax evasion situation came out in the open. They were talking a lot of money, and Jerry knew it was related to taxes on the Birch Hill Lodge and various property holdings. The government would probably want a complete audit, check out codes, discover errors, and the investigation would open doors to her other schemes—underhanded plots and twists and turns that even Jerry, as her former lawyer, didn't know about.

Thankfully, Jerry had insisted her accountant and bookkeeper do the dirty work and sign papers and whatnot. He was only there to advise her.

He showered before calling David Preece. The message itself was a mystery. Why would Preece call? No doubt it pertained to Russ's up-and-coming court hearing, his separation from Libby, and the child support.

Jerry knew Russ would not agree to a divorce. The flip side to the entire controversy would be that Libby, directed by JoAnne, would try to get everything: the house, their savings, all that she could bleed from Russ. Jerry had a feeling that JoAnne knew about Christine and would tell Libby soon.

He was set to call Preece, but the phone rang, and it was Preece himself, saying, "I was hoping you'd answer your message before noon, Mr. McPherson. It's almost five o'clock. Did you have a nice visit with Beverly Weyman in Standish yesterday?"

"So now you're following me?"

"No, following people around isn't my style," Preece admitted. "I have *other* people do it. And I didn't mean Standish, exactly. I meant the quaint farmhouse fifteen miles north of Standish. Is that right? Yes, I believe it is. Ah! She won't marry you? That's just *soooo* sad."

"You crooked fucker," said Jerry. "Why don't you slink on back to Florida or wherever it is you're from?"

"Because I have a thriving law practice right here in northern Michigan. Now, if you'd only take the time to answer your messages before you shower, not after, you'd know that you've been invited to dinner at the Birch Hill Lodge. JoAnne wants to get together with you for a quiet dinner meeting. We think we can come to terms without this awful mess going to court."

"If you have cameras in my house, Preece, I'll find them and sue your ass!"

"Come now, I'm not a novice at this." Preece paused for a few seconds. "But then neither are you. We think we can negotiate at dinner. Tonight, at seven o'clock."

"I didn't get papers to prove that Libby has filed for a separation."

"We have the papers. Libby filed the other day, but like I said, it's possible that we can make everyone happy without haggling in court."

"I doubt it. Unless, of course, Libby agrees to a reasonable child support amount. Russ said she can have the house. He'll gladly sign it over if she wants it. So that tells me there's nothing to meet about. The judge will decide support and visitation rights anyway."

"JoAnne has some very important business to discuss with you. Seven o'clock sharp. As you know, Mrs. Shaw doesn't like to be kept waiting."

Preece hung up. Jerry called Russ before heading to the Birch Hill Lodge. He told Russ about the dinner meeting and asked him if he'd had a chance to talk to Andrea. Russ explained he had met with Andrea, and as far as he could tell, she was on their side. She promised to look out for Libby, even try to confiscate the drugs before JoAnne had a chance to get more of them into Libby. Russ was convinced that once Libby got the drugs out of her system, she would give him another chance. Russ also explained what he found out about Edwin Mayfield. Andrea had all but admitted that Edwin had participated in the old woman's death.

Jerry and Russ talked for five more minutes before hanging up. Jerry was puzzled by the fact that Russ didn't understand Libby might never come "home" because he was having an affair behind her back all these years, with her brother's wife no less. It was only a matter of time before JoAnne would tell Libby about Christine.

Jerry dressed for the dinner. He wore a good pair of blue jeans, a long-sleeved shirt, and a brown corduroy sport jacket. It was cold outside, but it had stopped snowing. There was only an inch of snow covering the ground.

Apparently, JoAnne was advertising Scott's death to the hilt. The entire Lodge was still closed in mourning. The other parking area, to the right side of the Lodge, was empty too, except for Preece's silver BMW.

Right away Jerry noticed that all the candles in the cast-iron holders on the walls and tables were lit, and so were the old-fashioned gold-plated lanterns. Thanksgiving had just happened, yet there was a hint of Christmas décor at the Birch Hill Lodge. JoAnne had already started decorating with green wreaths and red ribbons, all the same shape and size lining the walls and arranged every couple feet near the windows.

The extravagant Christmas collection had been pulled out of storage. He wondered what else she would pull out of storage.

Edwin was leaning against the wall near the cash register, a toothpick sticking out of his mouth. He had both hands inside his pants pockets. He glared at Jerry, sucking on the toothpick, and turned and walked away.

Once Jerry entered the enormous dining room, he saw that the largest table near the front bay picture window was occupied by his dining companions. When JoAnne saw him coming, she lifted her wineglass in a toast. David Preece was the only other person with her. David stood up, indicated a chair at the other side of the table, the other side of JoAnne, suggesting for Jerry to sit there.

Then Preece smiled and fumbled with the buttons on his silk dinner jacket. He was so clean, Jerry could smell his aftershave; he could even smell the soap he had used to bathe with earlier: nutmeg and molasses, like a pungent liquor mixed with the herbs of dinner cooking in the kitchen.

"Have a seat," Preece said when Jerry remained standing. "We were having a sip of wine while waiting for you to arrive. Care for some? Or maybe a cocktail?"

"No thanks," Jerry murmured. He sat down, although he had only planned to stay a few minutes.

Of all people, it was Marilyn Clayton scurrying around the table playing the part of waitress, filling water glasses, laying down small crystal plates of butter, rolls, and jellies. She came back with a bottle of wine and filled Jerry's glass even though he had declined a drink.

As she moved away from him, her chilly fat arm grazed his wrist. He looked over at JoAnne and said, "What do you have for me? Keep in mind, I'm only here on Russ's behalf, so if you plan on discussing anything other than him, you'll have to contact *my* attorney."

"He's so clever," Preece said, sighing dramatically. He raised his glass in yet another toast. "Don't you think, JoAnne?"

"Indeed," JoAnne agreed enthusiastically. "But not clever enough to steal my best secrets." Her eyes sparkled and her voice scorched like fire. "Really now, Jerry, you pose as my attorney all this time just to get information on my son in order to help *him* get *me*? How completely backstabbing of you." As he expected, she clicked her tongue against her false teeth. Her delivery was so predictable and exaggerated. He hated the fact that he had fallen for this meeting even more than he abhorred the tongue-smacking.

Russ's attorney or not, this banter could have been handled over the phone. Jerry sat up straight but kept his sight on her. "That's a matter of opinion," he said. "And furthermore, it's only *your* opinion, which no one really cares about."

JoAnne drained her wineglass simply to pour another. "We need more wine, Marilyn," she shouted. "Go get it!"

Thus, when Marylyn Clayton disappeared, JoAnne put her skinny elbows forward against the tablecloth and propped herself upward, straight but wobbly. She had not been to the hair dresser in weeks, evidently. Her gray hair was combed this way and that, proving sporadic baldness. Or perhaps she had trusted a sticky, inferior hairspray to secure what she had left in place. It was an outlandish arrangement of wispy white and gray hairs covering a liver spotted forehead and scalp.

Not only are they both half-crocked, she's not well. Jerry gave her six months to live.

The very idea of JoAnne dying provided him with a burst of inspiration. He took a deep breath, becoming energized. Only then was he able to assess the way *she* breathed. Every time she inhaled air, her lungs rattled, hinting at a serious lung defect. After taking a breath, she would shudder. She closed her eyelids along with the shuddering and shook her head, all seemingly without intention.

Even so, she was center stage above anyone and everyone, as always. She looked back at him, and as she did so, her head shook uncontrollably. He knew then she was probably in the first stages of cerebral palsy, or some other nerve disorder just as serious. Things were finally getting to her at long last. Only sixty-nine years old, and she was paying for her chain smoking and conniving and all the demented vengeance spitting and brewing.

Marilyn returned with a bottle of champagne, and this time so quickly, Jerry knew her departure and reappearance had been staged.

JoAnne watched David pop the cork. David lifted the bottle to Jerry, indicating that Jerry should raise the empty crystal champagne glass beside his full wine glass. But Jerry put a hand over the tall-stemmed glass. He knew her ways. He knew Russ was right in suspecting her of drugging Libby.

"Goodness, as if we're out to poison you?" JoAnne exclaimed, her bony hands clamped together. "Oh, I love it! David, poor Jerry thinks we're trying to *poison* him with our exquisite Bordeaux. Isn't that...well, intriguing? He thinks we're..." she leaned sideways toward David and said with both bloodshot eyes wide, "*Murrr-derers.*"

"Intriguing indeed," Preece agreed, filling his glass, taking a hearty sip, and grinning at Jerry as if to say *if it were poison, would I be drinking it?* He filled JoAnne's glass and made a big production out of drinking more wine from his own. He said to Jerry in a jovial voice, "Do I look like I'm about to topple over, clutching my chest? Really!"

Preece and JoAnne laughed at the same time.

Jerry pushed his hands against the velvet chair and stood up.

But JoAnne snapped jauntily, "Sit the hell down!" And with her trembling blue-veined hand, she reached for a cloth napkin and wiped her damp forehead. "We haven't much time left. Let's talk. Libby wants to push the court date. She wants a divorce as soon as possible. Did you know, Jerry, that she now works here as my assistant manager? I thought it best to accommodate her any way I can. She's far more superior in intelligence and common sense, I'm afraid, than Russell."

Jerry was having trouble sitting back down in the chair. He felt a bit weak and tried to refrain from thinking of food. He knew she was going to serve lasagna. It was his favorite, and he could smell garlic and basil and other sauce-ingredients and Italian bread coming from the kitchen. She would try to impair his reasoning with lasagna, never mind wine; and he felt so light-headed already. He instinctively took a quick sip of water.

When JoAnne smiled at him, her powdered face shattered in tiny lines, and he wondered if he had made a mistake by even drinking the water. "Interesting," was all he could say in response to Libby, the teacher, working for JoAnne as the assistant manager of the Birch Hill Lodge.

He cleared his throat, stared at the glass of water, and back to JoAnne's painted face. Her tight black and pink pantsuit squeezed her bones in place. He said, "So the deal is Libby leaves Russ in exchange for taking over the Birch Hill Lodge. That's typical, manipulating your daughter-in-law to destroy your son."

"He has destroyed *himself*," JoAnne corrected. She pursed her dry lips. "Let me help you out with this, Mr. McPherson." Here her voice took on an exaggerated Scottish brogue, a feeble jab at his ancestry, which did not impress him in the least. She always used the accent whenever she deemed it fitting to mock him. "Libby makes her own decisions. Obviously, I need a successor. My children are useless idiots. They would run this place and all my other assets into the ground in less than a week's time. I will say this next part only once. Russ goes anywhere near my father's place, he'll be arrested. I have a restraining order out on him. So please, don't forget my friends in the sheriff's department, not to mention the city officials I have in my pocket. I hope I've made myself clear." She didn't wait for a response; she merely turned in her chair, as if on cue, to the side entrance where Claudia Bishop's high heels clicked against the wooden hallway and softened when she hit the dining room carpet.

"Look who we have here!" JoAnne cried, turning back to Jerry with a smirk dragging her chin muscles all the way down to her conclave chest. "What a surprise," she added, squinting hard at Jerry.

It startled him immensely when JoAnne pushed herself up from the table, thereby revealing she now used a cane. When she smiled at Claudia Bishop, it appeared that the cords in her neck shriveled with the strain of motion.

Jerry was speechless for several seconds. His throat felt constricted, and he wanted more water but knew to leave all liquids alone.

Claudia attempted to take part in the charade, although her acting ability lacked momentum. She came forward and held out a thin hand for JoAnne to pump.

Claudia looked the same as she did five years ago when she had lived at Grand Lake. The same long curly blonde hair, shapely legs, and the exact same beauty mark on her chin. She wore too much makeup though, just as Jerry remembered. The eyeliner and eye shadow were very thick and stark, and the lipstick, dark in color, gave her the swollen appearance of being immersed under water too long.

Jerry wanted to laugh at JoAnne's strategy, enlisting Claudia's attempt at helping or joining or whatever her part in this heinous horseplay was all about. But Jerry felt faint, and he was trying to figure out how JoAnne had sedated him. He hadn't eaten anything, and yet he felt sick even before taking the sip of water. Was her potion airborne?

He studied Claudia, primarily to focus on something, anything, trying desperately to keep his bearings. Keep alert, stay awake. Claudia wore a short skirt to accentuate her long legs; she wore an orange blouse with a matching orange jacket. Too orange. Too much orange and too much skin. *She's very attractive and young and it's a shame I even touched her, goddammit; how many years ago was it now?*

He turned to JoAnne, "And this means exactly what, JoAnne?"

He could tell JoAnne believed she had scored points. She relaxed inside her large chair and her hands stopped shaking. "You remember Claudia Bishop, don't you Jerry? Your little playmate from several years back?"

Jerry glanced over at David Preece who was pushing a piece of fruit around on his plate with a fork. Jerry straightened inside his chair, hoping to keep his vision focused, if not his reasoning. "It won't work, JoAnne," he said. "The case was acquitted."

Claudia took the cue and smiled. It was her big moment, her turn to speak on JoAnne's behalf. That is, if she wanted paid.

But paying her wouldn't be enough, Jerry knew, as there was no proof he had molested a minor. There was nothing damaging Claudia could contribute now.

It was all water under the bridge until she said, "I missed you, Jerry."

Furthermore, Claudia, as expected, was carelessly choppy in diction, although faultless in dialogue having been previously coached by JoAnne. Jerry saw in her oval eyes a subtle agreement between them. He knew Claudia wasn't out to dredge up the past. She was just trying to get information about JoAnne for her father, and if she could earn some money via JoAnne in the process, no harm done.

He told JoAnne, "Nothing she says now will hold up in court. Besides, we both know the truth of what really happened, don't we Claudia?" He knew to bump this subject for another before his lips turned numb. He said, lisping, "Let's talk about the papers you had drawn up regarding Russ's employment status a few summers ago. Drop those asinine charges now, JoAnne. I already talked to the judge, and well," he lifted his thumb and aimed it downward in explanation. "It isn't related to a damned thing. It's flimsy at best. A waste of everyone's time."

JoAnne tittered and grunted simultaneously, a sound he had tried to avoid in the past, a particular tone that always meant disaster. She placed a napkin to her lips and dabbed gently. "What'll you give me in return, Mr. McPherson?"

"First of all," Jerry began, "you amaze me with your thinking. The whole part about *you* giving the orders, playing judge and jury, even being your own attorney." He directed the last part at David Preece, who was still pushing peaches around on the plate with a fork. When David realized that Jerry had meant him, he stopped the arranging of fruit and peered outward with glazed eyes. Jerry shook his head in pity.

He decided to answer JoAnne anyway. "I'll drop the investigation into the murder of your father," he said. This offer was so out of line, so completely out of left field, even *he* couldn't believe he had said it. JoAnne, her face turning as white as the tablecloth, dropped her lower lip; it appeared as if she might scream in rage, but as usual, she checked herself in time. Out came a shriek of laughter instead, so spine-tingling and ear-splitting, even Preece winced.

JoAnne said, "*Murder?* My father died of old age, you simpleton! A natural affliction I'm sure *you'll* never achieve. You, on the other hand, *will* die young, mark my words! This preview into your warped, psychotic imagination proves it! You'll probably have a stroke, my dear, all this thinking up of outlandish scenarios and putting words into other people's mouths and creating actions from false motives! Accusations like this could get you—" She was about to say killed, they all knew it, but again, she checked herself in time and finished with, "an early grave, you stupid, arrogant boy!" She dabbed at her reddened eyes, this time smiling. "But you *do* entertain me Jerry, I'll give you that much!" she quickly looked to David for confirmation.

Preece shrugged; Jerry did too, thinking why not plunge forward: "Russ saw you do it, JoAnne," he said, his voice stronger than he thought possible. He expected her to gag on the fluids her throat had produced with hysteria, but she simply sat rigidly. "So much is coming out into the open," Jerry added without proper shuffling of his cards. "So much, so fast!" came the punctuation at the end of a slight slur.

JoAnne snickered again; she sat up to straighten her cracked spine. She placed both hands against the tabletop, palms downward, her mouth now a knot tied tightly, only to slacken. "I have no doubt Russ saw more than he should have, unfortunately," she said, surprising both Jerry and Preece. "Yes, I just might drop the charges against him for all the money he cost me a few summers ago. But you're way off about the murder allegations. I loved my father," she said, expecting to end the subject by feigning sorrow at his passing.

Claudia Bishop jumped in quickly, "Can I get a drink or something? A screwdriver would be nice."

JoAnne turned to her with a face laden with creases. "Certainly! David, see Claudia gets a drink, her check, and then get her the hell out of here!"

When JoAnne stood up this time her smile opened wide enough to taste the walls. "Look at this, will you? It's your future ex-wife. Come on in, Leeann. Do help us rake Jerry over the coals."

Right away Jerry could tell Leeann was outraged if nothing else. He knew this little meeting, or summons, put an awkward crimp into her schedule. She wore casual clothes—brown pants, a red blouse and black shoes. Her hair was arranged upward into a twisted bun of sorts, and her complexion was marred with irritation and worry. Jerry was surprised to find her appearance this bland, almost frumpy. Blurry vision or not, he was able to focus in on her, wondering at first if he was seeing an imposter. He knew Leeann was a woman obsessed with makeup and hair, especially when out in public.

This was practically a shocker, Jerry light in the head or not. Here a plain-Jane disheveled Leeann stood before him, both hands on her hips. "Jerry, what's this about you and Beverly Weyman having a child together? That would make our divorce very messy, and *very* drawn out too! Mrs. Shaw here says she has pictures, documents to prove you have a daughter! I want the truth! And *this* little bitch!" She indicated Claudia Bishop by pointing a mass of gold-painted nails her way. "What's this shit about proof that you raped her? I want the truth, and I want it now! If you've lied to me all these years, I'll take every penny you've got, you bastard!"

David Preece stood up on that note, trying to act as a barrier between Leeann and JoAnne. He was the attorney for both and seemed unable to decide which one warranted his attention the most. He took only a second to think about it, directing his loyalties to JoAnne, "I didn't know you were planning on calling *her* in. You didn't consult me on *that* one, JoAnne!"

"And do I consult you every time I blow my nose, David?" JoAnne shouted to all. She stared from one person to another and dropped back into her chair, her thoughts reeling. "Dear God in heaven!" she proclaimed, again fumbling with the gold necklace hanging from her shrunken neck. "Here are the facts. Jerry, we've been following you; We follow everyone involved. Why do you think we've employed Marilyn Clayton? For her profound beauty? Her extreme intelligence? No, for her cunning detective ability and her gift of taking pictures unnoticed and scrounging up pertinent documents without anyone catching on. She's found some interesting developments about Beverly Weyman and her hospital visit a year ago. The baby she wanted us all to believe is dead is in fact alive and living with her, *as we speak*."

Jerry fidgeted at the table. He managed to brace himself for a sluggish jump to his feet. "You know damned well that the baby is Russ's," he said, meaning to shout although his voice lost projection soon after leaving his lips. "Russ's!" he repeated, looking as if the name itself justified a pause or a prayer; if nothing else identification strong enough to stop the show.

"Then blood tests are in order!" JoAnne said in response to the name of her only son. "And what *you'll* do is talk Russ into it, asap! Now there," she was lining up her theories and ideas as if they were jewels determined by value. She paused, clearing her throat.

"Libby wants a quick divorce. I want Russ out of town. You, Jerry, can arrange both. I'm tired of being nice," she said, shaking again. Her violent, convulsive shaking made everyone flinch, even Marilyn Clayton, the brilliant detective standing in the shadows, had been caught off guard by JoAnne's fury. Marilyn Clayton was frozen, and intrigued, like the maids upstairs who were reduced to ears pressed against doorways and vents.

While JoAnne trembled from head to toe, she pushed on her cane until standing up again and pointed at Jerry with her free hand. "You are one sorry bastard for betraying me," she bellowed, panting. "Do this *my* way, or you're finished! Hand over the third copy of my father's will. I know damned well you have it! Hand it over or Russ loses his job!"

Jerry pushed his glasses further up the bridge of his nose. "Nothing doing," he heard himself say. "We'll take this whole show to court! Especially now that I know you *don't* have the third copy." He stood up with both hands outward, clapped, and screamed as if he had lost his mind: "Lights out, *baby!*"

JoAnne caught her breath, coughed, shook. She almost fell backwards by the force of Jerry's brazen audacity. "Who are you calling baby, you upstart son of a bitch!" she screamed. "Step a foot on that property and you're going to jail! You hear me, you childish, hideous im-be-cile!" Somehow, she lifted the cane, and at first it wobbled from side to side, hitting the table three times in her haste, but finally, the tip settled in Jerry's direction. "You and Russ! I'll see you *both* dead before this farce is over!"

"Dead?" Jerry asked, eyes blinking, his lips as numb as his hands. *"As in murder?"* he inquired in a high voice. He knew he sounded deranged as he imitated her enunciation earlier. "You mean *dead* as in how you murdered your father?"

When JoAnne stepped forward, now rasping and cavorting, David Preece ran to her, and so did Claudia Bishop, both attempting to steady her. But Jerry wasn't finished. "By the way, you can forget Brett Daniels. You wasted a grand on him. And you might be interested in knowing I have copies of your tax evasion shenanigans dating back to the early seventies. Yes! Brett kept all the records, JoAnne. He even kept the copies from his uncle Stephen, your former accountant. Not too smart of you to hoard that particular dirty laundry right in the Daniels' family home."

JoAnne tried to free herself from David and Claudia's grip and rush for Jerry. She pulled and tugged but got nowhere and retreated to the chair where she sat-crooked like a cloth doll ripped at the seams.

Jerry's mind, although suffering from a sedative, somehow had more vigor now than JoAnne; even though his vision had started to spin, he actually decoded how this had happened. It had to be the contact with Marilyn's vile skin, a powder of some kind that she had transferred to his skin from her *fat chilly arm*. And he knew it was imperative to exit before he passed out. He needed some air. He needed to hurry. Run, if he could. If he could!

JoAnne continued to scream at him as he walked toward the hallway. "You're *out*, Jerry McPherson! You hear me? There won't be a court hearing for you, mister! You had better spend every second of your life from now on watching your back!"

As he moved, trying not to trip or fall, Jerry brought forth a handkerchief and wiped his face and neck with it. He smelled lasagna, most assuredly, coming from the kitchen as he moved on by. He saw white Christmas lights twinkling, showing him the way to the back door of the Lodge. These lights defined the promise one more time—lights out! And now he was certain he had to prepare Russ's defense quickly.

He had to get through the heavy door for air first.

She'd lit all three fireplaces to torture him slowly.

What if he passed out inside the Birch Hill Lodge? They would then have him, finish him off. Lights out, indeed, for him, not her.

But he made it outside, thank God, and just in time. He took a deep breath and stumbled over to his car. He slid inside the front seat and locked the doors. He pushed up the cuff of his jacket and shirt and saw it—a powdery-gel, a residue stuck to the hairs on the skin of his arm. He managed to find an aspirin bottle in the glove compartment, empty it of the pills, scrape the tiny flecks of drugs, whatever it could be, into the bottle for analysis.

"I've got you now, JoAnne. You're going down."

Chapter 22

Jerry tried to figure out how Marilyn transferred the drug from her arm to his; why didn't she turn drowsy and disoriented like he did, and how could such a small amount affect him to the point where he almost passed out? He considered that maybe she had the powder—on closer inspection he determined the substance was more like a gel with dust-like particles throughout—on her blouse, which she rubbed against his wrist, and all he felt at the time was the skin of her cold arm as she moved away from him. Furthermore, what kind of sedative was it, and how strong? Would it cause permanent damage?

He took the sample to a lab, but because it was "out of curiosity," the analysis was not rushed; they told him he could come back in a few days for the results.

Meanwhile, as he searched for Russ, he confirmed that Brett Daniels would testify against JoAnne. He knew Brett's testimony was key to bringing her down; he saw the fear in her eyes when he mentioned the tax evasion evidence to her.

Because of this tactic, she could lose the land surrounding Birch Hill, all the parcels she bought up on Lake Huron, Lake Esau, and even the property she had acquired in Petoskey. Most of this land she had avoided paying taxes on for many years. For such a savvy businesswoman, she sure was dense when it came to the inevitable—following the laws regarding taxes and insurance payments.

Jerry knew she would try to blame it all on her accountant or banker, and in that way, prove she was unaware of the discrepancies. Or maybe it was Aaron, rest his soul, who had filed the wrong papers, signed on the wrong line, that useless bastard.

And *here* was how Brett Daniels explained her reckless plan to Jerry. JoAnne had purposely avoided filing payment on some properties, especially the newly acquired parcels. She paid off Brett's uncle and also paid Brett himself. True, Brett would be fined, might even lose his license for this daring transaction, but he was prepared to testify and expose himself to get JoAnne. He wanted to come clean anyway, or so he told Jerry.

Brett went over all the paperwork and calculated a grand total of eighty-five thousand dollars JoAnne owed in back taxes. Most of these parcels were close to the harbor land development, the very parcels she bought up through her tricky realtor out from under Tom Bishop's nose, land Bishop had wanted to buy to continue his developmental enterprise. She bought specific parcels, just to lock him out. Too bad she had to make the mistake of trying to avoid paying taxes on these parcels. They weren't too high at the time, but now with added interest, and with fines and so forth, she would probably lose over one hundred thousand dollars in land.

She might back off, Jerry hoped, and cut her losses. One way or the other, he would report her. He had suspected this in the past, and if she blamed him as her previous attorney, it would be her word against his.

Now he would concentrate on proof that she murdered Russ's grandfather. He had a feeling either Russ or Andrea witnessed the "falling down the steps," which led to Grandfather's death. He knew if Russ could remember, he would definitely come forth to get JoAnne. If not, Jerry might be able to talk him into hypnosis.

Or maybe Andrea knew more than she was saying.

Two days after the dinner meeting at the Birch Hill Lodge, he received papers from David Preece, stating Leeann's demands. She would settle for the house and their joint savings and checking accounts. They had purchased land as well on Lake Huron and had planned to build a cottage one day, but she willingly signed over the five-acre property, claiming it was of no use to her. She was planning on going on a cruise, and then to Europe when the divorce was settled, and she didn't know when she would be back. Jerry knew she wanted to sell the house and relocate. She wanted her half. End of story.

He wasn't a poor man by any means, but he had more money than she knew about because he had learned from his father, who had had also been an attorney and married three times, that it was prudent to hide assets, which Jerry had done. It was mostly stocks and bonds, but there were two bank accounts Leeann didn't know about.

Leeann, naturally, wanted to find out more about Christine. But Jerry knew that she really didn't give a damn if he were the father or not. She couldn't care less if he had had one affair or one hundred. He knew it was JoAnne who tipped Leeann off anyway, pushing her to claim adultery and heft up her chances in court. Unlike Leeann, JoAnne *did* expect Jerry to hide assets. She knew he had a stash of money into the hundreds of thousands, tucked away in secret places.

And, Jerry wondered if JoAnne was really capable of getting her son fired. Did she pull that much weight with the quarry, the largest manufacturing factory in the area?

Jerry would need to speak to Russ about the baby and Beverly and confess that he was in love with Beverly and wanted to help her. Obviously, the child was Russ's—or someone else's, but not Jerry's—because try as he might, he couldn't get Beverly to love him. He hoped he would be able to talk Beverly and Russ into altering the tests. He knew people in law enforcement, and specifically a lab technician, who would see to it that the lab tests were hushed, given to Jerry before Russ, and therefore Jerry could put his name on the birth certificate in place of Russ's. Altering documents was not too difficult if the right people were involved and payoffs promised.

Libby, as manager of the Birch Hill Lodge, posed another question. Had JoAnne already signed the Lodge over to her? Had she made Libby executor of her estate? Jerry had a feeling JoAnne already signed over other important papers to Libby as well, such as papers regarding Andrea being incompetent, and Russ too.

That sort of document, however, would require psychiatric evaluations.

Jerry knew one thing for certain, time was running out. Maybe all they had to do was kick back and watch JoAnne hang herself. But, sometimes the act of hanging and dying could take weeks, even months.

He had to find Russ.

● ● ●

Two evenings later, he found Russ at his grandfather's cottage on Grand Lake. Restraining order or not, Jerry had a feeling Russ would be there. He drove past Libby and Russ's house on the way. No *For Sale* sign posted yet; no Blazer parked in the yard either. He knew Russ would be looking for the third copy of his grandfather's will, even though JoAnne had warned him against setting foot on the premises.

Sure enough, Jerry found Russ's Blazer parked up the road from the cottage. He had parked it sideways into the ditch behind a birch tree. Jerry parked behind the Blazer. He got out and walked up the road to the cottage. The ground was lightly covered with snow, the air biting-cold. This darting around in the dark from one shadow to the next was a new activity for Jerry. There was a three-quarter moon, and he had to slink along the road from tree to tree until he found the gate to the cottage. Of course, the gate's hinges were rusted and squeaked when he opened it, but because no one came hurling in his direction, no flashing light beamed toward him, he knew he was in the clear.

But the pebbles in the path crunched beneath his shoes, and he had to tip-toe down the path, toward the log structure of the cottage. He moved a few feet and stopped to listen. He slunk behind a red pine; he actually put the side of his head against the cold, wide trunk to listen for footsteps, voices.

As he stood statue-like, he detected the beam of a flashlight inside the cottage and knew Russ was hunting through the contents of the rooms. Russ wasn't the type to crouch and crawl, but he was sensible enough not to turn on the lights, and so, with flashlight in hand, he was searching, just as JoAnne predicted.

Jerry went to the front door, changed his mind about entering that way, and walked around the side of the cottage to the bedroom, exactly where the flashlight beamed. He tapped on the window. It didn't take long for the window to snap open. Russ asked angrily, "What is it?"

"It's just me, that's what!" Jerry said. "You're not supposed to be here." He knew his words were useless. "And if you get caught, you'll get arrested! Remember the restraining order?"

"Who cares about *that*?" Russ said, shining the light directly into Jerry's face. "You think I give a shit about *that*?"

Jerry sighed and moved around the bushes. "I had a feeling you'd be here. Go open the front door. I'm not climbing through a window in my good clothes."

Russ muttered something under his breath about Jerry and his good clothes and motioned with the light. "Go around to the front," he said.

Jerry freed his pant leg from a snowy bramble bush and walked around the north corner of the cottage to the front door. He listened as Russ unlocked the cedar door, pushed it open, and stepped aside so Jerry could enter. Immediately Jerry noticed that the air smelled heavily of dust. At first, it was difficult to breathe.

Once he caught his breath, he reprimanded Russ again: "You can't be here. We have to play by the rules. You can't get caught!"

"What'll she do?" Russ asked, searching through a cupboard. "Hang me? Stone me to death? Shoot me?"

"She can't really do anything, per se," Jerry said, "But the fact is, it won't look good for you if you're caught violating the restraining order. Can you hear it? Russ Shaw *and* his attorney are caught sneaking around in the dark at the cottage—the very cottage a court order was issued to keep them away from. Get what I'm saying? Sneaking, breaking and entering...or did you make the copies?"

"Yeah, I copied them from her key ring. Don't you ever *listen* to me?" Russ moved the flashlight beam from Jerry's eyes down to his feet and over to the door, as if he had heard a noise.

In the other room, a candle was lit; the only other light came from Russ's flashlight. Jerry changed the subject: "We have to talk about Beverly. I know all about Christine. So, I'll get to the point. I could lie and say I slept with her around the same time you did. But I didn't. You don't care about Beverly. I do. We need proof of paternity. I was thinking that if you want out, we can put my name on the test results after the test is done. I know people," he added, although he didn't have to. Russ already knew Jerry *knew* people in law enforcement, in the medical field, and so on. "Think about it. We can also change the birth certificate. I'm offering."

"I have to sit down." Russ said. He found the rocking chair and slumped down into it. "No way in hell," was his immediate answer. "She's *my* daughter. No one else is going to claim her. But Libby, goddamn it, I don't want to divorce Libby! That's what you have to help me avoid, Jerry!"

"We could put my name on the birth certificate and falsify the records!" Jerry countered. "I care about Beverly. In fact, I've been in love with her for a long time now, even before I met Leeann. If you don't agree, you'll be paying child support for both children. Is that what you want? You can barely make ends meet as it is!"

"No," Russ said again, the fingers of both hands slanted into a triangle at his mouth. "I said *no!*"

"You pompous son of a bitch, you don't even *care* about Beverly!"

"But I care about my daughter," Russ said. "You're my attorney. You'll do what I need done! Another thing that needs done is selling the house. Libby told me to sell it; she wants to split the money. She said from now on, she and Olivia are living at the Lodge. JoAnne gave her a job as manager or something. Both of our names are on the deed, but I changed my mind. I want to keep it and buy her out. You work on *that*, if you want to help me!"

"I *am* trying to help you! Maybe we can make a deal with her," he said, referring to the sale of the house. "But you're so god*damned* impossible to deal with!"

Now that he knew Russ wanted to keep the house, Jerry could probably barter with Libby. He knew Russ would have to give her full custody of Olivia if he wanted the house. But that would be tricky. He had a feeling Russ would want joint custody if he agreed to the divorce at all.

Jerry changed the subject, "They drugged me the other night at dinner at the Lodge."

"You actually went there for dinner?" Russ demanded to know.

"Yes, to talk to JoAnne and Preece. I didn't eat anything and didn't drink anything. Well, I did have a sip of water. It was after Marilyn grazed my wrist with her arm, rubbing some sort of sedative on me. I had a sample tested; it was a strong sedative that can be transmitted through the skin. Anyway, it affected me badly because I hadn't eaten, and my resistance was down." Jerry could see that Russ wasn't interested in his half-baked theory on JoAnne having Marilyn drug him. Russ wasn't a middle-of-the-road thinker. To him, life was spelled out in black and white, no in between.

Russ did believe that JoAnne was putting drugs into Libby's drinks and food to sedate her, but a gel or powder on someone's arm, grazing that very arm against Jerry's to incapacitate him flew way over his head.

Jerry sighed, knowing Russ was thinking only of Libby. "I felt faint by the time I left there. Thank God I didn't pass out at the table. I was the main course, anyway. But I got out of there in time."

He had lost Russ completely. Russ was listening to something else, his face turned toward the log wall. "You hear that?" he asked. "A noise?"

"To sum things up," Jerry concluded, before Russ stood to go over to the window. "I told her we know about the tax evasion. We have copies, proof."

"That's good," Russ whispered so he could listen to the sounds outside. "We got her on that, eh? But the house and my visitation schedule are the two things most important to me right now. I want to see my daughter as much as possible."

"I knew this would happen," Jerry said, shaking his head with a finger to his lip for Russ to be quiet. He too heard the noises outside, a rustling coming from the road. "We've been followed. I knew it."

"Too late to blow out candles," Russ said. "Now what will we do? I'll be damned if I'm going to hide!"

"We'll just have a seat at the kitchen table and wait," said Jerry. "It's probably that Marilyn freak. Maybe we can talk to her and strike up a deal. Sit down at the table, I'll answer the door. Just act like we're sitting here having coffee or something."

Jerry opened the kitchen door to the presence of a cop, and behind the cop was David Preece. "We were just talking about you," Jerry told Preece, who was wearing a long overcoat and a wide-brimmed hat.

For once, Preece was expressionless. "I've got a court order here stating that a Mr. Russell Shaw isn't supposed to be within one hundred yards of this property," he said as he studied Russ. "You were warned so many times," he added. He touched his left eyebrow. "I guess it's off to court for Frick and Frack," he lamented sadly. "Write out a ticket please," he told the cop, who was probably in his thirties and no doubt one of JoAnne's *people*. "I have more important things to do this evening."

And with that, he turned to leave.

Instead of *Russ* losing his cool, Jerry was the one unable to control his temper. Jerry pushed past the cop to get to Preece, who was already making his way down the snowy path toward the road.

He shouted at Preece's fading back: "You enjoy spending another man's hard-earned money, you disgusting motherfucker?"

Preece turned with his hand on the handle of his BMW. Jerry could see him well now, due to the moon and the fact that both Preece and the cop had left their headlights on. Preece tapped his forehead with a finger in what appeared to be a gesture of false awe. He stared at Jerry and grinned, his perfect, white teeth glistening in the moonlight.

"Spend *your* money?" he asked Jerry. "That drop in a bucket chicken and pig fodder? That mere pittance fitting only for a low-life adolescent wanting to call himself a lawyer and a *man*? Come now, your meager settlement to Leeann wouldn't pay for the tuna to feed my cat!"

He opened the door to his BMW and slipped inside.

"Then to hell with agreeing to Leeann's terms!" Jerry shouted. He stepped backwards toward the house. Preece had already driven off with a screech of tires and was unable to hear Jerry's threats. "I'll fight it!" Jerry promised Russ, and the cop, who was still standing in the path. "She won't see a penny from me now! And we'll see who feeds your fucking cat!"

"Now what?" Russ asked, looking to Jerry for answers. "I don't even *want* a divorce!"

"We'll fight them all!" Jerry declared; the cop was already at the gate by the road, about to get into his squad car. "We'll get them all!" he said again, both hands in fists.

Quite abruptly, Jerry followed Russ back to the kitchen and opted for a chair at the table. He summoned a handkerchief and wiped the sides of his face. "I almost dropped dead on that outburst!" he confessed. "My number one rule out the window—stay calm and keep your fucking mouth shut!"

"Don't drop dead until you get me out of this mess!" Russ whined hysterically. "Now I'm cited for trespassing; but do you know what they can do with the citation?" He made a big production out of ripping the paper in half. "*That's* what they can do, and I'll mail this to them with a note telling them to shove it up their ass!"

But Jerry was silent, deep in thought. He was trying to figure out their next move. "We've got to find the copy of the will," he said. "I don't think it's here. Someone has it, and it's not JoAnne."

"I'll never let her sell this place, Jerry. And I *won't* sell my house!"

Jerry couldn't put his finger on the answer, but he knew the pieces were falling into place. He could feel it. He knew that the third copy of the will was closer than they both realized, but not here. Not in Grandfather's house. JoAnne *wanted* them to search for it. She had moved it, or maybe, just maybe, she had no idea where to look and she was using Russ to find it.

Chapter 23

JoAnne was glad that Olivia was in school part of the day. The child was becoming more difficult to deal with. She was always talking about her father and wanting to see him, wanting to talk to him on the phone.

The day before, recalled JoAnne with malice, Libby actually let Olivia visit him at the house. And yet JoAnne had instructed Libby to tell Russ to put the house up for sale. There he was, still living in their house on Grand Lake. He had moved out of the motel, and he was even doing house repairs. He had plans to add onto the boathouse and replace the roof of the front porch. Plans all for naught.

They were now into the Christmas holiday season, perhaps the time of year was to their advantage. Libby allowing Olivia to visit Russ more often over the holidays would make Libby look reasonable in the eyes of the court.

On the other hand, JoAnne worried that the divorce might not happen unless she worked on Libby aggressively while she was still in a daze. But Olivia became more and more of a nuisance. She whined day and night, demanding to see her father. JoAnne knew that her insisting to see Russ put Libby in an awkward position, drugs or not. Libby, by nature, was good-hearted, and more than likely, the child's plea for her father's attention would win her over.

JoAnne had already signed the papers of ownership of the Lodge over to Libby, and most of her estate as well. JoAnne had even given her medical and financial power of attorney. If Libby turned traitor, she would instruct Preece to strike her out of the will, but meanwhile, it was no secret that JoAnne was becoming physically weak. Her limbs shook at unexpected times, and her memory was dim.

Yet it was the holiday season. And she would rally enthusiasm for her favorite time of the year. Even if it killed her.

Just like every year, she insisted on playing Christmas songs in the Lodge all day long until they closed at eight o'clock at night. Piped throughout the Lodge were her most favorite carols, the classics and some contemporary versions of the classics. The music kept JoAnne going, long enough for her to accomplish what she had planned to do.

She counseled Libby on structure, routine, and inventory regarding the financial networks and records of the Lodge. Libby would sit at JoAnne's desk every morning while JoAnne instructed her on the credits and debits, and also the importance of keeping precise maintenance records. The computer helped. Libby had been trained in electronics and bookkeeping anyway. She had been a teacher, and to help pay for her college education, she had worked as a loan officer in a bank, so she had experience in the world of finance.

Despite the slight impairment caused by the tranquilizers JoAnne slipped into Libby's drinks and food, she was still adept when it came to managerial skills. She dressed suitably as well—the way JoAnne wanted her to dress—in skirts and blazers and pantsuits.

She was an asset to the Lodge in more ways than one.

She never mentioned Scott's death to JoAnne. It was as if she had put the traumatic episode out of her mind completely, although JoAnne knew she visited Scott's grave at least three times a week. Marilyn Clayton followed her whenever she left the Lodge.

"The divorce hearing has been postponed again," JoAnne complained to Libby one morning in the office. "Why are you allowing it?"

"Allowing it?" Libby asked, pecking away at a calculator. "What can I do? He wants joint custody of Olivia, and he won't agree to sell the house. I guess he does need a place to live, and he did put a lot of time and effort into the addition and repairs."

JoAnne steadied herself against the desk. She wore Christmas colors, shades of red and green beneath a bright maroon shawl. But her lipstick was crooked upon her lips, and her eyebrows, penciled on, were far too brazen. The combination made her look half-crazed. "No hurry you say? Are you serious? We have so much to do, and this can all be yours one day if you play your cards right."

"Play my cards right," Libby repeated, concentrating on the figures projected on the calculator. "I see."

"Yes. You divorce Russ, so he can't claim any of the assets. And after what he's done to you? Think of it, that Beverly woman pretending to be your friend! A sister. And here she was sleeping with your husband behind your back. Then to make matters worse, they have a child! How can you forgive him of *that?*"

JoAnne could tell by the slight sliding from left to right of Libby's eyes that she had once again struck a chord. It seemed as if Libby kept trying to put the idea of Russ fathering a child with Beverly out of her mind. She was using her new job as a deterrent, a way to block her fears from her thought process.

JoAnne proceeded. "*Now* is the time to sell the house. You want to set up a trust fund for Olivia like we talked about, don't you? I'll match whatever proceeds you get from the house. Believe me; it will be wonderful to have a trust fund tucked away for her future. I see her excelling in medicine; perhaps veterinary medicine, she loves animals so much. Maybe she'll become a research scientist, or God forbid, an attorney. Nonetheless, it's imperative that you set up a trust fund for her."

JoAnne shifted her weight—all ninety-eight pounds—against the support of her wooden cane. She observed Libby, sleek and confident, working the keys of the calculator as if it were a piano and she a concert pianist. Libby, Susan's daughter. Why didn't she have a daughter like Libby? Why was she cursed with Andrea?

After all these years, JoAnne still couldn't get over the curse bestowed upon her, *that* girl child. She knew from birth to the present moment, Andrea had been working against her.

Absentmindedly, she told Libby, "I should just give Andrea some land. Maybe a suitable trust and tell her to leave. Take that no-good riffraff husband of hers and move to another state. Yes, that's what I'll do."

JoAnne appeared to be miles away, herself *in another state*; in fact, she was also thinking that after she spoke with Marilyn Clayton about the turn of events regarding Brett Daniels and the tax situation, she had a very important meeting with Edwin Mayfield. But she had to retrace her steps, rewind her days and think very hard. Exactly where was she to meet Edwin and at what time?

The boathouse at three o'clock.

"Now Libby," JoAnne said, patting Libby's arm while Libby's fingers clicked the keys of the calculator, "You tell Russ you want to sell the house or he can't see Olivia anymore."

"I don't know," Libby said. "Olivia would throw a fit."

"Oh! I know all about children and fit-throwing, my dear! You must ignore it and press on. Believe me, her best interest is at stake, and once Russ does what he's told, he can see her again. It's called leverage. Use it."

"Maybe," Libby said.

"Now drink up," JoAnne pushed Libby's glass of water closer to her elbow. "You look thirsty."

"Yes," Libby said, pretending to concentrate on the calculator.

Libby took the glass while JoAnne watched her, but as soon as JoAnne walked out the door she turned and saw Libby go into the small bathroom off the office. She wondered if Libby poured the contents down the drain.

• • •

JoAnne found Marilyn Clayton in the back yard gathering pine branches to make more wreathes for the interior of the Lodge. JoAnne waited for her to notice she was at the fence, and she was instantly infuriated by the distracted, childish manner in which Marilyn selected and bundled the pine boughs.

Marilyn placed her bundles upon one of the picnic tables and walked over to JoAnne. She wore a black wool coat with a hood over a tight red cap. She did look like a warthog.

The cap pressed her hair upward and out of view. Her bushy eyebrows were concealed as well, over eyes that bulged and were dry and transfixed. She was stiff-moving, acting completely distracted when summoned, even as she towered over her emaciated boss.

"Get Brett Daniels today," JoAnne ordered as the cold air cut through her words. "What did I tell you? We must stop him! We must pay him—whatever it takes—or I'll ruin his company."

Marilyn looked as if she were sleepwalking, like an impartial bystander lost in a dream. She tried her best to help JoAnne keep upward by placing a hand beneath her pointed elbow. "You'll have to cut your losses with Daniels," she said. "I tried, JoAnne, believe me. But he insists on staying with McPherson."

"What a devious bastard!" JoAnne snarled. "I paid him for the copies! Didn't we receive them yet?"

"No, remember I told you he tricked us? He took the money and gave the papers to McPherson. It was a matter of choosing. And he chose the other side."

JoAnne bit her lower lip. "It's his word against ours," she said. Her eyes warped at the memory of him standing before her desk in her office. She had known Brett since he was a child; she had known his uncle all her life, and this was his way of repaying her for trusting him with her business?

Hadn't she offered him an exorbitant amount to keep his mouth shut?

She'd have to take care of him. He's next in line after that backstabbing McPherson.

And then, just by looking at Marilyn's square, bumpy face, she knew she had lost her "detective" as well.

"Well, Marilyn, so much for that. One accountant down, as they say. You know a lot about me. But always remember, I know even *more* about you."

"What are you saying, JoAnne?" Marilyn asked. "Are you threatening me?"

JoAnne attempted a grin, but she suddenly realized her feet were about to give out on her. She grasped the wooden gate of the fence surrounding the yard. "I must go inside now," was her answer. "You go back to collecting your pine boughs. And consider yourself a maid from now on."

"But JoAnne," Marilyn protested. "I did my best to help you," she said in a forced whisper.

"You just get on back to Lansing or wherever you're from!" This, as everyone knew, was one of JoAnne's favorite sayings to either keep people at bay or fire them. Whenever she said, *Go back to wherever you're from!* she meant it.

255

"Perhaps you can find more lucrative work *there*," she ranted, her hot breath making swirls in the cold air. "I won't allow traitors in my organization!"

"Well, I don't approve of some of your methods!" Marilyn fired back. "And your term organization? That's *hilarious!*"

JoAnne shook her head and moved toward the front door of the Lodge. She took her time. The sidewalk was slippery, which made her wonder where the maintenance man—also known as Edwin Mayfield—was hiding. He was supposed to take care of hazards such as icy sidewalks. He was also supposed to shovel snow and repair wiring and plumbing—all tasks he claimed were within his capabilities.

But, he was nowhere to be seen. What if a customer fell on the sidewalk and broke a few bones? What if they sued the Birch Hill Lodge?

She remembered she was to meet Edwin at the boathouse at three o'clock.

She picked up her pace toward the back door of the Lodge. Everything she attempted to do lately was profoundly frustrating. Never in her life had she expected such sluggish mobility. She had always been spry and agile.

She found the clock in the foyer of the Lodge, thinking about the diamond and emerald wristwatch normally upon her left wrist. The expensive watch Aaron had given her on her fortieth birthday. When she looked down at her arm and checked her wrist, the watch was gone. She realized for the first time in years she had forgotten to put on the cherished watch. Immediately, she thought of her valuable collection of jewelry tucked away in the top drawer of her dressing table. Specifically, the watch, and the gold necklace that her hand would automatically reach for in times of distress. Her most expensive pieces were stored in her safe deposit box in Alpena, but the box she hid in her dresser contained some very pricey diamond bracelets and rings, as well, also an emerald necklace, a large ruby stone encased in a gold band, and three strings of pearls.

She felt threatened, as if *her jewels were as exposed as she felt. There for the taking.*

The Lodge itself was humming with activity and conversation. It was another full lunch crowd. She could always count on doing well between nine o'clock in the morning until two o'clock in the afternoon. Afterwards there was a lull, but the activity picked up again at five o'clock for the dinner crowd until eight o'clock when the restaurant closed.

Meet Edwin Mayfield.

On the way to the side door, she decided to get a heavier coat, which she kept on a hook by the stairs, Libby detained her. Libby held out an envelope for her to take. "This is for you," she said. "I've got to go upstairs and see how Olivia is doing. She just got home from school."

Libby turned, skirt swaying, and headed for the stairs.

JoAnne leaned against her cane and opened the envelope. She was not surprised to see it was a note from Marilyn telling her she was giving her a two-weeks-notice.

"That stupid woman," JoAnne said, turning with the help of the cane to go search for Edwin. "What a costly mistake, Miss Clayton!"

There was no waiting for three o'clock to roll around. There was no time for napping or searching for a heavier coat. She would have to find Edwin and seal her next plan.

Along the way, she found Andrea, who was shoveling the driveway. There were snow blowers for such a purpose, and a truck with a plow for heavier snowfalls and drifting, but Andrea was using a shovel, pushing the snow to the sides of the driveway.

"That's what I have a maintenance man for," JoAnne shouted. "Your useless husband. You're supposed to help out in the kitchen!"

Just like JoAnne used a cane, Andrea used the shovel to lean against. She walked toward JoAnne, and as usual, she wore outdated, drab clothing. She had on a long sweater-jacket, frayed jeans, knee-high boots, and a canvas cap concealing most of her greasy blonde hair. She looked anemic in the face, but because of the cold air and her physical exertion combined, her slanted cheeks were splotched pink.

Andrea said, "I had to come outside for some air."

JoAnne recalled the doctor said her baby, Andrea, had difficulty breathing at birth. She had also been a breech birth, problematic from the start. It took JoAnne weeks to recover from the grueling delivery. She was hospitalized for one full week afterwards and didn't want to nurse or see her new baby.

JoAnne remembered wishing that the baby had died. She remembered Aaron had been drunk the night

Andrea was conceived. It had been the first time JoAnne was overpowered, lost control to another person by force.

JoAnne stood before Andrea now and breathed deeply. Andrea's explanation for being outside "for some air," struck JoAnne as ironic. She had wished for Andrea to die at birth. Sometimes, like now, she still wished it.

Stop breathing, she told her baby.

"Where is your imbecile of a husband?" JoAnne inquired; all she wanted to do was talk to him, set her next plan in motion, and go back inside and sit by the fireplace where the cold could not pick her brittle bones.

"He's at the Harbor buying cigarettes." Andrea looked concerned, as if she had revealed too much. "But he'll be right back."

JoAnne clutched her cane as if she wanted to squeeze the ornate brass handle into dust. "When he gets back, tell him to meet me in the boathouse. If he doesn't appear within the hour, tell him he's fired. I'm not putting up with people taking time off to buy cigarettes when they're on my clock!"

"Yes, Mother," Andrea said, and not passively this time.

"Tell him to get here immediately!" JoAnne crooned, spitting at the end of her last word.

"Yes, Mother," Andrea said again, mockingly.

"And don't call me *Mother*," was JoAnne's final remark before she turned and stumbled away.

"Yes, Moth-er," Andrea said under her breath. She watched JoAnne disappear around the corner of the Birch Hill Lodge.

While waiting for Edwin in the largest boathouse on Lake Esau, JoAnne could see herself nineteen years earlier on the day she found Aaron, locked in the arms of Susan Weyman. JoAnne was in her forties, and so was Aaron. Susan was the youngest, only thirty-seven.

The *episode* happened one summer near this very boathouse. A secret uncovered only because JoAnne had returned home early from a trip to the Upper Peninsula, where she had been visiting friends. She caught them. But it was Susan more than Aaron who begged her for weeks thereafter to *forget* what she had seen.

And now she was waiting for the unsavory character, Edwin Mayfield, an accessory to the murder of an elderly woman, widowed and childless and living alone on a remote road in her cottage near a river.

Edwin and two other men had intended to rob the woman but ended up stabbing her repeatedly in the chest, all because she had put up a fight by trying to defend herself, her land, and a mere two hundred and thirteen dollars.

JoAnne shuddered, thinking about the woman lying on the floor bleeding to death. Or did she shudder due to the bone-chilling cold? She wanted to have a heating system installed in the boathouse. After all, not only did they store the boats here used during the summer and early fall, there was a workshop in one corner as well. The workshop had been Aaron's retreat. She kept it the way he had left it. Apparently, Aaron had used the boathouse for more than woodworking and tinkering with radios. He'd had other hobbies, including *tinkering* with Susan Weyman.

JoAnne sat down on a maple trunk that had been her father's, the man she blamed for her mother's suicide. Her father went behind her back and put the cottage and property into Russ's name. She couldn't accept this turn of events, how her own father had betrayed her, first by causing her mother to kill herself and last, but not least, putting the property into Russ's name when in fact, he had promised to give it to JoAnne. He knew JoAnne needed this particular lakefront acreage to fill her quota of a thousand acres on the eastern side of Grand Lake. She had all but her father's five acres, no thanks to her son, whom she vowed would never own this land.

She tapped her cane against the cement floor, *waiting, waiting* for Edwin Mayfield. She heard him enter, not quietly, but with a loud slam of the side door behind him. "Lucky for you, Mister Mayfield," she began, knowing it irritated him when she called him *mister*, "I was about to leave, and that would mean you'd be out of a job, maintenance or otherwise."

"And better off for it," Edwin said. "Working for you is giving me an ulcer."

"Oh pity," JoAnne scoffed; she slid her bony hips upon the maple and wrought-iron chest. One of the clasps had pinched her right thigh, making her even more irritable. "A pity and a shame you should actually *do* some work!"

Edwin stood, humped-over due to his posture. His eyes were half-closed, his face speckled with acne. He dared to suck on the cigarette and blow smoke around her. She could see a light-red, maybe a pink hue, rise in skinny patches up his cheeks across his forehead. He was wearing one of Aaron's coats of all things—without her permission. JoAnne had noticed quite a few of Aaron's items had been missing since Edwin and Andrea had arrived, mostly clothing and tools, and JoAnne wondered if they had already taken some of her jewelry. But for now, she didn't have time to question him on the subject of thieving. She would get to that later.

She could tell by Edwin's jerking gestures—smoking the cigarette rapidly and pacing, not to mention the darting of his tiny eyes—that he wanted to get on with things.

"Nonetheless," JoAnne continued. "You can leave here *after* you do what I hired you to come here and do. And you'll do it soon, preferably tomorrow night. You have his address?"

"Yeah, I know where he lives. And I already know a way inside."

"Good. Do it; then take Andrea and leave. I don't want to see either one of you around here again."

"Ah, but can't we come to your funeral?" Edwin asked, his eyes twinkling. "I sure wouldn't want to miss that."

"Come to my funeral, and you'll never have a moment's peace again! Just do what I say and leave here. Leave for good!"

"I want the money now, or the deal is off."

"I figured you'd say that, you spineless lunatic. I should think all the jewelry you've stolen from my bedroom would suffice. It should more than pay off the balance!" She wanted to find out how he would respond to her mentioning the jewelry.

"It helped," Edwin said. He stood by a rowboat with one arm propped against the frame. It was obvious he enjoyed smoking in front of her; that he knew she didn't approve of smoking. She was taken aback when he said again, "I want the money now, or the deal is off."

"How typical, you useless rat," JoAnne countered with a heated glare. "Again, I should think diamonds and rubies would more than pay for the job."

He pushed away from the rowboat, smoke fanning out around them both. He repeated, "I want the other fifteen grand now, or the deal's off."

JoAnne poked around inside her coat pocket. "As I said," she began, "you get rid of Jerry McPherson and leave. Take Andrea with you. I don't care where you go, just don't ever come back *here*!"

Edwin noticed JoAnne was studying him as he smashed the cigarette butt with the heel of his boot. "I would think you'd want Russ taken out instead. It would make more sense."

"Kill my son?" JoAnne asked, her bony hand touching her chest. "What on Earth do you take me for?" She held out a check, the balance of fifteen thousand dollars and waited for him to come forward to take it. "McPherson's the one who betrayed me. I want him to pay! I treated *him* like a son, and he repaid me by stabbing me in the back!"

Edwin nodded and stuffed the check inside his pocket. "I want the keys and registration to that green sedan you got parked in the back garage too."

"I suppose that can be arranged," JoAnne said. "But remember, you must get all the papers in his office *and* his condo before I grant the perks. I need all the documentation he has on me, from taxes to land and property deeds. Any notes he has on me as well. Do what I ask, and you can have the car and keep all the jewelry I know you stole."

"No kidding," he said listlessly. "That's awful generous of you."

"Hah! You better quit while you're ahead *Mister* Mayfield!" JoAnne warned, her hands shaking from disgust and the cold. "And when you leave, take that damnable cigarette butt with you!"

Edwin grinned at JoAnne. He pinched the end of the cigarette between two stained fingers. When he was satisfied the butt was out, he put it inside his pocket. The money was tucked away, the job as good as done.

JoAnne watched him leave. She clicked off the tape recorder in her sweater pocket, stood up from the trunk, and stumbled toward the back door of the boathouse. She wasn't sure she could make it back to the Lodge, but she did, taking several exhausting strides. She thought about Edwin and what he was about to do for her. Then she went a step further, thinking about her mother, her father, and Susan Weyman.

And she would never forget what she had witnessed behind the boathouse.

Chapter 24

Jerry paid the fine for the trespassing stint, but the other charges were still pending. He doubted they would have to go to court over the matter. The word around town was that JoAnne had dropped the charges. She had more important things on her mind, such as dying some said, and Claudia Bishop, whose father was also dying. Claudia was Bishop's only heir and would control his entire estate.

Russ knew it was inevitable that JoAnne would find out about the daughter he shared with Beverly, hence Libby would also find out. Russ and Jerry had a plan, one which developed the night Russ broke into Grandfather's cottage in search of the will, a plan they conjured up at the kitchen table after their encounter with Preece.

The following Monday morning, they took off for Standish in Russ's Blazer. Although Russ had not been to Beverly's new place and had not seen Christine in several weeks, he asked Jerry to go with him for directions and moral support.

On the way, passing through Oscoda toward Tawas City, Jerry brought up the question of Christine's paternity. "We will do the testing and prove that you're the father. Have you ever considered maybe you're not?"

Russ nodded while making a wide turn at the intersection. They had already passed Tawas City and were heading for the small city of Au Gres. Next would be Omer, all four locations parallel with the magnificent Lake Huron shoreline. The trip was incredibly scenic, if nothing else. Russ said simply, "She's mine. She has my hair."

"Beverly probably had several lovers," Jerry continued, wishing he had been one of them. "We can alter the blood test records, if she agrees, saying Christine is mine just to get you out of child support."

"No," Russ said for the third time in two days. "Maybe Beverly did sleep around, but if Christine's mine, I want custody. Libby can't have more children, and Beverly isn't fit to raise a child."

"Oh, listen to you, the model of parenthood! You won't get custody of Christine. Giving the father custody is extremely rare; we probably won't be able to prove Beverly unfit, and even if we could, I won't be a party to it! She needs someone to help her. She *can* straighten out. *I'll* help her."

"Huh," Russ said, shaking his head vigorously. "You don't know what you're saying. She's way too much for *you* to handle!"

"Both Libby and Beverly will take you for everything you've got!" Jerry continued, moving around in the passenger seat. "You'll lose everything!"

"Do I look worried?" Russ asked. He turned to look at Jerry but then quickly back to concentrate on the road. They were on Interstate 23 South, all the way from Alpena to Standish. "Libby will come back to me. She'll forgive me. That's the way she is!"

"Oh, damn you!" Jerry seethed, feeling his heart pump vigorously. "You don't want Beverly! You screw around with her, get her pregnant, and that's it?"

"I *love* Libby," Russ said, his facial expression making him look closer to fifty than forty. "I always have and always will. And I don't have to explain myself to you or anyone else!"

"I want to *help* Beverly," Jerry said for what he hoped would be the last time. "I want to take care of her."

"She's a disgusting drunk! Right now, she's probably passed out on the kitchen floor. I just hope that cousin of hers, or friend, or whoever the hell she is, is taking care of Christine. When I called her the other day to tell her I want to set up blood tests at the lab, she sounded drunk. If something happens to my daughter, I'll have her thrown in jail!" Russ glanced over at Jerry again; he wanted a reaction. He knew that he was responsible for adding to Beverly's problems, but that didn't mean she could wallow in a drunken stupor; if she wasn't responsible enough to take care of a baby, Russ knew he could talk Libby into fighting for custody. Libby wanted another child, and she was heartbroken that she couldn't conceive again.

Russ was on a roll regarding Beverly's state of mind. "The last time I talked with Beverly on the phone she was crocked. So, if Christine's mine, like I said, I want custody of her. Olivia needs a sister anyway."

"You fool!" Jerry blurted while squirming around in the seat to find a more comfortable position. "Don't you ever pay attention? Libby's attorney, the infamous David Preece, has petitioned for a court hearing. The divorce is in motion, and we all appear in court in two weeks to discuss child support, division of properties and other holdings! Libby wants out!"

"Libby will come home," Russ said confidently. He wanted a cigarette but wouldn't buy them anymore. He didn't have a spare pack tucked inside the visor like he used to. It was his habit, particularly when agitated, to reach for the visor, but instead he reached for the travel cup inside the cup holder and drank some hot coffee. "Libby will come home to me," he said again.

"You don't even *want* Beverly. I want to get her into a treatment center. I *want* to help her!"

"Well, good luck. All I *want* is my family back."

After going through the city limits of Standish, Russ veered left onto M-76 and then turned again onto South Huron Road. There wasn't as much snow this far south, only patches here and there. When they finally arrived at Beverly's farm, the friend was there. She was an attractive woman in her late twenties. Her name was Amanda. She had short black hair and petite, evenly-spaced features on a smooth round face. She wore no makeup, but her clothing was casual and new, not threadbare or mismatched. She talked very little and smiled a lot, but it was her, not Beverly, feeding Christine at the kitchen table.

Beverly was sitting nearby on a stool drinking black coffee from a pink-and-white-striped mug. Right away she told Russ that she was coming off a two-day drunk.

Amanda didn't even blink when Beverly said this. She merely concentrated on the beautiful baby in the high chair.

Jerry waited in the Blazer for Russ; it was his suggestion to do so, not Russ's. Amanda finished feeding Christine, cleaned her mouth off, and wiped the tray of the highchair with a washcloth, then she left the kitchen, carrying Christine with her.

"I don't really want to go to this appointment today," Beverly told Russ. Her head was tilted to the left, caught upward by her shoulder, it seemed. Her hair was messy, but glossy, as always. Her light blue blouse was stained.

She stared down at the table, her eyes focused on a fork. She was groggy from the alcohol, and yet she managed a bewitching glow, a swirling abyss among the mystery of her that Russ had fallen into before.

She tried to sit straighter in the chair, as if a stalwart position might improve her speech. She leaned her chin against her left hand with her elbow against the tabletop. "We all go down to the community hospital and have some blood drawn? They will do the DNA test, or whatever. The woman I talked to on the phone said it will take about a week to get the results."

"Yes," Russ said, agitated that he still felt like an awkward teenager around her. He wanted to hold back. Part of him wanted to say *Never mind the tests, I believe you.* But no, he knew what he had to do.

"Jerry's waiting outside," he said, as if Jerry's name alone gave him strength to move forward. "Libby knows about this, and so does my mother. Everyone knows. Now I need proof."

"To hell with you all!" Beverly lashed out, but just as quickly, she started to cry. "I don't care what you want! *I'll* decide what happens next, you hear me?"

"You can't make decisions in your condition," Russ said, feeling stronger against her now, thinking primarily of the child in the next room and of Jerry McPherson waiting in the Blazer. "You need help," he added when she sneered at him. "But no one will push you! And no one will threaten you, I promise! We all want what's best for Christine."

"If she's yours, then what?"

"Then we'll talk about custody."

"Will you leave Libby and marry me?" She was still staring at the fork, but her voice had weakened.

"I told you from the beginning that I would never leave Libby," he said. "If I get Libby back and Christine's mine, I want custody of her."

"And what if she's Jerry's?" Beverly asked him.

Russ cleared his throat. "Then it's all up to you and Jerry," he said. "And good luck with that!"

"Funny how no one even considers she might be Scott's," Beverly said meekly. "After all, I was married to him when I conceived her!"

"That won't work with me," said Russ; he wiped his mouth to control his temper. "Libby told me a long time ago that Scott was impotent. Libby knew you had an affair when you got pregnant and had the baby. Now we all know why Scott started acting strange. He already knew you were fooling around behind his back. He just didn't know who you were fooling around with. No wonder he went crazy and shot himself when he found out the baby was alive. We can thank my mother for that one too!"

"Yes, your mother!" Beverly said vehemently. "I hope she rots in hell. If it wasn't for her, we would be getting along just fine!"

"You think we'd be together?" Russ stood up from the table. He was done talking. "Get ready, and let's get this over with!" he said. "I have to get back to Grand Lake. I have to go to work tomorrow."

"When I finish my coffee," she said irritably. But he was waiting at the door for her. He handed her a coat that was hanging on a hook.

They went to the Community Hospital in Standish to get their blood drawn. They would not know the results for 4-5 days, said the phlebotomist and the social worker Beverly had known from volunteering at the hospital.

When they got back to the farmhouse, although apprehensive, Russ left the baby with Beverly, knowing that Amanda, the responsible friend, was going to stay with them for a few weeks until Beverly decided if she wanted to sign herself into a treatment program. The closet facilities, however, were south of Standish in Saginaw or north at Alpena General. The social worker, Russ found out from Beverly on the way back to the farmhouse, was helping by providing a babysitter when Amanda was unavailable and connecting Beverly with substance abuse counseling and hopefully rehab.

But Russ sensed that the entire "counseling" maneuver was a smokescreen to make Beverly look good in court. *Classic David Preece.*

Russ and Jerry drove back to Grand Lake. Jerry smoked several cigarettes while Russ drove, and they both drank too much coffee. Russ had to pull over to four different gas stations so they could use the restroom.

"I'm fighting for custody," he told Jerry again when they got back into the Blazer after a stop and were off onto US 23, heading north. Nothing else was said between them for another fifty-five minutes. By then, they had reached Alpena and had pulled into the parking lot of Jerry's condo. "Well, I'm going to make sure Beverly gets some help," Jerry vowed. He was jumpy thanks to all the caffeine. "I love her. And one day I'm going to be with her!"

"It's your funeral, pal," said Russ after parking the Blazer. "That looks like my sister sitting on your steps. Now what?"

They got out of the vehicle and walked over to her. She was crouched forward, trying to shield herself from the northwestern wind coming off Lake Huron. She wore a red hat, a quilted coat, thick black pants, and a thicker gray sweater. "I've been waiting all afternoon for one of you to show up," she said. "I've got important things to tell you."

Russ helped her stand up. She was clutching a leather case and shivering from the cold. "You should have waited in your car," he told her when he noticed that the Jeep JoAnne had given her to use was parked by the dumpster. "You are lucky you didn't freeze to death!"

Jerry pushed the buttons of the security system. He held the door open for Russ and Andrea, and they quickly entered the building, if for no other reason than to thaw Andrea out. Before getting into the elevator— Jerry's apartment was on the fourth floor—Andrea said in a frantic tone, "I can't ride in elevators! Don't try to talk me into it!"

They elected to take the stairs, all three of them out of breath by the time they reached the fourth floor. As usual, whenever Jerry entered his apartment, he was relieved to find it untouched. He constantly worried that Preece would hire someone to ransack the premises for materials relating to JoAnne. After all, Preece claimed to have pictures.

Jerry attempted the role of host. "Sit down," he said. "I'll make coffee to warm you up, Andrea." He studied the kitchen counter and searched for opened cabinets or anything out of place. He put a paper filter in the coffee maker and scooped coffee from the can into the filtered basket. He poured in the water.

Andrea looked nervous and exhausted. She sat down on the couch. Russ sat down directly across from her on the edge of the coffee table and watched her.

But she was silent. All they heard was the coffee maker gurgling at the end of the counter where Jerry stood, flipping through his mail. "Look at this," he said, drawing their attention to him. "A mysterious envelope with no return address."

He sliced the end of the envelope with a knife. He held up pictures, and then he held up a skinny round disk. A small video. "There's a note attached," he added. He tapped his glasses further up the bridge of his nose and read out loud. "Here are some photographs you might be interested in. Enclosed you will also find a video of David Preece. I've taken from JoAnne's office. They are of no use to me. M.C."

"Marilyn Clayton," said Russ. "She must have jumped ship!"

Jerry thumbed through the photos, his smile increasing as he sorted and studied. "Hmm, a few incriminating pictures of you and Beverly, but they are the ones I gave her. And some real explicit shots of Preece." At this point Jerry smiled. The pictures were vivid and clear. "Looks like a couple of guys in bed with Preece. Next, we have two of Preece and my ex-wife, who I would know anywhere, of course, in any position, naked or otherwise. Preece is finished now," emphasized Jerry, "thanks to Marilyn Clayton."

He walked over to Russ and handed him the envelope of photos. Russ wasn't happy with the nude shots of himself and Beverly, but there were only two; the third simply showed them kissing in the doorway of her house.

The pictures of Preece, however, were very explicit. He was with Leeann in bed, with Leeann in the shower, and on the living room floor. Other shots showed him partaking in a male threesome. One picture was just Preece and a man in his early twenties, all subjects naked. "Well, well," said Russ. "What a busy son of a bitch."

Andrea interrupted, "I knew Marilyn was going to leave; JoAnne kept yelling at her. But I'm here to tell you more about Edwin. I overheard JoAnne talking to him in the boathouse. She is paying him to murder you, Jerry. Here at your apartment, and it's supposed to happen tonight."

Both Jerry and Russ laughed. Then Russ shrugged and leaned more of his weight against the hand still propped against his knee. "Well, that *is* interesting," he said. "So, you actually heard this? You heard JoAnne asking Edwin to kill Jerry?"

"Yes, now I think that's why JoAnne wanted us to come here. It wasn't so I could be at Scott Weyman's funeral, it was because JoAnne had a job for Edwin. He was with the two men who were convicted of stabbing that old woman years ago. He served time for it because he was there. But it was a robbery gone bad. The old lady fought them after they broke in. Edwin stayed in the car. Anyway, I'm not sure if he would actually go through with murdering you, Jerry. But I wanted to warn you."

"Thanks for telling us," Jerry muttered. He turned to Russ, "You feel like setting up an ambush tonight?

"Sure, nothing better to do but sleep, like normal people. I doubt I'll be doing much of that for a while."

Russ was going to ask Andrea more questions, but she cut him off. "JoAnne told me you accused her of pushing Grandfather down the stairs and that you didn't see her do it. Well, I did. She didn't know I was in his room, reading to him. She called him to the stairs, said it was urgent and he told me to stay in the room. But I went to the door anyway; I just didn't like the sound of JoAnne's voice. I knew she was going to hurt him. And I saw her push him."

Russ rubbed his forehead. "I knew it," he said. He looked at Jerry, pleading." I remember coming into the room and there he was lying at the bottom of the stairs, unconscious."

"Yes," said Andrea. "And then we all took him to the hospital. We brought him home, but he died a few days later. A blood clot in his brain, I think it was."

Russ couldn't speak, remembering.

"Grandfather gave me something before he died," she said. "He told me to only give it to you. He didn't trust JoAnne." She held out the leather folder. It was tied with a tan ribbon. Russ reached for it and held it for several seconds before opening it. He stared at the document and closed his eyes. When he opened them, he had to read it over two more time. "The third copy of his will, Jerry," he said.

Andrea sipped at the coffee Jerry handed her. "JoAnne killed him because we saw her push Susan Weyman off the break wall," she continued. She paused for another sip of coffee. "She killed her in broad daylight."

"*What* did you say?" Russ asked, staring at her, as was Jerry from the counter.

"Grandpa and I were fishing out on Grand Lake in his boat. You know, his favorite boat, the white Lyman. We were out by the reed bed near Macomber's Island. It was a windy day. We were about to pull anchor and go home, but we saw JoAnne and Susan fighting; they had walked out onto the break wall. They would do that, walk out there sometimes to talk. This time they were fighting, and JoAnne grabbed her and pushed her into the water. She said Susan fell into the lake before she got to her and that she tried to save her, but it was too late. It's a lie. Grandpa and I saw her shove Susan into the water. JoAnne ran off. *We* tried to save her but we were too late, Grandfather and I."

"My God," said Russ.

"Grandpa told JoAnne he saw her. He didn't tell her I was with him, but after that, she made things harder for both of us. I begged Grandpa not to tell her what we saw. He wanted her to know she hadn't gotten away with it."

"She killed Susan because Susan was having an affair with Aaron," Jerry said, thinking out loud. He had pieced that much together long ago, a result of things JoAnne had mentioned, but he had never intended to bring the subject up to Russ or Andrea.

"Libby might be interested in knowing JoAnne killed her mother, and indirectly, she killed her brother too," Andrea added. She put down her coffee cup and pulled her coat around her waist. "There. You have the will. The land's yours. You know to watch for Edwin tonight and that I am a witness to Grandpa's murder and Susan Weyman's too."

"Why did you keep this to yourself all these years?" Jerry asked her.

"Because I was worried she would hurt Grandpa. But she did anyway. I have something else to settle with her now. Asking me and Edwin to come back here after all these years was the biggest mistake she ever made."

She got up from the couch and left them sitting speechless in Jerry's condo. They ordered a pizza, had a few drinks, and waited in the dark for Edwin Mayfield.

Chapter 25

Jerry and Russ waited half the night for Edwin Mayfield. They waited in the dark and discomfort, with Russ crouched behind the headboard of Jerry's bed, close to the wall, and Jerry ready to step into the closet, out of view. It was after three in the morning by the time they heard a noise at the front door. A picking sound—lock picking, they knew. Jerry made it easy for him by not chaining the door. He also left the downstairs security system off. He could do this with his main key, and his intention was to re-lock the front lobby door after they caught Edwin Mayfield.

"He's stupid enough to use the front door," Russ observed. "And he didn't notice the security system in the lobby has been deactivated. I would have tried the back door or a side window, even though you're on the fourth floor. Here the son of a bitch comes in the front. He might as well ring the doorbell."

"Be quiet," said Jerry, clicking off the flashlight. He wasn't sure how professional Edwin could be with sneaking and prowling; robbery might be how he made a living, if one could call it that, even though JoAnne claimed she hired him to do odd jobs at the Lodge.

"Where is he? I wish he'd get on with it," said Russ, not whispering anymore. "I've got to work tomorrow. By the way, they've cut my hours. I want you to call there tomorrow and find out what's going on."

"Yes," Jerry whispered. He was focused on the noises coming from the living room. He slid along the bedroom wall and stopped at the door. He leaned into the direction of sounds. It had to be Edwin.

Hopefully Edwin has a weapon, that way they could prove he broke in armed with intent to do bodily harm. He would be arrested and charged, especially with his record. Andrea indicated she didn't care about him anyway, so maybe putting him in prison would give her a chance to start over.

"I've got an idea," Jerry whispered. He went back to the bed, slid under the covers, and pulled them up to his chin so he would be hidden from view. For a professional thief, he thought, Edwin was making a terrible racket. Jerry could tell exactly when Edwin entered the kitchen area because a stack of papers fell off the counter. Then he heard a drawer in the filing cabinet slide open. No doubt, Edwin was flipping through folders and papers.

"Let's just go in there and get the bastard," Russ said. "I'm getting a cramp in my hip. We can take him!"

"Quiet," said Jerry as he peered toward the direction of the opened bedroom door.

He waited for the shadow of Edwin's body to wobble in and out among the dim orange of the night-light. He waited for the beam of Edwin's flashlight to announce his entrance.

After the drawer of the filing cabinet closed, the beam of the flashlight finally appeared. Jerry could hear him breathe, in and out; pause, breathe in and out. Edwin stood in the doorway, trying to douse the light behind his leg.

Jerry could see the long-bladed knife Edwin had in his right hand. The knife was close to his side, and the papers he found for JoAnne were tucked inside his jacket, visible near the opened zipper.

Russ had wedged under the bed, trying his best to stay quiet near the headboard. Jerry could feel the pressure of Edwin's stare, and he knew Edwin was trying to determine if Jerry was actually asleep. Ambushing a man while asleep was as bad as shooting a person in the back.

The moment finally came when Edwin lunged forward. The motion was so quick, Jerry barely had enough time to turn over on his side, but turn he did, and he kicked Edwin's arm with his foot, near the elbow. Edwin shrieked and dropped the knife to the floor.

"No way!" exclaimed Edwin when he could speak again. "You tricked me!"

Although the cramp in Russ's side hindered his mobility, he jumped up from under the bed at the exact second Jerry flipped on the light. Edwin had dropped to his knees on the floor, clutching his wrist.

Once Jerry was able to catch his breath, he warned Russ to calm down. The last thing they needed was Russ attacking Edwin, especially now that they had caught him red-handed. "You son of a bitch!" Russ yelled at Edwin. "You're a thief and a murderer!"

"I might be a son of a bitch," Edwin yelled back, tears in his eyes. "But I'm smarter than you are by a long shot!"

Jerry confiscated Edwin's long-bladed knife and handed it to Russ. "Let's see, Edwin," he began. "Attempted murder. Possession of a deadly weapon," he continued, although he knew there was no way Edwin could have orchestrated the break in and intent to murder on his own. He had no real motive. JoAnne was the one with the motive. Edwin was only interested in cash.

"She made me do it!" Edwin cried, the words all pushed out in one breath. "She paid me fifteen grand!"

Jerry couldn't believe it. "I'm only worth fifteen thousand dollars to JoAnne Shaw?"

"Fourteen more than I am, probably," Russ said.

But Edwin wasn't in the mood for their wit. He searched for a chair to fall into. When he realized there wasn't a chair in the bedroom, he settled for the edge of Jerry's bed. "Listen here," he groaned. "The bitch knows I need money! She's insane! She's dying too. She wanted me to do this favor for her and take Andrea and leave here for good. She promised me a car."

"You don't need a car," said Jerry, sick and tired of the whole thing. "You aren't going anywhere!" He went to the phone at the bed stand and started to dial the police. "The only place you're going is to prison. Think I'm going to let you off easy after you tried to stick me with a knife?"

"Goddamn it," cried Edwin, in a higher pitch now. "Give me a break! I wasn't really going to hurt you! I was just trying to scare you! And make her think I did the job so I could collect the money and get out of town! She paid me fifteen grand and said I could have a car. I was going to demand another ten from her, or I'd go to the cops myself!"

"I'm not buying that!" Jerry shouted, trying to maintain his professionalism. "We all know about your past, and what happened here tonight won't look good for you at all. Not to mention I'm sure you're on probation."

"Wait a minute," said Edwin, still on the edge of the bed. "Maybe I got some information for you. Maybe we could make a deal. I'll tell you what I know and in return you don't make the phone call."

"I don't want you anywhere near my family," Russ yelled from the doorway. "And you stay away from my sister! She's the one who tipped us off to your little plan tonight. She overheard you and JoAnne talking about it. What do you think of that?" He stepped forward and leaned in so close to Edwin's face; Edwin closed his eyes.

Then Edwin looked up at Russ. He said, "If you let me collect the balance from the old hag, I'll leave Andrea here. How's that? No offense, but she's dead weight to me anyway. I guess I only married her knowing JoAnne would kick in some cash now and then. She wanted me to take Andrea away from here. She didn't want her own daughter around!"

Jerry placed the receiver back to the phone on the nightstand. "What's this information you think we might be interested in?" he asked.

Edwin crossed his short legs when Russ glared at him. He said, "Marilyn Clayton left. She got sick of JoAnne's bullshit."

"We already know," offered Jerry. "You'll have to do better than that!"

"Did you know she's giving Libby drugs, but Andrea said she caught onto it, Libby that is, and quit taking them? Dumping out juice and food?"

"Glad to hear it," said Russ. "Libby's too smart for JoAnne! I'm going over there first thing in the morning and take both of them out of there!"

"Good luck," said Edwin. "Libby is running the Lodge. Seems JoAnne gave her a lot of pull around there. Andrea thinks JoAnne's leaving everything to her. JoAnne's been training Libby to take over when she dies."

"Is there anything else?" Jerry prodded impatiently. "We know this already!"

"Did you know Thomas Bishop, the owner of the Harbor Resort, died yesterday?"

"Now that's news," Jerry admitted. He started to pace. "Wonder if Claudia will sell to JoAnne."

"You mean Libby," Edwin interjected quickly. "It's Libby running things now!"

"I've had enough of this!" Russ shouted. He turned to Jerry. "I'm going to the Lodge. I need to talk to Libby. You let me know the second the lab tests come back."

After Russ left, Jerry carefully explained things to Edwin. "You can have your money from JoAnne, and you can also keep your mouth shut! Then you leave town, or we go to the police, understand?" He gestured for Edwin to get up off the edge of the bed and head for the door. "You will leave town and never come back!"

"What about the car?" Edwin insisted. "I got to have a dependable car to drive! The one I drove into town is a hanging wreck. It won't get me to Flint!"

"I'll call Russ, and he'll arrange for you to get a car at his house in the morning. By the way, I want the folders you stole from my files. Hand them over." He waited for Edwin to give them up. And Edwin did, but reluctantly.

Jerry pushed Edwin Mayfield out into the living room and all the way across the floor to the front door. He knew that once Edwin got the car and more money from JoAnne, they would never see him around Grand Lake again.

• • •

Early the next morning, around nine-thirty, Edwin showed up at Russ's house. Russ woke up at eight; he had already been to the bank to get the title out of the safe deposit box for the '98 black Grand Am. The Grand Am was a spare car he owned. He decided to give it to Edwin; he would do almost anything to get Edwin to leave town. He also called work to tell them he would be late. Risky, yes, under the circumstances, because they had already cut his hours, but Russ needed some time off.

Edwin stood waiting at Russ's screen door. It was a chilly December morning, and Russ was dressed in heavy clothing, but Edwin was not. Edwin wore a thin jacket, thin pants, and a tan t-shirt. He wore tennis shoes and no hat. "Andrea locked me out," he explained. "She won't even let me get my clothes!"

"Time for you to leave town, Bub," Russ said in no uncertain terms. He didn't feel sorry for Edwin Mayfield and never would. "I am giving you one of my cars." But he decided to keep the title. "You have no reason now to go back to the Lodge." While looking at Edwin, Russ thought about the woman who Edwin and his cohorts had robbed and murdered. Edwin was not the one who murdered her, but he was in the car waiting, which made him part of the horrific crime. Russ knew Jerry was planning on reporting the break in to the police and that Edwin had planned to commit murder. Edwin was too stupid to realize he was trapped. He wouldn't give Edwin the title, and it would appear that he had stolen the car.

Down went Edwin Mayfield.

Chapter 26

Russ couldn't believe Edwin headed for the Birch Hill Lodge anyway, no doubt to try and collect more hush-money from JoAnne. Even after Russ allegedly gave Edwin his car and told him to leave Grand Lake, Edwin drove off toward the Lodge, and Russ followed him.

Judging from the number of vehicles in the Lodge parking lot, there was another large breakfast crowd assembled. Russ knew it wouldn't look good for business if the sheriff arrested Edwin in the Lodge dining room, or anywhere on the premises. But he hoped the sheriff was already there waiting.

Russ had called the sheriff's office before he left his house, anticipating that Edwin would head for JoAnne before leaving town. While waiting down the road near the Birch Hill Lodge entrance, Russ noticed the ropes of pine and the wreathes with large red ribbons. How could she celebrate Christmas with all her dirty deeds unfolding, murder at the top of the list?

The holiday display was impressive, but really, how could she go on with life, seasonal activities and celebrations, year after year? He decided she must not have a conscience, or she was able to bury crimes too graphic to recall.

He waited in his Blazer, waited and watched as the sheriff's car pulled up behind Edwin in Russ's Grand Am. Edwin sat slumped at the wheel, too paralyzed to move. Russ watched the sheriff go up to the window and wait for Edwin to roll it down. Edwin turned and searched for Russ, knowing Russ and Jerry had planned the ambush. He got out of the Grand Am, turned for the handcuffs to be placed upon his wrists, still searching the tree line near the front path to the Lodge and studying the area past the stone wall, far and wide, yes, looking for Russ.

Russ watched Edwin leave in the patrol car. He drove around to the back parking area of the Lodge. He had to speak with Libby right away. He had to tell her what he knew. Andrea witnessed JoAnne pushing her mother off the break wall. It wasn't an accident as everyone believed. Andrea actually saw JoAnne push Grandfather down the long stairway of the Birch Hill Lodge after he confronted JoAnne, after he told her that he witnessed her push Susan off the break wall. JoAnne pushed her and stood by while Susan drowned. Grandfather and Andrea were too far away to help Susan, but not too far away to witness what had happened.

When Russ walked through the main entrance, the dark and foreboding cedar-logged archway, down the hallway past wreathes and strings of white lights outlining desks, fireplaces, and the walls, he found Andrea behind the front desk. She was talking on the phone, writing down reservations.

He was surprised she was dressed up, for her, at least, in a light-blue dress with a black jacket covering her thin arms. Her hair was tidy, combed away from her pinched face, but at least her hair was caught neatly in a wide, silver barrette.

Russ didn't want to bother her. He turned and left her to answer the phone, take on a new occupation, anything to get her mind off Edwin Mayfield. The police would question her soon enough. He heard the breakfast commotion coming from the dining room, alive with conversation and clattering silverware, pots and pans banging from the kitchen. The customary smells of breakfast. He stayed focused on finding Libby. Directly inside the expansive foyer, he noticed an eight-foot Christmas tree, colored lights bright and blinking, and he couldn't help but think of the waste of electricity. But then again, the Birch Hill Lodge was a haven of business, and the beautiful colors and red bows and ribbons and green lush wreaths attracted customers.

He stared at the Christmas tree and listened to the music piped throughout the Lodge, up and down the stairway, throughout the hallways, meandering bells and violins and harps floating in and out of the enormous main dining area. Christmas carols piped through speakers, one in each corner of every hallway. It made him shiver.

The holiday fever and mood.

He didn't notice Libby was behind him until she stepped up next to him, holding clipboard and pen. She said, "Looks pretty, don't you think?"

He was startled by the sound of her voice. For a second, he didn't recognize her. She was slimmer; her beautiful long auburn hair was pulled up to the back of her head in a wispy fold, and her outfit was a mauve-tinted suit and black shoes with four-inch heels, and a cream-colored silk blouse with a ruffle at the neck.

Libby? he almost said. *Where's Libby, the woman I married?*

"Russ, what do you think of the decorations?" she asked, as if he should care. As if he dropped by regularly for a cup of coffee and a Danish.

"Oh," he said. "It's nice."

"It was fun to decorate this year," Libby said, studying the Christmas display. "What do you want? Olivia's still in school. If you want to see her, you'll have to come back later."

"I really stopped by to see *you*. I don't want a divorce, Libby."

"And I don't want to get into that *here*," she said, her smile gone. She moved forward to adjust a glass ornament on the tree. An elf, maybe an angel. It was glass, that much he knew. Then she stepped back beside him again, to examine the ornament from a distance.

"It's about your mother," Russ said cautiously. "Something Andrea saw with my grandfather years ago. And she gave me the third copy of Grandfather's will. She had it all along. He told her to keep it for me."

"That's amazing," said Libby, still admiring the tree. "So, the place is yours now."

"Yes, according to the will. Jerry says it's iron-clad."

"I'm happy for you, Russ," she said. "I know how much the cabin and land means to you," she added, her voice subdued. "Now what's this about my mother? I have a lot to do; we're having a Christmas party here this weekend. All the business owners in the area are invited."

"I can't talk about it here, honey," he said. "Please come outside for a minute, and I'll tell you what I know."

There was really no privacy at the Birch Hill Lodge. Not in the attic, the basement, a dark corner anywhere in the entire structure, not even outside behind the hedges. But she agreed to get her coat and go outside with him. She agreed to sit in his Blazer and let him tell her what was on his mind.

He made sure they weren't followed, but as they moved toward the back door by the back porch, Pat, Libby's faithful companion, stepped in line behind her. Once outside, instead of going toward the Blazer, Libby stopped near the deck and folded her arms, "Hurry up and tell me, Russ. I have a lot of work to do."

He pulled the collar of his coat up around his neck. He felt a chill, and it wasn't only coming from Lake Huron or Lake Esau. "Andrea and Grandfather saw JoAnne push your mother off the break wall. That's how she drowned. JoAnne pushed her," he repeated, waiting for Libby's reaction.

Libby brushed a strand of hair away from her eyes. "JoAnne pushed her," she echoed, considering this information. "I see."

"Yes," Russ said. "If you don't believe me, ask Jerry. He was there when she told me. And JoAnne pushed Grandfather down the stairs, as I've always suspected, because he saw her murder your mother. The story goes that your mom and my dad were having an affair. JoAnne found out, and that's why JoAnne is so twisted out of shape over Beverly and me."

Now Libby's lips were pressed together, and little red patches surfaced on her cheeks, even her forehead. "You and Beverly," she said, almost whispering. "That *is* a big deal, Russ. A big deal to *me*." She paced up and down the snow-covered area near the deck, Pat sitting still and watching her. "And this child," she continued, noticing Russ shivering in the cold breeze, "You have a child with her? How could you when all this time you knew how upset I was about not being able to have more children? How could you keep something like that from me?"

He reached for her, but all he got was the brushing of her arm against his hand. "I wanted to tell you, Libby. But she started threatening me with big support payments. As it was, I was paying her about three hundred a month. I didn't want you to find out about it. I wanted to find the right time to tell you myself."

He felt sick, right then and there. Everywhere he looked there were reminders of his childhood: the deck and cookouts, the horseshoe pits, the tennis court. The Christmas tree.

"Libby," he pleaded, trying to catch her as she walked past him. "Please try to understand. All this with my mother, she tried to sue me and get me fired from my job. Don't you see what she's doing? She is trying to take you and Olivia away from me. She told Scott about the affair and the baby too. She pushed him over the edge, and he killed himself! Now we have a witness who says she killed my grandfather and your mother! And we know she's been drugging you."

Libby smiled at him; she leaned against the wall. "Yes," she said. "I believe she killed my mother. Mother told me she was seeing another man. But I had no idea

JEAN DeGARMO

it was Aaron. I think she knew she was in danger. Yes," Libby reflected, nodding her head. "It all makes sense now."

Russ was tired of standing out in the cold. And he watched large snowflakes fall from the dark sky, floating in the crisp breeze. He wanted to either leave or go back inside the Lodge. "She's a murderer," he said, "You and Olivia need to get out of here, now!"

"You know, Russ, I was looking through some papers the other day, and I found a trust fund for you, set up by your grandfather. You can have the money any time you want. I'll fax the document over to Jerry. It's approximately sixty-thousand dollars. He had a lot of stock. Maybe JoAnne is planning to give it to you when she dies. But you can have it now. I have the authority. It will help you with bills and court costs." She turned to him, tears in her eyes and added, "And child support for this child you didn't tell me about."

She shifted and said, "Well, I have things to take care of inside. I need time to think about all this, and I need you to take Olivia for four or five days, and Pat too, if you can arrange it."

"Sure, but I'll have to get a babysitter. Maybe Andrea can stay with her." He was encouraged that Libby had asked him to watch Olivia. And the trust money, that bombshell was enlightening too. He couldn't help but ask, "Are you going somewhere?"

"Never mind," she said. "Just take care of Olivia and Pat for a few days. What you do about the little girl is your business. But Olivia is my daughter too, and I want to be sure she's safe while I'm gone."

He could do nothing but watch her walk away, back to the Birch Hill Lodge.

Later that week Jerry called Russ to tell him that the blood tests proved Russ was Christine's father. He also wanted to tell Russ that Libby had faxed documents regarding a trust fund that Russ's grandfather set up for him.

Russ said, "Libby reminded me about the money earlier today."

"You be careful what you say to her!" Jerry ordered. "Don't trust anyone right now, especially not Libby!"

"She wants me to take care of Olivia for a few days. She didn't tell me why. I think she's up to something."

"Exactly!" Jerry shouted into the phone. "And precisely why you say *nothing* to her! Understand?

"I also have news about Beverly," Jerry continued. "Right now, Christine is staying with Amanda. Beverly's in bad shape; I'm going to take her to rehab in a few days. I think I have her convinced she needs help. The center's in Standish. I'll stay at her house for a few days to be close by if she needs me."

"What *in* the *hell!*" Russ yelled back. "You are going to find yourself in over your head, my friend! Believe me. I know what I'm talking about!"

"She wants to dry out," Jerry said, trying to explain in terms Russ could understand, or at least accept. "If she doesn't, she'll lose custody."

"You listen here, Jerry!" Russ was so worked up now, he was perspiring. "I'll prove her unfit if I have to! I want custody of Christine!"

"How in the hell are you going to be able to take care of a child?" Jerry asked. "You have to work, and you have Olivia to think about!"

"Libby's coming back to me," Russ insisted. "I can feel it. Like I said, I talked to her earlier today. I told her what Andrea saw, JoAnne pushing Susan off the break wall and murdering Grandfather too, just to shut him up. Joanne told Scott about me and Beverly."

"Very noble of you," Jerry said in response to Russ's speech. "But I think the only person to convince Beverly about custody of Christine is Libby herself. And after she sobers up, I hope to God she can get *you* out of her head!"

"Well, Scott's the one who ruined Beverly, if you ask me," Russ said, nursing a drink and wondering what he should fix for dinner. The house was cold. He needed to stoke the fire and turn up the heaters. "Scott married her and then ignored her. She gets pregnant with Christine and kept her from me for leverage. Trust me, Beverly is all about money! And you think you are in love with her? Good luck with *that*, pal!"

"Let's change the subject *right* now, damn it!" Jerry said. He wanted to punch Russ in the mouth, so it was a good thing they were miles apart. "I have other news. Claudia Bishop is going to sell to Libby. She says she'll wait until Libby has full control of JoAnne's estate. That means, if you do get Libby back, you'll be a very wealthy man. You and Libby will end up with the entire estate and all JoAnne's investments, minus the tax evasions, penalties, and fines. JoAnne's entire scheme will backfire, *if* you do happen to get Libby back. But don't count on it," here he took the liberty to imitate Russ's earlier sentiment, complete with sarcasm, "my friend!"

"Time will tell," said Russ. "I have to stoke the fire and get something to eat." He ended the conversation with, "I'll call you later."

Russ hung up, and so did Jerry.

Chapter 27

"I don't understand why you have to leave," JoAnne said to Libby. JoAnne was sitting on the couch in her living quarters with large pillows supporting her thin body up, so she could see straight and concentrate. She wore a blue sweater over a white blouse, a heavy wool skirt, knee socks over hosieries, and still, she complained about the cold. "Tell me again, dear," she said, positioning her slumped spine as upright as possible. "Why do you have to leave for a few days?"

Libby sat in a chair across from her. She wore heavy clothes too, but she had instructed the maintenance man, an experienced, reliable person hired after Edwin Mayfield was taken away, to crank the heat throughout the entire Lodge.

"Because I have business in Ann Arbor," Libby lied. She wasn't about to tell JoAnne she was going to see Beverly in Standish. She wanted to convince JoAnne that she was proceeding with the divorce from Russ; for now, that was the plan. The last thing Libby needed was for JoAnne to change her will. As things stood presently, Libby was the executor of JoAnne's entire estate, not to mention primary inheritor of her assets and most importantly, the Birch Hill Lodge.

Libby refrained from confronting JoAnne about the matter of her pushing Susan off the break wall. Libby wanted to interrogate her, make it clear that she knew the truth of what happened to her mother, and she wanted JoAnne aware of the fact that there had been two witnesses—Russ's grandfather and Andrea. But she held her ground for now.

Let her pay the price in due time.

Libby would soon own the Birch Hill Lodge, but the divorce was something else entirely, and there was no rush. The decisions regarding Russ, Beverly, the child they had together, child support, and so on would be determined as she went along. She needed to speak with David Preece as soon as he arrived, and she would speak to him alone, without JoAnne present.

"What a unique Christmas present for Russell," JoAnne continued, her voice irritatingly squeaky. She pulled a shawl up from her lap and adjusted it under her pointed chin. "But he made his bed, as they say. Merry Christmas, dear one," she chided. "Happy divorce to you!"

Libby didn't respond to JoAnne's sarcasm. She was anxiously waiting for Preece. She had something very important to tell him. Moments earlier, she had signed a paper at JoAnne's request that proved Libby owned the Birch Hill Lodge. It was the deed, signed over to Libby, fully notarized. A done deal. For this to happen before JoAnne's death, obviously, JoAnne was convinced that the marriage was over between Russ and Libby. She had Libby's word that she and Olivia would continue to live at the Lodge. Libby would control everything in JoAnne's estate. She would leave Russ lonely and destitute.

JoAnne wasn't aware that Andrea had come forth with the third copy of her father's will. Russ now legally owned his grandfather's cottage and land; also, Libby had arranged through the bank and Jerry McPherson for Russ to receive the trust money his grandfather had left him. JoAnne had no idea that Libby found the trust document he'd made up for Russ. Libby had acted on it quickly, transferred the document to Jerry, and now Russ had the money in his bank account.

No matter what happened to them in the future, Libby decided, she would be fair with Russ. For now, she had to tie up loose ends before JoAnne died. She had to convince David Preece he needed to set up his law practice elsewhere.

JoAnne, from her wool and cotton nest among the cushions of the couch, asked Libby in a childlike voice: "Where did you say Olivia is today, dear?"

Again, Libby knew she had to lie to JoAnne. She must make JoAnne believe Russ was out of the picture. "She's staying with a friend. She'll be back in a day or two. I'll take care of everything."

"All right, dear. Turn the radio up for me before you leave, will you please? I do love Mozart, and I can't hear the music very well with the furnace running so hard."

Libby went to the wooden table and turned up the radio. At the same time, she heard Preece climb the stairway. With the music loud and JoAnne's hearing impaired, Libby could talk with Preece in the hallway without JoAnne overhearing the conversation.

Libby left JoAnne's rooms and found Preece at the top step about to turn toward the direction of JoAnne's living quarters. He seemed startled to see Libby. He tugged at his blue and gray tie; he cleared his throat and cautiously moved toward her. As always, he was dressed to the hilt, the loud, bright tie, the immaculate silk trousers and polished shoes, the silver wavy hair, sprayed into place. He looked suited-up for Las Vegas, not the small isolated community of Grand Lake.

Libby had always suspected Preece was trying to conceal his true identity. She researched him and discovered he, indeed, owed several unsavory people large sums of money. Libby decided that the future owner of the Birch Hill Lodge could and would do without this particular lawyer.

"How's JoAnne today?" Preece asked, merely as a tension breaker.

"Oh, she's sitting on the couch, complaining she's cold."

Libby was dressed in traveling clothes—jeans, a sweater, a jacket, and boots. She wanted things wrapped up before Olivia's Christmas vacation began in a few days.

She waited for Preece to speak. She looked at him, waiting.

But he said nothing. Libby continued. "She's preoccupied with Mozart right now," she was drawing out the suspense, making Preece think things through before speaking. "I didn't appreciate the way you helped her drug me, David. It's a good thing I caught on and poured the drinks out, dumped the food."

"I assumed as much," Preece said listlessly. He sensed he was in for a pink slip. "I was hoping so too."

"It was stupid of you," Libby added. She was still shaken up by the matter. To think her mother-in-law and attorney would attempt to drug her. "And I want you to know that once I am in full control, I'll be hiring another lawyer."

"I'm sure you will," Preece said. He pulled at his cuff links, one at a time. He always pulled at an article of clothing whenever agitated, like now. "I expected as much."

"JoAnne knows I'm divorcing Russ, and I've known for a while now that you have been trying to convince her to make you executor of her will. Please don't continue with that notion. Hear me clearly. I found a video JoAnne had Marilyn Clayton took of you and Leeann McPherson. On the tape, there's you and Leeann in action with two of your boyfriends. I know Marilyn already gave a copy to Jerry and Russ. The video would ruin you around here. I suggest you go in to JoAnne right now and tell her you have a job offer elsewhere. By the way, your plan with Claudia Bishop backfired too. She's reserving bids for her father's property at the Harbor for me. So really, why should you stick around?"

"Actually, I do prefer to keep on the move," Preece admitted. He shivered dramatically and collected the lapels of his jacket. "It *is* the best strategy."

"Yes, and we all know why, David. You're trying to hide from…certain people."

She played that card forthright, not sure of the impact, but when she saw a frown escape Preece's tight facial features, she knew she had been correct. He was running from dangerous interactions, possibly the law as well.

"Handing me my walking papers, are you, Libby?" he asked, trying to smile.

"That's right," she said.

"I want the tapes before I go," said Preece. "Even the one McPherson has, so you'll just have to retrieve them for me."

"Tapes? What tapes, David?"

"You know, the videos; *the tapes! Whatever!* You just now said—"

"Maybe I'll give them to you as a going away present. Now go on in there and convince JoAnne that everything is wonderful, and then go home and pack your bags. The game's over. Even Marylyn Clayton has left town. You do the same."

Preece fidgeted and fingered his clothing, lastly his thin belt. "Taking after the old bitch, I see. How fitting. She's threatened me enough already; I guess it's your turn. I've sucked hundreds of thousands of dollars out of her, anyway. I guess it's time to move on to fresh pickings."

"Yes, and I know you're just hanging around, hoping to find the third copy of the will. I know JoAnne promised to pay you dearly if you found it. So, did you?"

"No, I don't think it exits."

"You're probably right," Libby agreed. She knew better than to tip her hand to Preece, but she had one more thing to say. "When you get to your new location of fresh pickings, send me your address. Then and only then will I send you the videos and pictures. You'll just have to trust me the way I trusted you."

"Hmm," Preece murmured. "Trust is something that simply doesn't exist between you people. I was only playing along." He had his hand on the doorknob, ready to enter JoAnne's rooms. "I found that out right off the mark!"

"And *you* should know precisely why I'm coming in with you. I want to make sure you tell her you're leaving town *tomorrow*. Tell her everything's in order and Russ is out of the picture.

"Certainly," said Preece, opening the door for Libby, even bowing to her as she passed. "I'm sick of you people, anyway."

• • •

Later that afternoon, on her way to see Beverly in Standish, Libby recalled the meeting she previously witnessed between JoAnne and Preece. Immediately, JoAnne instructed Preece to turn down the music. She knew right away, by the frown distorting Preece's face, that something monumental was about to take place. After the radio was turned to low, JoAnne ordered Preece to sit down beside her on the couch. Libby recalled that JoAnne's face turned from pale to opaque when she heard the news. Even the age spots on her neck and arms retreated to a lighter shade of brown. She had trouble believing David had a better offer in…he chose…Alaska?

"You're not happy in my employment?" JoAnne asked him anxiously, pulling her shawl. "Have I not paid you enough?"

David assured her that it was simply time for him to move on. But if she wanted, he would be available long distance via fax machines and phone for legal consultation. He would forever be in her debt, literally, he knew. He looked at Libby and shrugged.

JoAnne finally conceded to the plan of David's self-preservation, his moving on to more lucrative territory. What could she say to that?

Now thinking about JoAnne's expression, her dismissal of her right-hand man and favorite attorney, David Preece, Libby drove along Route 23 South toward Beverly's farm and she realized JoAnne Shaw didn't have much time left.

She was grateful too that Marilyn Clayton had given her Beverly's new address before she left town. Marylyn informed Libby she was going to provide certain information to Jerry for Russ too, incriminating photos and videos and evidence pertaining to Beverly Weyman's involvement with Russ.

Driving along the highway with a clear view of the Lake Huron shoreline, it began to snow, but only in delicate shafts. Libby found the road leading to the farmhouse and there was the friend, Amanda's, car in the driveway, near the garage. She was surprised to find Jerry McPherson's Passport over by a large apple orchard. She parked next to Jerry's car. When she stepped out onto the driveway itself, snow-covered gravel crunching beneath her boots, a Golden Retriever came forward from the expansive front porch to greet her. As soon as she knocked on the front door, Jerry McPherson showed her inside; apparently, he had been standing by the front window and saw Libby's van approach.

Libby said quickly, "I came to see Beverly."

Jerry looked exhausted; there were dark circles beneath his eyes. His clothes, office attire as usual, were creased. His tie hung loosely from his neck, his sleeves were rolled up to the elbows. "Yes, I know," he said. "I was here on business, on her behalf I might add. She's resting right now. We're trying to convince her to go into treatment tomorrow morning. It's all arranged, but now she's balking. So, I really don't think this is the right time to discuss Russ," he said Russ's name in a brash crescendo, a surge of hot air that conveyed nothing pleasant about the name or the man.

"I'm not here about Russ," said Libby. She would push past Jerry if necessary to get to Beverly. "I'm here about Russ's daughter."

When Libby turned, she could see Amanda at the kitchen table cleaning up the baby. The baby was quiet while Amanda wiped her face with a dishrag. Libby moved closer, toward the child. She could see right away that the baby had Russ's curly brown hair and large blue eyes. Libby smiled and touched the baby's soft cheek. "Well, you're just beautiful," she said. She abruptly turned toward Jerry, who had been wringing his hands by the stove. "Jerry," she said softly, but nothing more came to mind. Instead she turned to Amanda, who looked to be in her early twenties. "Are you a professional childcare giver?" Libby asked her. She didn't like the fact that the baby, Christine, was wearing only a flimsy nightshirt and a diaper.

"I'm just here helping out Beverly," said Amanda. "My mom's her best friend."

"Where's Beverly's bedroom?" Libby asked. "You watch the baby, Jerry," she ordered in no uncertain terms, "while she shows me Beverly's room."

They walked down a musty hallway, through the living room, sparsely decorated with only two chairs and a bookshelf. The entire downstairs area was too large and drafty. They came to a stairway and climbed up. Libby told Amanda she wanted to speak with Beverly alone. She explained that Beverly was her sister-in-law, and they had personal matters to discuss. After Amanda left, Libby opened the bedroom door without bothering to knock. The room stank of alcohol and cigarette smoke. Right away, Libby noticed an ashtray filled to the rim with cigarette butts and ashes on the table by the bed.

She also noticed that Beverly was almost naked, wearing only underwear and a bra. She was sprawled out across the large queen-sized bed.

Libby walked over to the window and lifted the blind to catch what was left of the wintry afternoon sunlight. The blind opened in a loud crack, which made Beverly sit up in the bed, a startled look across her wan, blushed face. She grabbed the sheet and attempted to cover herself. She squinted at Libby from behind a hanging hedge of bangs. And presently, she licked her lips to ask, "What are you doing here, Libby? Did you come to shoot me or something?"

"I'd love to shoot you, Beverly," Libby admitted, "but I came here to talk instead. I don't fight over men."

"Well, good for you," said Beverly, attempting to smile. She had all she could do to sit up straight. "I do. I *love* Russ."

Libby scanned the messy, stinking room and made a big deal out of bending over and searching beneath the bed. "I don't see him here," She said to the dust circles beneath the bed. "Are you down there, Russ?"

"Go to hell!" Beverly shouted. Apparently, the shout, the very movement of her lips and throat, had cost her. She clamped a shaking hand to her right temple.

"No," Libby shouted back at her. "You're the one going to hell. Not because of Russ, but what you did to my brother! Russ can sleep around if he wants to, God knows that's *his* business; I don't believe in hanging onto a man who doesn't want me. Although let me see, Russ is at *our* house at Grand Lake and not *here* with you. That should tell you something."

"His daughter's here!" argued Beverly. Tears came to her eyes, and her face turned scarlet-red with tiny lines collecting around her mouth and across her forehead. "She's Russ's and mine, and he'll come back to us!"

"Like I said," Libby sighed, her breath drawn out. "That's *his* business. I see it this way: we're all free spirits, and if he wants you, by all means, he's free to divorce me. I won't try to stop him. To hell with the house we built together and all our plans. I'm not a dreamer. I know things and people can change at the drop of a hat. Look at me. I am about to inherit the Birch Hill Lodge. But Russ?" She put a finger to her lip. "Is he here, helping you with the baby? Trying to talk you into treatment? No, he's at Grand Lake, taking care of *our* daughter, Olivia. And why? Because that's what he wants to do, and that's *where* he wants to be."

"Shut up," Beverly yelled, wincing again. She tossed her bare legs over the side of the bed and sat there a few seconds before reaching for a pack of cigarettes. Her hand trembled as she lit one, and her chest rattled as she inhaled and exhaled. She glared over at Libby. "Russ will want Christine," she said with slow, pre-picked words, "even if he doesn't want me."

"I know that," Libby said, watching her smoke the skinny cigarette. "That's why I'm here. First, I have something to say about Scott." Libby moved toward Beverly, and it was all she could do to keep from grabbing her around the neck and choking her. "Did you know that Scott was impotent?"

Beverly laughed but continued to draw on the cigarette, exhaling a long stream of smoke and staring at Libby now with intense suspicion. "Well, he didn't tell me directly," she said.

"But you suspected?" Libby made a face of mockery. "Huh! That's what I thought when you tried to pull off the routine of his daughter dying. I knew then that the child wasn't his, and so did he. We talked about it, but he said he loved you and would let the lie go." Now it was Libby's turn to laugh. "Let it go? He should have let *you* go, and he might still be alive."

"Scott always was spineless," said Beverly, now smoking with greater conviction. "I married him for his money. But Russ is the man I've always loved."

"I doubt you know much about love," Libby pointed out. "If you did, you wouldn't be sitting here drunk or hungover or whatever you are right now while your daughter's downstairs with strangers."

"Amanda and Jerry aren't strangers!" Beverly insisted. "Far from it!"

"And not her mother either!"

"Here we go," sighed Beverly, smoking the cigarette to the filter and searching for an empty ashtray. She drained what was left of the whisky in a glass and shook her head, watching Libby hard. "Perfect Libby throwing stones again."

"If you loved your daughter," said Libby, "You would get help. It's that simple."

Beverly closed her eyes. She was exposed and wilting, the truth of herself draining upon a stained bed. "Exactly what do you want from me, Libby?"

"I want to take Christine back with me to Grand Lake. Olivia and I live at the Lodge now. I'll take good care of her for you."

"Even if Russ leaves you, you'd still want my daughter?"

"I want more children and can't have any," Libby said, her voice matter of fact and not the least bit self-pitying. "Christine is Olivia's half-sister; the DNA tests prove it. I'll take care of her as if she were my own while you get help. Let Jerry take you tomorrow morning for treatment."

Beverly's face fell into a contortion of scattered splotches and grief. She covered her eyes and cried into her hands. Sadly, Libby knew that it would be easier for Beverly to give up her own child than it was to give up Russ.

"I'll take care of her for you," Libby repeated. "But I'll need you to sign papers giving me guardianship. And who knows, maybe Russ will come to you, in the end."

With that thought in mind, Libby sat down next to Beverly on the bed, despite the damp sheets. "We'll have Jerry draw up the appropriate papers for you to sign right away. And tomorrow, you'll go into the rehab center."

"But I want Russ," cried Beverly, unwilling to shake him from her heart. "I didn't mean for Scott to die! I only wanted to be with Russ!"

Libby put her arm around Beverly, feeling awe instead of pity over Beverly's devotion to a distorted, unreasonable love. Poor Beverly. Russ was at Grand Lake, and he would never leave it. Not for her. Not for Libby. Not for anyone.

Chapter 28

Libby took Christine home to the Birch Hill Lodge. Amanda and Jerry helped her load the baby's clothing and portable crib, toys, and so forth into her van. It wasn't difficult to set up a nursery for her in the bedroom connected to Libby's master suite, and of course, Libby could afford the essentials for the child: medical care, clothing, and other items necessary to take care of her properly.

She was still legally married to Russ, although the divorce hearing was scheduled for the day after Christmas. If it came to that, a divorce, Libby wasn't sure what would happen. She didn't need child support on either child, and she would not pursue it through the court; she was considering adopting Christine if the divorce actually happened, and according to daily reports from Jerry, Beverly was not cooperating in rehab, so it was unlikely that she would be able to support and care for a baby. Jerry confided to Libby that he didn't think Beverly wanted the child back. If rehab taught her anything else, it was the fact that Russ was out of the picture. She must live without him. If she couldn't have Russ, she didn't want his child either.

This was the exact opposite of Libby. Libby would want Christine with or without Russ.

The following week after Libby visited with Beverly in Standish and took the baby home with her, Jerry arranged a quick hearing for a judge to appoint Libby as Christine's legal guardian. There was absolutely no objection from Beverly, and Russ also agreed, as her legal father. And the fact that Libby and Russ were still married, although living separately for the time being, and that Libby could well afford to take care of the child helped her case as well. It was clear to all that getting pregnant with Russ Shaw's child was Beverly's attempt to trap him once and for all. Not through child support. She truly believed he would leave Libby and marry her. Now the baby was Libby's, and so Libby believed in her mind that she had two daughters.

Russ continued to live in the house on Grand Lake. He called Libby almost every day and dropped by as much as possible to see his daughters. He was so involved with work and getting his family back, he didn't even notice that JoAnne was failing fast and confined to her living quarters most of the time.

However, JoAnne would still shuffle down the hallway and have her morning coffee with Libby in Libby's office. She would force herself to get dressed at six o'clock and stagger down the hallway, sometimes down the long arduous stairway, to inspect the kitchen and check the dining room area, make sure the holiday decorations were in order, make sure Andrea was living up to her new temporary status as hostess for the Lodge, and conclude her rounds by visiting Libby in her office.

JoAnne would sit down, directly across from Libby's desk in the only chair provided. She would watch Libby move her slender bejeweled fingers down a calculator or through the files in the file cabinet.

"You're going to adopt Christine yourself and still divorce Russ?" JoAnne asked Libby every morning since she discovered Libby's plans for parenthood. "Is that even possible with our present court system?"

"Anything's possible, JoAnne," Libby said somewhat absently as she concentrated. "You of all people should know that."

"I'm so afraid you will weaken and go back to Russ," JoAnne admitted. Libby studied JoAnne thoroughly. She appeared so frail. Still, she knew not to underestimate her. "You won't do that, will you, Libby?"

"Not a chance," said Libby. It had become annoying trying to convince JoAnne daily that there was a court date scheduled for the day after Christmas, whereby the divorce decree and dividing up the assets and child custody issues would all be discussed and settled.

Libby was more determined than JoAnne to conclude the terms of separation if nothing else, and especially now the baby was involved, but she'd been so busy running the Lodge and taking care of her daughters, she hadn't given much thought to Russ.

She examined a list of phone numbers for local lawyers while continuing the usual morning banter with JoAnne. "It's Christmas anyway," she said to JoAnne with a genuine smile because she knew how much JoAnne loved the season. "Let's get through one event at a time. Don't worry about the divorce. As far as I'm concerned, I divorced Russ a long time ago." She paused and smiled again, "It's not for *you* to worry about, JoAnne."

"I don't think you should allow him to come here every day," JoAnne droned on in a whispery voice but with harsh enunciation. "Allowing it makes him think he can come back into your life to stay! Haven't you learned anything from me? Haven't you yet learned the art of playing hardball?"

Libby wanted to say, *You mean like murder, as in pushing my mother off the break wall because she was fooling around with your husband? Like shoving Russ's grandfather down the stairs because he knew too much? Telling a hideous destructive secret to my brother that drove him to suicide?*

Libby kept these thoughts to herself though and did some research to match names and phone numbers of attorneys with the list Jerry McPherson had given her. She knew JoAnne was almost finished with her morning pep-talk, and as JoAnne stood up, the scent of cinnamon candles and holly radiated from her shrunken body. "Russ is a loser and a scoundrel," JoAnne proclaimed, shouting back at Libby from the door. She had obviously decided it was her main task on this Earth to remind Libby of the fact. And here on her last note of fervor, JoAnne would shake uncontrollably and turn purple in the face. The veins in her neck would pop out and throb, and Libby would think that she would collapse any second, fold up into a crumbled shell of bones and deteriorated muscle, and fall to the floor, dead.

But no, JoAnne would just stand there, supported by her cane and the door until Libby agreed by nodding, and only then would JoAnne push herself off the doorframe itself, and stagger back to the dining area where, if up to it, she would converse with the patrons. She didn't even notice Libby was wearing her mother's exquisite gold chain.

Libby knew fully well that JoAnne didn't care about Christine. JoAnne, in fact, acted as if Christine were a temporary client. A visitor, if you will. Or maybe an associate of Olivia's who would soon go home and perhaps come back to play another day. Libby couldn't tell if JoAnne understood who the baby was or not. JoAnne would nod as she passed the children, attempt a sly smile, and once she did ask Libby, "Now who is this beautiful child with the big blue eyes?"

Libby stared at her, thinking that she knew damn well who Christine's parents were and that she was jerking her around, as she did so well. As was her style, even in her delirium.

• • •

Christmas Eve day, Russ called Libby to ask if he could have Olivia and Christine over for the day, and maybe they could stay the night. But Libby told him they had Christmas Eve dinner already planned, and if he wanted to, he could join them.

"No thanks," he said to the offer. "Not with JoAnne staring me down with a loaded pistol concealed under the tablecloth." Then he hung up on her.

Libby wondered what to do about him as she put away her work. She recalled that Russ stopped by two nights previously, out of breath, explaining to her that he had commissioned a local building company to add another bedroom onto the house this spring. The bedroom would be off the hallway by his office. He would have plenty of room to accommodate both of his daughters when they visited him. Now Libby was irritated, as she had not necessarily agreed to Russ keeping the house. Then he proceeded to inform her that he was going to have the master bedroom remodeled. There were leaks in the shower and the ceiling above the doorway, and he also wanted to replace the windows on the porch. He wanted to tear down the boathouse and build a modern one. He told her if they sold the house later, the repairs and remodeling would increase the value.

But Libby could see right through this maneuver. She knew Russ was anxious to reconcile, and he was only trying to confuse her with thoughts of additional plans and projects.

The holiday season put everything in his favor temporarily. He knew Libby was a sentimental person, and therefore vulnerable during Christmas. He would be able to see the children more often this time of year; and that way, he could also be near Libby. But he also knew she would turn maudlin and weepy right after New Year's Day. He'd have to work on her quickly. Time was running out.

He called again on Christmas Eve about an hour before he knew she would get the girls ready for bed. Christmas Eve dinner at the Lodge would be long over with. "I want to come over tonight," he told her. "I have a gift for you. Meet me on the front porch around ten."

"I'll think about it," said Libby.

"It's the sapphire bracelet you wanted, the one you showed me last summer before all this bad business started. You remember, in the window display at Pierson's Jewelers?"

"I remember," Libby admitted. But it would take more than a bracelet to empty her of the pain of her brother shooting himself. Never mind the fact that she would never be able to trust Russ again. "I'll meet you later tonight," she said. "Merry Christmas."

Andrea helped Libby take the children upstairs to their bedroom. They had the room joining Libby's, one story up from JoAnne's living quarters and Andrea's room. Then Andrea told Libby she was going to take a walk and get some fresh air, but that she would be back in an hour if Libby wanted to join her in the dining room for a Christmas Eve drink. Libby noted Andrea was in an unusually cheerful mood.

Libby read the children a story and watched them drift off to sleep. She allowed Pat to stay in their bedroom, but of course, she left their door open and the door to Libby's room. She knew if anything out of the ordinary happened during the night, Pat would awaken her. Pat suddenly lifted her head. Right away Libby knew she heard something down the hallway, a sound out of place. "All right," Libby told Pat. "Something's going on, and you want me to go check it out. Stay here with the girls."

Pat watched Libby leave the room, and when satisfied she was off to check out the intrusion, the large Labrador laid back down between the crib and the twin bed. Libby walked quickly down the hallway when she realized a bell was ringing. It had to be the bell JoAnne kept on the stand next to her bed in case she needed something. JoAnne's rooms were on the floor directly below Libby's, and so Libby descended the stairs. As she came closer to JoAnne's bedroom, she heard voices. JoAnne's voice was one, yes, and at first, she couldn't place the other. But both voices were female, perhaps one of the maids or assistant cooks was pestering JoAnne for a raise. Meanwhile the bell rang again, and then the ringing stopped. JoAnne yelled out, there was a sliding sound, a crashing and banging of furniture against the wall.

Libby's first reaction was to knock on the door, but if she knocked, she would interrupt the commotion going on inside. If she waited and listened, she would be able to figure out what was going on and who was in there, threatening JoAnne.

"It's all over," said the voice, not JoAnne's. "This is the end for you."

"You damned simple idiot of a girl!" JoAnne cried; her voice sounded like a belch or a muffled squawk. Nonetheless, in Libby's opinion, her voice was a last plea for help.

A storm of trouble brewing.

"You stupid freak of nature!" JoAnne managed to spit out. "I never wanted you, never! Your father is the one who wanted children! He insisted on *two* children! I didn't even want *one!*"

Libby opened the door just in time to see Andrea grab JoAnne by the shoulders of her cotton nightgown and jerk the fragile bag of bones upward. Andrea looked insane with anger. Her hair was tossed around her shrew-like face, and her arms and hands shook as she slammed JoAnne against the headboard of the canopy bed.

"Call me whatever you like," Andrea said, spitting and jeering, "but I've had enough of you. I saw you kill my grandfather, and I saw you push Susan Weyman off the break wall. You're a murderer, and you should have paid for it a long time ago!"

"You're brain dead, child!" JoAnne stammered. She didn't even attempt to pry Andrea's fingers from her shoulders. She was weak, and what's more, she was too shocked to retaliate. "Let go of me this instant, or I'll have you put away in an asylum! Something I should have done when you were much younger!"

Andrea clamped both hands to the sides of JoAnne's quivering head. She leaned down and stared into JoAnne's dark eyes. "You told Scott Weyman about Russ and Beverly too. Admit it!" she started to slap the sides of JoAnne's face, several times, furiously, until JoAnne murmured an affirmative confession. Then after twisting and turning beneath Andrea's grip, she surrendered physically, but still she was able to screech, "Let go of me you crazy little lunatic! I'll have you arrested for assault! If you don't leave the premises immediately, I'll have you put away where you belong!"

"Where I belong?" Andrea asked, and next she feigned laughter. When JoAnne attempted to drag her legs over the side of the bed to get out of it, Andrea shoved her foot against her thigh. "You think *you* know where I belong, Mother?"

"You're hurting me!" JoAnne shrieked. "Any minute now, someone will come! Libby will come! You'll see!"

"Like you hurt *me*, JoAnne?" Andrea pushed harder with her foot while watching JoAnne's facial muscles contract in pain. She sighed and gasped. Andrea grabbed her by the hair and forced her to look into her own eyes. "Like you had that doctor cut out my ovaries, so I wouldn't be able to have children?"

"You don't know what you're saying," JoAnne screeched, trying to push Andrea's foot away. "You had tumors on your uterus, and it was taken care of by a specialist!"

"Taken care of?" Andrea asked, pulling JoAnne's frizzed hair even harder. "Maybe I *wanted* children and you took that choice away from me!"

"I didn't want you to go through what I went through," whispered JoAnne, attempting justification. When she turned her head, Libby could see tears slide down the crevices of her leathery face. As soon as she managed to turn away, Andrea jerked her upright, to full attention.

Then Andrea took a syringe out of her skirt pocket and held it up for JoAnne to see that it was filled with a clear liquid. As soon as JoAnne saw the syringe, she squirmed with all her might to free herself from Andrea's grip. She jerked her head side to side, but only wasted what little energy she had left in the effort.

She simply wasn't strong enough. "And it was up to *you*?" said Andrea. She held up the syringe, tapped it, and lowered it to her knee. "I hate you. You killed my father, my grandfather, and Scott and Susan Weyman. You're a mass-murderer. No wonder Dad went to Susan. She was much prettier than you, and she didn't nag him day and night. I'm glad he had some happiness with her."

The mention of Susan's name made JoAnne convulse beneath the weight of Andrea's foot, still pressed against JoAnne's frail leg. JoAnne came alive again with a surge of energy and power. If not for Andrea thinking quickly and placing a pillow over her face, JoAnne might have overtaken her, if by no other method of retaliation than sheer rage. Andrea took one hand and pressed down, hard, against the pillow, watching JoAnne's reflexes shudder to a stop. She waited for the very breath to expel from the old woman, and while waiting, she contemplated the syringe again.

Libby noticed Andrea's hesitation. She walked into the room, up to the bed, and took the syringe from Andrea's hand. "Take the pillow off her face," Libby told her. "I want her to see me."

Andrea did as Libby said. She pulled the pillow off JoAnne's gray face, and they watched JoAnne lying still, her lungs pumping slowly, her breath raspy, all but spent until only one finger twitched. She was dead, almost.

Libby leaned down close to JoAnne's ear and was surprised JoAnne smelled sweet, and somehow, Libby felt strangely validated by this knowledge. "Can you hear me, JoAnne?" she said into her ear, nudging her thin shoulder. "It's me, Libby." Libby stuck the needle into JoAnne's skinny yellow arm and stared down at her as her opaque eyelids stopped fluttering, and finally JoAnne's labored breathing, although reduced to small swirls of air, stopped completely.

Libby stood up and tucked the quilt around JoAnne's emaciated, lifeless body as if wishing her pleasant dreams. "We'll wipe the fingerprints off the syringe, put the fingers of her right hand against it," she said to Andrea, "and put it on her bedside stand here. She's been so distraught lately, the poor thing overdosed."

You have made your bed, thought Libby.

"Yes," said Andrea, standing beside Libby now, eager to cover their tracks. "And isn't it just like Mother to ruin everyone's Christmas with *her own* suicide?" Andrea shook her head regrettably. She diligently wiped off the syringe with a tissue, and as Libby suggested, pressed JoAnne's fingertips against the syringe, her own fingers holding the syringe with another tissue.

Libby looked down at JoAnne's bloodless face, as if admiring her in death. So stately, so out of commission, never to hurt anyone again. Libby consulted her diamond and emerald studded wristwatch, the one she had stolen, along with numerous other expensive pieces, from JoAnne during her recent reign as the manager of the Birch Hill Lodge.

"Well then," she said, emitting anticipation all around, knowing a new beginning was upon them, a brand-new year only a week away. "It's time for me to meet Russ. He's coming over tonight to give me a Christmas present. He's so thoughtful."

Andrea followed Libby out the door and closed it, a whisper of wood against wood, hoping not to disturb JoAnne even though she was reduced to a corpse, covered with her quilts, her favorite one on top—the old-fashioned wedding ring design she and Aaron received as a gift. They left her Christmas decorations surrounding her, spreading the holiday cheer throughout her coveted Birch Hill Lodge.

"Let's have that drink before you meet Russ," Andrea said, her mood improving as the night wore on. "After all, it's Christmas Eve."

"Sure," said Libby. She led the way down the long stairway and turned the corner to the massive dining room. It was quiet for a change, except for "Silent Night" piped from the walls and cathedral ceiling. "All is calm, all is bright." All is well, and it's a good night to pause with celebration, Libby thought, although her plans to get even were just beginning.

Made in the USA
Lexington, KY
27 October 2018